Frayed Promises

PROMISED DESTINY
BOOK TWO

LYNN U. WATSON

Lynn U. Watson
stepping through time
stitching stories of faith

ISBN: 978-1-7329281-6-9 (print)

ISBN: 978-1-7329281-5-2 (ebook)

Dedicated to the Staff and Volunteers

at Life Choices of Memphis, Inc.

A man's heart deviseth his way: but the Lord directeth his steps.
~Proverbs 16:9

German Word List

GERMAN NOUNS ARE ALWAYS
CAPITALIZED

Apfel – apple

Apfelwein — cider

Auf Wiedersehen – goodbye (literally until we see each other again)

Backhaus – bakery (often with a coffee shop)

Bauernfruhstuck – farmer's breakfast

Bitte – you're welcome

Danke – thank you

Das Königliche Gänsespiel – The Royal Goose Game

Doktor – doctor

Dreikönigstag—Three Kings Day

Erntedank – Thanksgiving

Federbetten – feather bed

Frau – Missus/woman

Fraulein – young lady(ies)

Freund(e) – friends(s)

Gasthaus – guest house, inn

Grossvater -- grandfather

Gut Apfelhof – fine Apple Home – community (Gut commonly used with the community's name – residents under the protection of the Gut Herr of their home village/town)

Gut Herr – Nobleman of the Gut, Good Sir, or Good Lord

Gut Herin – Nobelman's wife

Guten Morgen – good morning

Herr – Mister/man

Ja – yes

Kartoffel(n) – potato, potatoes

Kinder – children

Kirche — church

Kirsche — cherry

Kleinkind—little child

Komm, Herr Jesus – Come, Lord Jesus

Lass uns essen — Let's eat

Lehrer – teacher

Marktplatz – marketplace

Mutter – mother

Mütter – mothers

Mütter' – mothers'

Mutti – mom

Nein – no

Oma – grandma

Onkel – uncle

Opa – grandpa

Sehr gut – very good

Sie schwanger sind? – Are you pregnant?

Spätzle —egg noodles

Tante – aunt

Vater – father

Väter – fathers

Vater Gott – Father God

Vati – dad

Wein – wine

Wiener Schnitzel – meat cutlet

Zeitung – newspaper (*Illinois Staats Zeitung* – Illinois State Newspaper)

Zimf-Streuselkuchen – cinnamon crumble cake

.

Characters

Gut Herr Kraig Reinhold—Baron of Gut Apfelhof

Gut Herrin Lydia Reinhold—Kraig's wife

Clara Reinhold Becker—oldest Reinhold daughter, twin to Curt, and wife to Daniel Becker

Curt Reinhold—oldest Reinhold son, twin to Clara

Hannah Reinhold—17-year-old daughter

Emmaline Reinhold—13-year-old daughter

Wilhelm Reinhold—11-year-old son

Oma Dorthea Reinhold—Kraig's mother, the children's grandmother

Daniel Becker—Reinhold family carriage driver, Clara's husband

Tante Adeline Walther—Lydia Reinhold's sister

Onkel Martin Walther—Adeline's husband

Tante Caroline—Sister to Kraig Reinhold's father

Onkel Knut—Tante Caroline's husband

Lillian Denzller—Curt Reinhold's love interest

Mamsell Lotti—Reinhold's Mamsell

Alice—Clara's personal maid

Dora—Reinhold cook

Fritz—Reinhold doorman

Henry—Reinhold household servant

Rosa Becker—family seamstress, Daniel's mother

Jost—coachman

Hans—coachman

Megs Wolff Schmitz—Clara's best friend

Mrs. Hardy, Mrs. Spalding, Mrs. Pullman, Mrs. Miller—clients of Megs' dressmaker shop

Edmund—Walther's doorman

Trude—Walther's cook

Nina—Tante Adeline's personal maid

Helene and Katrin—two of the Hearts ladies

Max Engel—friend of Onkel Martin

Sandra Blum—Tante Adeline's seamstress (traveled with Clara)

Belinda—Sandra's daughter

Hilda—Sandra's granddaughter

Bertha, Eliza, Freddy Strauss—passengers on ship

Louise—passenger on ship

Theodor Strauss—Bertha's husband and the children's father

William Willigerod—Captain of the S.S. Elbe

Archie—telegraph delivery boy

Egon Hess—Owner of Hess Trust Bank of Chicago

Frances Hess—Egon's wife

Zilla Hess—Frances & Egon's daughter

Arthur Hess—The Hess' grandson

Agnes—The Hess' neighbor

Secrets. Lots of secrets nearly destroyed my family. The treasured secret I snug to my bosom promises to put an ocean between us. Oma's last warning spins like a tempest around me threatening to shipwreck my joy and fray every promise we've made.

~from Clara Reinhold Becker's sketchbook

Chapter One

THE OLD ABANDONED COTTAGE, Gut Apfelhof, Württemberg, Germany, *Thursday, 10 November 1881*

CLARA LAID her head against Daniel's chest, her curls tingling and her body quivering with joy. "Six weeks already, and nobody knows."

"Shh. No need to announce our private nuptials." He silenced her with another delicious kiss.

Oma stood in the doorway of the old cottage. "What's the meaning of this?"

Clara wiggled her way loose from her husband's arms and the sheets entangling them.

"Get dressed now."

They both scrambled into their clothing.

"Oma, I can explain." Clara pushed the curls from her eyes.

1

Daniel buttoned his shirt, looked down at his bare feet, and nodded to Clara's grandmother.

Oma stepped toward them and clasped Clara's hand. "What I have to say is for both of you."

"Are you guilty of something, meine Kinder? I don't read minds, but your shakiness rattles my arm. You worry your curls senseless?"

"You caught us together. Will you tell Vati?"

"The genuine admiration and love between the two of you glows. It has for years. A beautiful thing, and I'm sad for you. This old lady's opinions don't count for much in our world, though."

"You believe Daniel and I shouldn't see each other anymore —at least not like this."

"I'm not my children or my grandchildren's judge. You must decide whether to follow your conscience or your heart. Often conflicts rage between our desires and the still small voice whispering into our ear the right thing to do. Clara stared at her shaky hands and pressed them over her stomach. *Maybe I can hold my nervous flutters inside.* An eerie silence draped itself around them.

Daniel finally spoke. "Clara and I are married."

Pinching the bridge of her nose, Oma drew a breath. "Onkel Martin's responsible?"

"With Curt's assistance." Clara nodded. "They surprised us at the Erntedank festival by having everything ready. We needed only to say, 'I do.'"

Oma's arms crossed over her bosom. She frowned at the couple.

"You don't share our excitement, Oma?"

The older woman took another deep breath and rubbed her fingers between her springy white curls. "Your decision creates grave difficulties ahead for the two of you."

"But you'll not speak a word to anyone. Promise."

"I'll keep your secret. But, Clara." Oma looked her granddaughter in the eye. "Choices carry consequences."

IN THE GARDEN, Gut Apfelhof Estate, Thursday morning, 24 November 1881

CLARA LAID one hand on Brigette, the salt-and-pepper Schnauzer, who nuzzled close. With the other, she held her tummy. Clara pulled a warm blanket around herself and leaned back on her favorite garden bench. "No one else out here to have a conversation with. You're going to hear it all today, my furry friend."

"A lemon drop for your thoughts." Her twin called to her.

Clara gagged.

"Oh my – your green face. He helped her lean forward and lose her breakfast on the ground rather than the blanket or the dog.

"Help me back to my room. Please."

They plodded their way to the house, Clara leaning on him.

I'm leaving you here in the kitchen. Dora keeps ginger root. Chewing some always helped our upset tummies."

Dora studied Clara up and down. "I saw you two coming." She shook her head at Clara. "I will handle this from here, Curt." The Reinhold's cook handed Clara a bit of the herb. "You have eaten the same things we have. Bad food hasn't made you ill. How many days have you felt poorly?"

"About three weeks now. Today is the worst."

"Have you been up to something? I notice your absence from the big house on Thursday afternoons."

"You keep track of my activities?"

"I notice things, Fraulein."

"Then you know I've disappeared on Thursdays for several weeks. Why so much concern today?"

"By your admission, you've been ill for three weeks." Dora peered down her nose at Clara. "Those many Thursdays ago concern me most, Fraulein. It would be best if you disappear to your room. If my instincts are correct, you'll be spending extra time there, especially in the mornings. Mamsell mentioned your peaked appearance as you headed out to Bible class yesterday, the same as she'd observed for several mornings prior. Your malady promises to be with you for a while — weeks even months."

"What a scary thought. I confess I threw up on my way to Bible class yesterday too. Nausea has swathed me like a steamy rag every morning for many days. Why would nausea and an upset stomach last so long? You are teasing, right?"

"I'm merely a servant who knows you well and cares about you even more."

Clara reached for Dora's hand. "I know caring for us is duty for staff, but danke for your kindness."

"Bitte." Dora lifted her eyebrows and laughed. "Here. Take extra ginger with you. I asked Alice to keep the water pitcher in your room filled. A cool rag to the back of your neck will stem the nausea."

"You are going to much trouble. After a nice rest, I'll be good as new." Another wave washed over Clara. "Am I dying?"

Dora's tummy jiggled to the rhythm of her laughter. "Nein. Most women do not. But you went from being fine to dying in a hurry."

More porridge sloshed over her tongue and soiled her clean dress. Dora's meaning dawned clearer than a bright blue sky. But the sky wasn't bright at all. Dry heaves assaulted her like a terror in the night. Consequences.

"Take the back stairs. They'll be the quickest. There is one thing you could do to make it all go away. I don't recommend it, but if you'd like we'll discuss it later."

Clara trudged up the stairs to her room colliding with her personal maid as she reached the landing. Alice held out a pan just in time to collect her mistress' next soggy heave. She pointed to the bedroom door, and Clara turned the doorknob letting them in.

"Would you like to sit down by the window, Fraulein? We'll open it and let the autumn breeze cool you."

She responded with a barely audible "Ja. You know?"

"I handle your laundry, and I've suspected for the last couple of weeks."

"Maybe it's not true? I would need to be married for it to be true." Clara silently reprimanded herself for the lie, but no one could ever know — at least not until she and Daniel were on their way to America.

"Clara." Alice groaned. "Best to be married, ja. And maybe you're not in a family way, but probably you are. Ja? Usually, a woman requires a few weeks more than you have taken opportunities before she knows for sure, but your sickness and one other thing—you've placed no women's needs among your soiled items for weeks. It is true, Clara, whether you're married or not."

Clara covered her head with both hands and wept. "Who else knows?"

"Dora and I have spoken only to each other on the subject of your secretive whereabouts on Thursday afternoons. Family and the rest of the staff may also be observant." With a sly grin on her face, Alice added, "But no one else is privilege to your intimates."

"Thank heavens! Dora mentioned something to make it all go away?"

"But *it* is a baby, Clara."

"Maybe not. I haven't felt anything moving inside me."

"Many think there's no baby until the woman feels the quickening. I believe differently, and so do you. If you make the choice you heap up a bigger helping of shame and guilt on yourself."

"But I must hide this from Mutti and Vati."

"Or if you become more ill from ingesting the tea, what then?"

"Guilty accusations scream in my head. There's no easy remedy to the punishment I have brought on myself."

"Pardon my forwardness, but punishment? Or natural expectations?"

"You'll help me keep it quiet from anyone else?"

"I'm quite impetuous, you know, but I'm obliged to keep my lady's business a private matter." Alice slipped a hand in her pocket and twisted the fabric around her finger. "I predict you have a few weeks, at best, before it becomes obvious. People suspect now."

"Danke, Alice."

"Get your rest. Your Vati, the great Baron of Gut Apfelhof, will expect you at dinner. The evening promises to be a fun one with your family. Mamsell has Fritz setting up the game table in the parlor now."

"I do love when the family plays games together. I better rest or I'll be yawning through the evening."

"I'll be back to help you dress."

Clara curled in a ball atop her lavender Federbetten and picked at its embroidered daisies and roses. *O Lord, why did you allow Oma to find us? Even though You know we're married, we face the consequences of our secret and our intimacy. Why does such intoxicating pleasure bring such difficult trials and result in such sobering illness?*

Chapter Two

THE OLD ABANDONED COTTAGE, *Gut Apfelhof,*
Thursday afternoon, 24 November 1881

CLARA TOOK the long way around. The now barren branches
of the orchard trees shook their long fingers at her. Grateful
her morning sickness eased after lunch, she ignored their
warning, lifted her skirts and petticoats, and ran as quickly as
her feet would carry her. She prayed they wouldn't be caught
again, then flew through the open door of the cottage and
into her husband's waiting arms. Her very favorite place for
her heart to rest.

"How long can we meet like this?" Her chin quivered and her
eyes stung. "Oma knows we're married. She promised not to
tell, but…"

"Oma's knowledge didn't stop us last week, my Lovely
Lady."

"Because she was off visiting her own love interest. Vater and Curt accompanied her. There was no one here to catch us."

"She gave us a serious lecture. You trust Oma with our secret?"

"I trust Oma, but her promise not to tell Vati depends on our trusting God, and doing what is right. And secrets find us."

"And what is right, my Lovely Lady? We are married."

"Loving someone can't be so wrong, but God commands us to obey our parents. We ignored another law in His book when we said, *I do*. Life hurts too much like this. Guilt torments me, yet I prayed all the way here for God to happily allow us to do exactly what goes against His word."

Daniel pulled a ribbon freeing her curls to float down her back. "Forget all your worries for now."

"We've worked so hard to make this place cozy again. Alice had no idea she laundered fabric pieces for pretty curtains." Clara squeezed her hands together and drew in a tense breath. "She freshened the bedding too, believing it for a neighbor in need."

"You arranged it all handsomely. And, thankfully, the pigeons are gone! But what about you and me?"

"I'm scared, Daniel. I'm grateful Vati's agreement with Georg is history and his pigeons with him, but I'm petrified for what comes next. How quickly can we leave for America?"

Daniel's arms comforted her well. "I live for Thursday after-noons, and for you. Eight weeks we've embraced wedded intimacy. I don't want us to end—ever." He let go only to lead her into the waltz position they loved. While humming quietly in her ear he eased them into smooth twirls. Dizziness landed them atop the pretty peach and green quilt. One kiss had them wiggling from their encumbering garments, and all those same wonderful tingles and sizzles from last Thursday and the Thursdays before enraptured her whole being once again. The quivering in her heart rejoiced her spirit and sent all pricks of conscience to the abyss.

Pure joy flowed between them before reality pierced her thoughts once again. "What if Vati finds out, what then? And he expects me at dinner."

Daniel caressed her cheeks, groaned, and kissed her again. Long. Gentle. Lingering. He moved her face out from his. "I love the sparkle I see in your eyes. Our time together is worth the risk, ja?"

She blushed. "Ja."

A knock sounded at the door.

THEY JUMPED up and hurriedly dressed.

"It's me. Oma. May I enter?"

"Just a moment." Clara smoothed her hair. "Come in."

Clara kept her face hidden from Oma's to avoid the pain she already knew filled her grandmother's eyes. "Go ahead. Say it, Oma. You're right to tell my parents."

"And what will I tell them?"

"Daniel and I disrespect them with our actions, despite our marriage. So, my heart is full of sin and wickedness and void of all holiness."

"Loving someone is far from sinful or wicked."

"Then what else are you thinking?"

Daniel shuffled in place. "It's my fault, Frau Reinhold. I encouraged her devotion, and eagerly agreed to Onkel Martin's offer to officiate."

"You haven't coerced my granddaughter against her will—not into marriage and not into the trysts you two share." Oma shook her head.

"It won't happen again until Clara and I leave for America. I give you my word." Daniel cleared his throat.

"Your word has always been good, but do you realize how difficult your promise will be to keep? You're the best carriage driver Gut Apfelhof has known. Quite a disappointment to me if my son must let you go."

Clara followed Oma away from the cottage and from her dear husband.

"My heart, too, once belonged to one I couldn't have. Then I met your Opa. I never forgot my first love, but I would not have traded my Otto for any other. I see true love for Daniel in your eyes. I see his for you. I feel your pain as if it were my own heart breaking once again. But no more warnings. You asked me to keep a secret, but your behavior makes it a challenge to continue hiding it. Others will realize what you're doing. Come to my cottage with me. Splash cool water on your face and use a comb on those unruly curls. Smooth your garments before you return home."

Clara sniffed loudly. Her hanky was drenched. She straightened up as best she could. Her voice raspy, she answered, "Ja, good idea."

With Clara's appearance improved, Oma rubbed her palms

on Clara's shoulders. She peered into the girl's eyes. "Imagine a new dream. Pray about it, meine Kind. Watch God work."

"Danke! I'll imagine Daniel and me on our way to America. My prayer—God works quickly."

She waved to Oma and scurried back home. Hoping to avoid family, she snuck in the back entrance and quietly took the servants' stairs. Her bedroom door stood open, and rustling could be heard coming from the room. Her legs went stiff and her hands trembled. With her back against the wall, she inched closer for a peek. Who would be in there?

"Fraulein." Alice whisked a gown from its hook on the wardrobe door and placed it on the bed. "We must get you ready for dinner and family games. Have you rested today?"

Clara inhaled, and a smile spread across her face. "Ahh. Dora's preparing Wiener Schnitzel for dinner."

"You're avoiding the question. Will you be falling asleep at the table this evening and missing Dora's delicious cooking?" Alice clamped her teeth over her lower lip.

"I'm refreshed." Clara stifled a yawn and gazed across the room at the brass clock beside her bed. "Is it that late already? I'm so sorry. Danke for having my gown ready."

Alice worked quickly readying her for the evening, then shooed her out the door.

Emmaline and Hannah greeted her in the hall.

"Where have you been? We waited for you and now we're all late." Emmaline frowned.

"Tsk. Tsk." Hannah wagged a finger in Clara's direction, then tugged on her sister's sleeve. "Let's go."

The three hurried to the dining room and seated themselves just before Vati joined them at the table.

"We're all here. Let's thank God for the food and the cooks. And I can't wait to beat you all at Das Königliche Gänsespiel after dinner." Vati folded his hands. "Komm Herr Jesus, be our guest, and bless what You bestowed on us."

Everyone joined in the "Amen."

"This all smells so good, I can't wait to taste it. Lass uns essen." Vati motioned for their staff to serve the food so they could eat.

Henry and Dora filled the family's plates with the Wiener Schnitzel and German Spätzle.

Vati wiped a crumb from his mouth. "It's so quiet around the table.

"I'm enjoying my meal. These bread dumplings are the best accompaniment with the veal cutlets." Clara devoured all that was on her plate. "May I have seconds, please?"

Family members nodded their agreement. Dora and Henry refilled several plates.

Hannah, seated next to her, poked an elbow in Clara's side. "They are delicious, but you won't be able to fasten your gowns if you eat too many."

Clara laughed. "Rosa will need to fix them then."

"Vati, is it true the scarecrows in our orchards won an award?" Wilhelm asked.

"Where did you hear that, Sohn?" Vati grinned.

"Hans told me when I helped him shine the carriage."

"Well, the scarecrows are outstanding in their field."

"I thought they were in the orchards." Wilhelm's eyebrows squished together."

"Hans was pulling your leg. It's a play on words. Ask Lehrer Frederick to explain those to you during your lessons tomorrow. For now, who's ready to play The Royal Game of Goose?"

"Clara, I'm going to beat you." Wilhelm ran to the parlor and arrived at the game table first.

The rest of the family joined him.

"When you land on my goose's square and knock me off, I'm going to go take a nap." Clara placed her goose at the start and added four of her dozen counters to the center of the board. The others joined in doing the same.

Wilhelm crossed his arms over his chest. "That won't be much fun, Clara. We all have to play."

Mutti tousled the lad's hair. "She's teasing you. We'll all play and all have a great time."

As he had predicted, Vati won the first game. Clara held a small lead on her younger brother, and she was close to the finish line in the second one. Wilhelm rolled the dice again—a double six—and moved his goose to join Clara's."

"Oh-oh." Curt laughed. "Looks like you're headed back a long way. And you both get to place two more counters in the center. I'm going to win the jackpot."

"Then I'm thankful we're not a betting family." Clara added her counters to the pile.

"My bets are Dora has warm pretzels for us when we finish the game." Mutti reached for Vati's hand. "I did see you bring some of those from the Backhaus earlier?"

"Ja. The Frankens insisted I take them knowing how much all of you enjoy the treat."

"With hot Apfelwein. Mmm mmm." Clara rubbed her tummy.

Henry brought in the small plates with the pretzels. Dora poured each of them a cup of the cider.

Lifting hers to drink, the aroma sent a wave of nausea over Clara. Her eyes widened. She gulped back the bile. *This isn't happening in front of my family. No.*

FRIDAY, 25 November 1881

"GUTEN MORGEN, FRAULEIN." Alice's melodious greeting sounded a bit too cheery.

"I hope it turns good. It's beginning as awful as yesterday."

"And yesterday didn't end well either."

"I'm so sorry you had to clean the mess up last night and now again this morning."

"Let me rinse this pan before we dress you. I'll get fresh water, too."

The maid returned to Clara's room a few minutes too late. Alice rolled up the soiled coverlet. "Don't you worry. I'll launder it and hang it by the basement fireplace to dry. No one will see it there."

Clara moved to the rose-velvet chair by her dressing table, and took a tiny piece of ginger, hoping Alice could shape her appearance into one worthy of her role at Gut Apfelhof. She prayed she wouldn't mess it up with another spewing disaster. The ginger had always warded off an upset tummy when she was a child, but the herb had proved to be of little help now.

"This dress isn't so fitted — cinched only by the sash. We might tie the bow a little looser. The neckline rests lower, too — a couple of inches above your bosom."

"Perfect, but no corset, please!"

A perusal in the looking glass before her assured Clara, like Cinderella's fairy godmother, Alice had woven a magical spell. Except for the dark circles of weariness under her eyes and the continuous churning and nausea, Clara believed she almost resembled herself again.

A light brushing tap at the door — Rosa's signature knock. Gentle blue eyes peered at Clara through the barely opened door and assured her of Rosa's tenderness and love. What will she think when she knows? *What do I even think? Too late to think. It's done. Maybe not.* Alice said it might not be true.

"Guten Morgen, Fraulein Clara."

Clara smiled. Her first in a few days. "And to you as well."

"Have Hannah and Emmaline modeled their new gowns for you yet?"

"Nein, but they asked to see me yesterday."

"You turned them away?"

"I was resting and reading."

"But you were here. Emmaline was correct. You're gone every Thursday afternoon — over two months now. No wonder she groaned with disappointment."

"How does everyone know?"

"We're not blind, Clara. And Proverbs 10:9."

Clara grimaced. "Share the wisdom verse with me. I am certain I need to hear it again."

"He that walketh uprightly walketh surely: but he that perverteth his ways shall be known." Rosa's voice was barely a whisper.

The words would settle in her mind and work in Clara's heart in God's perfect time. Clara grabbed a wet cloth to hide her reddening cheeks.

"Shall we start on your Christmas gown? We have the beautiful turquoise and ivory striped silk from Paris or the rich and flowing purple velvet. Or do you have a different preference?"

"Remember the verse you shared on the train to Paris a couple of months ago. Another Proverbs verse when we talked about new styles designed to avoid these painfully tight undergarments."

"Of course! *Clothed with strength and dignity — a woman can laugh at the days to come."*

"I fancied the styles with a bent to the aesthetic look — looser and free flowing. Please create one from whichever fabric you believe best."

"The rich purple fabric will lay gently over your curves and accentuate your hair and eyes. I'll take your measurements and get started."

"The fabric and style are settled then, but new measurements are unnecessary. Use those you took for my last gown."

Rosa tapped her fingers to her temples. "This seamstress' peepers see things others might miss. I noted the taut strain on the bodice fabric of your dresses. A recent development. Ja, new measurements are necessary."

"Are my dresses able to be let out in the bodice? I would welcome the looser feel. The look is up-and-coming, and I do enjoy seconds at dinner."

Rosa crossed her arms, took two steps back, planted her feet and stared at Clara. "The aesthetic look? Welcoming the looser feel? Refusing to allow measurements? This isn't about the latest fashion or eating extra Spätzle. May I have your permission to ask questions?"

Clara averted her gaze while she fought down the next surge of nausea, but she nodded her agreement.

"You dry heave even as we speak. Your quilt's missing, and a most pungent smell assaulted me when I entered your room. You inquired if I might alter your gowns. Is there something I, as your seamstress, should know?"

"This was not meant to happen. It may not be true." Clara sank on her bed.

"Did Georg do this to you?"

"Do what?"

Rosa pressed steepled fingers to her lips. "Please look at me, Clara. You're in dire need of my help if I'm correct?"

"Oh Rosa, I tell you all my secrets. Georg's a most despicable man who acted very untowardly with me, but as much as I'm certain he would have desired it, he never had a man's way with me. I would've told you."

"Danke. His usual behavior and the signs you show worried me. I fear to ask further, still I must. My son disappears every Thursday afternoon during his free time. You've been missing the same time. Is it a child of love?"

"It's not a child unless I feel it move. I haven't."

"And you won't for a while yet."

"Maybe it isn't true?"

"Clara, precious Fraulein, your breasts are swollen, you're ill every morning, and when was your last time of women?"

"I haven't counted, and it's difficult to be honest with myself about it." Clara shrugged. "Alice reminded me it was before Erntedank — middle of September, soon after we returned from Paris."

"Gracious." Rosa fished in her pocket. "I brought a calendar with me. She poked a needle down the rows and counted. "Eleven, twelve weeks your time hasn't come?"

"It still might."

Rosa pushed her spectacles down her nose and shot a piercing glare at Clara right over the top of them. "When was the first time?"

Clara smiled brightly between her sobs. "October sixth. I'll never forget — my forever dream come true."

Some women discover their condition much later than you have — the ones fortunate enough to avoid the unpleasantness of the morning sickness. It's easy for them to deny the change in their bodies. You celebrate the date, and you've been so sick."

"This can't be happening! I understand now why some women end it. Maybe I should do what it takes to bring my time back."

"Regardless of your marital status, God knows all the days he has for your little one since he knit her together — when He cast on the first two stitches of her life. She was conceived in love, even if not in matrimony."

"We promised each other to keep it a secret, but has Daniel shared with you that he and I are married? Maybe not so perverted as you say." A strange combination of guilt and fear swallowed her joy.

Rosa's eyes widened. She clapped a hand over the squeal—or was it a scream— about to escape. She hugged Clara tight. "This baby is my grandchild!"

"If I'm truly with child, then ja, tis true."

"Oh, what a conundrum. No one else knows?"

"Oma knows we're married."

Rosa sat beside Clara on the bed and rubbed her brow. "I won't tell, but Proverbs 10:9. It still applies.

"You referred to Psalm 139 again. We studied the Psalm a few months ago in our Bible class. Is God punishing me? I deserve it if He is. Daniel and I sinned against God when we ignored my parents and you about the rules."

There was no way the pan Alice carried back into Clara's room would be large enough for all her tears and the next course of nausea. Rosa grabbed the vessel anyway. "Just leave this with me, Alice. I'll take care of Clara this morning."

"Danke, Rosa. Mamsell Lottie asked for my help. I'll be on my way." Alice exited the room, and her footsteps could be heard scurrying down the hall.

Steady again, with a cold cloth pressed to the back of her head, Clara said, "I disappointed Oma. She found us and knows our secret now. She even guessed Onkel Martin performed the ceremony. She promised not to tell but warned of consequences of our deceit.

"Daniel accepted the blame. He tried convincing her that he pressured me into the ceremony. But Oma knew my eager desires. She knows the depth of our love for each other. He failed to convince her that he alone was at fault. She encouraged us to stop. Keeping secrets means you must avoid possible consequences.

"Secret-keeping is hard, and knowing we're married at least in the eyes of the state, every minute of those afternoons filled me with ecstasy I never imagined existed. Why is there no way for us in the eyes of the church? I love Daniel with all my heart."

"As he does you. You carry my granddaughter."

"You make it sound like a fairytale. Mutti and Vati will see it as the greatest tragedy ever. And why do you say it's a girl as if you can peek through my belly?"

"Pray, pray, and pray again. We will watch and see what God will do. He's in the business of giving impossibilities beautiful endings."

"What if Mutti asks me to drink the pennyroyal tea — so Vati never needs to know? Oh, I don't want Mutti to know until

Daniel and I have the funds to leave for America, but I can't hide this for long, can I? And the tea killed Sarah. As if I am not nauseous enough, my thoughts bombard me aimlessly from a hundred directions at once. Rosa, you always know what to do. Help me."

"Does this mean you acknowledge you are indeed with child?"

"My wishfulness has served me poorly. You, Dora, and Alice have all forced me to note the changes and admit the truth."

"Who already knows?"

"You, Dora, and Alice for sure. Mamsell most likely. Oma will not be surprised at all—the consequence she warned of. Quite a lot of people to keep a secret. As soon as Mamsell is sure, she'll tell Mutti, but only you and Oma know this baby was conceived in a legal marriage."

"Would your Mutti welcome your honesty before she's informed by a servant?"

"Pray for extra courage for me. I must tell her, but the words will be between her and me alone. If possible, this conversation will be more difficult than the one about Georg, and you'll not be at my side."

"I'll pray while I make the alterations. And, Clara, Psalm One-O-Three." Rosa rubbed Clara's back before scooping up several gowns and slipping from the room.

BEFORE RETIRING FOR THE EVENING, Clara lifted her Bible from the bedside table. She trailed her finger in curlicues through the dust settled on its cover. The servants ignored this while cleaning or had intentionally left her a message. *Lord, I have not touched this book since before Erntedank when Daniel and I married against all the rules. When Curt and Onkel Martin suggested the secret ceremony, we didn't object. We showed no respect for our parents or the church. I am ashamed but not enough to regret it.*

When You look on me—I imagine Your pity. Instead of studying Your word, the Wednesday morning Bible class has become a sewing circle making reticules for Megs' shop. I've had no need to open this book to direct the task. You trust me to lead these ladies in studying the Bible. I can't think of one reason You would place this grand responsibility in my hands.

You know I don't regret marrying Daniel, I only regret becoming with child so soon. We could have hidden our marriage until we left for America if this hadn't happened. No one would've known our secret. I would've adored carrying Daniel's baby then. You do everything in Your time, but as much as I love children the timing of Your blessing could have been more convenient, Lord. I hear Your voice now. 'Clara, you and Daniel could've waited on my plan. You're both My children, and I work all things for good for those who love me and keep my commandments.'

I haven't kept them well. I'm ashamed to open Your book now. I understand why Tilly believed You hated her—believed she couldn't be forgiven, even though it was despicable Georg's fault. She didn't deserve the horror she faced. I feel punished, but I deserve all You've allowed! What a wretched sinner I am. Send me away. Vati will when He learns."

"Clara, I'm waiting for you." The still small voice.

Gently turning the pages expecting them to crack from her slightest touch, she heard the voice again. *"Psalm One-O-Three".* Exactly like Rosa said.

Clara found the chapter and read slowly until her eyes rested on verse ten. She took in verses eleven and twelve, as well. She needed to soak up every little bit of God's words to her. They were for her, right?

H E HATH NOT DEALT *with us after our sins; nor rewarded us according to our iniquities. For as the heaven is high above the earth, so great is his mercy toward them that fear him. As far as the east is from the west, so far hath he removed our transgressions from us.*

H ER DEEP GROANS stirred the persistent nausea. Twitching lips hindered her words—ones she preferred to not admit. *Removed from me? I carry the growing evidence. Soon everyone will know. My family will bear the shame. Please let Your mercy fall on me, but how dare I even ask when I'm only sorry we've been caught?*

In truth, I desire to share this pleasure again and again with the man I love—the one I am legally married to despite the rules for my noble family. Maybe it isn't true about the baby. Oh Jesus, but I know it is. Daniel's baby. Our baby. We'd love her so. But take our child if you believe it's best. I place her in Your hands.

Rather than another queasy mess, peace washed over Clara. She laid the Bible to her side, and fell into a deep restful sleep.

S ATURDAY, *26 November 1881*

"A LICE, how many more days like this?"

"You'll know when it stops."

"I wish I could laugh."

Alice pirouetted across the room. "At least smile. Daniel has returned!"

"Has he asked about me?"

"He waved to me from the drive when I stuck my head out the door this morning. He readies the carriage as we speak. I overheard Mamsell talking to him. Your parents are attending a state affair tonight and will return tomorrow afternoon. Maybe you could greet him from your window before they pull away."

"Your suggestion tempts me, but I fear him witnessing my messiness. He's another I need to tell."

"Do you believe he'd welcome the news he'll be a Vater soon?"

"What future does his child have? It would be better for Daniel if he connected with any common girl instead of the daughter of the Baron. Tilly has always secretly admired him."

"But he loves you."

"I'm glad he is taking my parents away for the weekend. I'll attend church without Vati's eyes on me, and their absence provides additional time for me to gather enough courage to tell Mutti."

"Very well. Rosa sent one of your gowns back. Shall we try it today?" Alice offered her a simple loose petticoat, then lifted the gown over Clara's curls, bouncing extra wild this morning. A few ribbons tucked them in place.

"Rosa added panels in the sides and lifted the waistline. It falls softly over my mid-section. She did this all since yesterday?"

"Ja. Rosa's skills with a needle and thread amaze me over and over again. She is very efficient about it, but…"

"But what?"

Alice shrugged. "Just my imagination running wild. We'll talk about it another time."

"Whatever it is, I trust Rosa punctuated every stitch with prayer while she implemented serious modifications. People might notice my clothing style has changed."

"You asked for the more aesthetic look. She delivered. Your blooming body is grateful, ja?"

"My blooming body is grateful, but currently I'm not at all grateful for its blooming."

"Attempting to stop the condition now, would bring on a greater sadness. Every child is special."

"Some people say there isn't a child until the woman feels it move. Besides, I told God, He could take it back. He knows what's best."

"Clara, how could an *it* without life do so much rearranging of your body?"

"Your words are logical, I admit. But it's all so hard. Why did I choose pleasure over waiting on God's plan? My choice is causing my whole life to be reshaped? Do you think I learned a lesson? Truth be told, I would make the same choice again a thousand times over."

"I'm sorry you find yourself trapped between your love for Daniel and the few choices open to a woman walking in your shoes—especially one born to nobility. Could you have gone to another city or country where no one knows you, and married?"

Clara's cheeks grew warm. She turned her face from Alice to keep it from betraying the growing bundle of lies. If others had known of their marriage perhaps this would have been easier. She would attend church tomorrow. Monday Clara would face whatever consequences announcing their news to her Mutti would bring. She deserved to know.

But when Sunday morning arrived, Clara's best efforts to rise and dress for church fell short. Heaves rose and sank in rhythm with her failed attempts to sit upright. Monday proved worse. Dora had said she'd be spending a lot of time in her room. The words proved true.

Chapter Three

ST. *LUKE'S KIRCHE, Sunday morning, 11 December 1881*

THE THREE SISTERS donned warm wraps and took a leisurely stroll to St. Luke's Kirche. For Clara, the crispness in the air kept her malady at bay, but not before she had created more laundry for Alice earlier this morning.

Three candles were lit on the wreath this third Sunday of the Advent season. The pink one was added to the two purples today. Pink—a color of rejoicing with the shepherds for the joy announced to them. Joy about a Baby born to save mankind from their sin.

The girls chose seats at the back of the sanctuary. Clara studied the hem of her dress. Bending over the rigid corset stays poked at her midriff, and her thoughts pierced her heart. The Mutter of her Savior had been an unmarried woman. Except for a few everyone believed she was, too. Her condition no comparison, but Clara related to Mary's difficulty. How had Mary told her Mutter? Clara hadn't told

Mutti like she'd promised herself she would two weeks ago. Had Mary's Mutter believed her? Clara's condition hadn't been the result of an immaculate conception like Mary's. She knew everything she and Daniel had done, but she had failed to find remorse for their secret marriage and for shrouding their life as a married couple. The fact should have been a warning sign. Had it been fair to hope for God's forgiveness? Today Clara would sit at the piano and make the ivories sing joyful praise to Him. Tomorrow she would tell Mutti.

MONDAY MORNING, *12 December 1881*

"MY SICKNESS HASN'T LEFT."

The corners of Alice's lips twitched downward. "I'm headed to the laundry with the evidence now. I pray the symptoms leave you soon, and you'll find joy in new life."

"Ask my Mutti to come to my room, please." Clara almost choked on the words.

"On my way, Fraulein. Any message you wish me to deliver?"

"Nein." *Father God, I must do this alone. I trust You're with me. I need Your guidance and Your grace.*

"What's wrong, Clara?" Mutti rushed to her daughter's side.

Sitting together on the bed, Clara held onto Mutti as if her life depended on it. It did. "I fear to tell you what I'm afraid you already know."

"Except for family dinners, you've kept yourself apart from the rest of us for weeks. My imagination has created many possibilities. My worst fear, Georg did you more wrong than we knew."

"I assure you, Mutti, if Georg having a man's way with me is your worst fear, you've nothing to worry about. But you may find the truth more disturbing. As distasteful as it would have been, I could've married the noble Georg Wolff with everyone's blessings."

Mutti stared quietly toward the window. Clara watched her eyes widen in full realization of what her daughter's riddled answers conveyed. "Are you sure?"

"The signs are present. Do I need to list them for you?"

Mutti studied her daughter up and down. "You're wearing a new gown?"

"Mutti, please, this is difficult enough. Rosa altered the dress to allow for changes. The bodice squeezed me tighter than a corset. And lacing a corset as tight as Frau Wolff on our Paris trip is an action far from possible now even if I wanted to."

Mutti patted her daughter's springy ringlets and her slightly rounded tummy. "Perhaps you've eaten too much kuchen, ja?"

"If only Kuchen was to blame. Besides my expanding bosom and thickening waist, I've been sick to my stomach for a couple of hours every morning for over two weeks now. Nausea already consumed me for a couple of weeks prior. Ask Dora and Alice for details, if you like. My last time of women visited in September—three months ago. Do you require more evidence?"

"If it's not Georg's, then whose? Your Vati will take care of him."

Clara mumbled and heaved again. "Please don't tell Vati. I wish no harm on Daniel."

"Our carriage driver did this to you? For all the warnings…" Mutti shook the closest bedpost. "Why? How could you disrespect your Vati?"

Her voice quivered. "No one did this to me, Mutti. I love him. He loves me. I knew at twelve years old he was the only one I'd ever choose for my husband. At Curt's and my sixteenth birthday party, Daniel and I promised each other we would find a way to be husband and wife despite the rules."

"Friendship, ja. Even with our servants, friendship poses no threat. Marriage. Forbidden. And you and Daniel chose to make it worse playing like you had walked a flower-strewn path to the altar."

"Erntedank. Behind a tree rather than along a flower-strewn path, Mutti, but Onkel Martin married us in the eyes of the state. Curt witnessed our vows." Unintentional giggles escaped her mouth followed by a deafening silence. Clara awaited Mutti's response.

"I see the trouble this brings and find little tolerance for your feelings or your sinful choice to disrespect your Vati."

"We did go against his wishes." Clara twisted the stray curl and rolled her lips between her teeth.

"And against the rules, Clara. If this becomes known your Vati will lose his title. Lose Gut Apfelhof. Lose everything."

Brigitte bounded into the room landing in Clara's lap. She rubbed her behind the ears. The frisky schnauzer was exactly what Clara needed to boost her courage to say the rest. "Man's rules. God declared every person equal in His eyes. And why does Vati ignore this verse? *Fathers, provoke not your children to anger, lest they be discouraged.* We waited long enough for the impossible."

Clara's heart shuddered while she watched Mutti worry her crooked fingers. A sigh erupted from where Clara could only imagine was the deepest place in Lydia Reinhold's soul.

"Rosa predicts a girl. Your granddaughter."

"I'll ask Dora to send up the pennyroyal tea. Drink it each evening. Your time will return soon. You've not felt it move yet, have you? There is no life until you do."

"I thought of all these things, Mutti. I considered the tea. I cannot. I recently read and taught Psalm 139 to the women's class. I helped one of them through the aftermath of exactly what you suggested. I experienced Tilly's grief and pain alongside her. Every morning I believe the sickness is a passing thing, and I will be well the next morning, but every morning it remains. My body changes daily. I know Sarah died because Georg forced the tea on her. I wish to live, and I pray the same for my baby—mine and Daniel's baby."

Silence blanketed the room and hung over the bed for endless minutes. Mutti walked to the window. She ran her fingers down the edge of the drapes brushing stray threads away. Clara's body groaned with more of the morning sickness.

Mutti pivoted, grabbed a towel from the washstand, and handed it to her daughter. "Send a letter to Tante Adeline. Ask if you may be their guest for an extended holiday."

"I expect Vati to send me away when he finds out, but not

you. When do I have to leave?" *Maybe Daniel and I have time to make our getaway?*

"As soon as possible. Write the letter today. Don't expect me to lie to your Vati, but I won't tell unless he asks."

"What if she says no?"

"Your persuasiveness with Tante Adeline is no secret—you're her favorite niece. The arrangement buys you some time. Protects Daniel for now." She kissed her daughter's cheek and exited the room.

Chapter Four

CLARA'S ROOM, *Monday, 19 December 1881*

CLARA ACCEPTED the wire from Alice.

"I hope it's good news." Alice lifted a basket of soiled items and exited the room.

Fingers twitching Clara unfolded the telegram.

DEAR CLARA,

Onkel Martin and I are delighted to have you as our guest for as long as you like. Your situation did not surprise us. You married. Then come babies. You are always welcome in our home, as is Daniel.

We will visit Gut Apfelhof at Christmas. Plan to travel back with us.

Love always,

Tante Adeline.

Clara refolded the paper and fanned at another rising stream of nausea. *Over a month now.*

Will this ever end? Christmas is Sunday. So soon. Will I ever be able to come home? I must tell Daniel my dilemma. Vati keeps him busy and unavailable. If he doesn't know, how will we make a plan of our own? Will Rosa deliver a letter to her son? She rushed for paper and pen and prayed for patience to make her message and her writing clear. Stepping from her room, into the hallway Clara bumped into Rosa. "You're the person I'm looking for!"

"Are you ready for your dress fitting?"

"I'd prefer the privacy of my room rather than in the sewing room, please."

Rosa had fumbled with and dropped the gowns earlier. Clara prayed she would be steadier today. But Rosa hobbled off to retrieve them. Several minutes elapsed before she entered Clara's room. The fabric confection flowed from Rosa's outstretched arms, a basket dangling from her arm with the necessary tools to pinch, nip, tuck, and otherwise mark the dress for the required compensations. *She's not customarily so short on breath, and I'll be adding more for her to worry about.*

"I'm leaving with Tante Adeline and Onkel Martin after Christmas. With Christmas only a week away, how many more gowns can you alter by then?"

"How long will you be gone?"

"Long enough to feel the baby move at least. No matter what Vati asks it will be too late to drink the tea as Mutti suggested. My refusal spurred the only other option. An extended visit with Tante Adeline, if she and Onkel Martin would allow it."

"Have you told Daniel?"

Clara shook her head. "Nein, but I wrote a letter requesting to see him. Will you deliver it for me?"

Rosa accepted, sliding the note into the basket among her sewing things. "What would you like to do, Clara?"

"As difficult as my situation has become, what I want means having Daniel's baby, and I want her with Daniel. Sweet little babies follow a wedding."

Rosa pressed a hand to her heart. Tears flowed. "Exactly what I'd like, too, but no solution occurs to me. I continue to pray for the best for you, my son, and my granddaughter."

"You'll be astounded if she is a he instead."

"I'll love the child the same."

"You brought my Christmas gown. May I try it on?"

Rosa carefully gathered the full panels over Clara's head. Her arms slid into the wispy sleeves. The dress glided down to cover all her curves including the newest one emerging at her waist.

"I love the wide curving neckline." She brushed her hands down the soft fabric folds in front, experiencing the freedom from binding dresses and intimates in a refreshing new way. "These aesthetic designs are a gift to any woman. I'm especially grateful. The gown fits to perfection."

Rosa bit down on her lip. "Oh my, but your bodice is already full. I'm grateful I allowed ample seams. I'll be sure to consider your future needs before adding my finishing touches."

"Will the style arouse Vati's suspicions?"

"Your dinner dresses are altered to a similar look. If he asks, educate him on the new styles for women."

"I make a point every evening to be seated before he arrives at dinner, and to leave quickly."

"If you see Hannah and Emmaline after their lessons, ask them to come find me. I'm eager to see their gowns." Clara smiled. "And bring me Daniel's reply."

FAMILIAR KNOCKS TAPPED at her door. "Come in." Clara grieved the little time spent with her sisters the past few weeks. Before she became ill, they read together, played duets and trios on the piano, and stitched beautiful gifts for their Mutti and Oma. *I danced atop a beautiful world. How quickly it spun upside down with repugnant grievances from my own body.*

They twirled around the room. Crescents of lace trailed down the sleeves of Emmaline's rich red gown. Additional flounces of the lace created a cape-like frill around her shoulders and neck. The colors and style accentuated Emma's dark coffee eyes and caramel curls.

"Hannah. Emmaline. You're modeling your Christmas gowns!"

Sandy-haired Hannah chose emerald green. The bodice fabric crisscrossed just below her womanly flesh. The skirt flowed long and free. Clara laughed hard, and happy tears trickled from her eyes. "We all opted for the highly stylish aesthetic look for our new gowns!"

"Put yours on, Clara." Emmaline bounced across the room.

"Turn your backs and no peaking. I'm unaccustomed to doing this by myself, but for you, I'll try. Cover your eyes. You should be as surprised with my gown as I was with yours. She would need to be as efficient as a quick-change stage artist to avoid their prying eyes. She moved slowly in front of them. "Now!"

"Clara, it's beautiful! Rosa's new creations will attract all eyes to us on Christmas Eve."

"Danke, Hannah, but what's the concern I'm seeing in your eyes."

"Vati always comments on our new dresses. Will he approve of the new style?"

"We'll inform him Rosa suggested these for all of us."

Emmaline's arms swung side to side letting the loose fabric swish freely. "I'm so glad she did. It's just like when we were little Mädchen, and she made us matching gowns. I especially loved the time they were exactly like Mutti's."

Clara's hands rested over her tummy. "Let's change back into our day gowns. Ask Dora for a basket of apples and meet me at the dining room table. We'll tie pretty ribbons on them for Mamsell to decorate the Christmas tree."

While they ran to change, Clara reveled in Rosa's foresight. The skirts of their gowns fell the same. To the undiscerning eye, Clara's secret would remain well-hidden and unsuspected. Who was she fooling? What man had an undiscerning eye when observing a woman's body even if it belonged to his daughter? Vati would notice. Requiring modesty of his girls, he paid attention to those details. Ignoring the thought, she smiled and headed for the stairs to join her sisters.

"Rosa provided miles of ribbons when we returned our gowns to her care and keeping." Emmaline ran her fingers down the length of a peach satin streamer.

Hannah set the apples on the table. "Clara, where do you go on Thursdays?"

"I've been here the last three."

"And hidden away in your room," Emmaline frowned. "You're not sad about losing Georg, are you?"

"I hope they keep him locked in jail forever." Disgust shivered up Clara's spine, and her skin prickled. Only two years hardly covers the atrocities he has done to women, especially Tilly.

"Hannah, you studied me from my head to my boots earlier. You're doing it again Why?"

"You look different. Your lips, nose, and eyes are puffy."

Clara gazed into the looking glass above the polished sideboard, patted her curls, and shrugged. "It is the same me standing here in front of you."

"But you're different, and I admit jealousy. I only wish my bosom was as voluptuous. The womanly part of you is puffier, too. And you say you've not noticed?" Hannah chose a velvet ribbon from Clara's dressing table and wound it around her fingers. She scrunched her brow. "I don't believe you."

Emmaline's pointer finger rested on her cheek. "We love the style of our new dresses, but why did Rosa insist we all dressed the same?"

My sisters will have many questions when I disappear from Gut Apfelhof I want them to hear the truth from me. "I'll be leaving with Tante Adeline and Onkel Martin after Christmas, staying with them for at least a couple of months. When I feel the baby move, maybe I'll come home. Vati won't ask me to take any extreme measures. He knows as well as anyone there's a baby when the woman feels it move."

In her customary way, Emmaline jumped with delight. "We're going to be Tantes!"

Hannah, much more reserved, asked, "Is it Georg's?"

"Nein. There's not any possibility this is Georg's baby!"

"But this is why you leave on Thursdays?" Hannah's head tilted to one side, and she squinted her eyes.

"It's not why but because of my Thursday adventures. Daniel and I have found a way to be together. Our choice exacts a high cost."

"Should you be sneaking around to do this?" Hannah pressed.

"Hannah, please accept this as my warning to you when you meet the man you love. Coming together exhilarates your senses on every level, but it's worth the wait until you are united as one in marriage. Daniel and I are married."

"We're going to be Tantes and we have a new brother-in-law!" Emmaline's eyes widened.

"Sh. You must keep my secret." Clara pressed a finger to her younger sister's lips.

"How did we not know? When? I would have been your maid of honor." Hannah's shoulders slumped.

"Onkel Martin married us behind a tree during the Erntedank party. Curt witnessed our vows. Vati will be furious if he finds out."

"But if you waited, you and Daniel would've never had the moment you longed for," Hannah said.

"It's true. But we'll leave a hole in each other's lives now, and in the life of this little one. Maybe it would have been better to drink the tea and return life to the way it was."

"And you and Daniel would still seek each other's presence beyond all else. It could happen again?"

"Mutti knows. She suggested the time with Tante Adeline. Mutti's also very angry. This must remain a secret from Vati. Keeping the secret will be most difficult since most of the staff have been observant enough to discern my condition. I believe even Henry's aware, but he hasn't asked. Will the two of you walk with me at least to the garden on Thursday afternoon so no one suspects where I'm headed? I'll tell Daniel then. I'm counting on your help to keep my secret."

They agreed.

Now if I can keep my promise to myself to tell him, but not allow myself the pleasures I so desire. In the afternoons, I am well enough I would welcome it with my whole being. But we flirt with the consequences of the half-truths we are living. O Lord, my flesh is weak.

∾

TUESDAY, *20 December 1881*

. . .

INHALING holiday aromas from Dora's cherry hazelnut
shortbread cookies delighted Clara. She descended the stairs
to peek in on the kitchen staff preparing the Reinhold
Christmas feast. Her enchantment turned sour a few seconds
later.

"Clara, I simply don't have time for your illness today." Dora
handed her a damp cool cloth. "Press it to your forehead until
the feeling passes."

Henry pinched his chin. His eyes widened as he looked at
her. He knew. Clara would be forever grateful he exercised
prudence and hadn't asked embarrassing questions. She
needed to share the news with Daniel. What if someone had
blabbed? In her note, Clara had asked Daniel to meet her.
Would she be able to meet him without incident?

Rosa appeared at the kitchen door. "Clara. Let's head to your
room."

Clara followed Rosa. "Is this the last time I'll see you? You,
Megs, and Tilly are my best friends. Megs is gone, and now
I'm leaving. This is all too hard."

"I pray it's not the last. I spent the night making new accom-
modating lines in your gowns. I wished to deliver them to
you here, along with Daniel's response." The folded
stationery slipped from Rosa's hand.

Clara smiled at the musical notes floating across the outside
panel as she retrieved Daniel's note from the floor. She
cradled it in her hand before slipping it into her pocket.

"I counted the weeks the best I could, over and over, and
compared them to what I know of the journey you're on."

Rosa showed her a calendar with the dates nearly worn off. "Expect to be with Tante Adeline until sometime in February."

"Thank you for the gowns and your encouragement. I'm struggling to believe this has happened."

"When you expose yourself to love's fountain, you must be ready to accept all it offers."

"In the confines of marriage, a beautiful offering, but I didn't expect to be expecting so quickly. I ignored the possibility altogether like I ignored the rules."

"There is beauty in the act when shared between a married couple. Chapters four and five of Song of Solomon describe the intimacy in stunning imagery. You and Daniel made those vows. When your Vati learns of them, I fear he'll dole out punishments rather than celebrate nuptials and a grandbaby."

"For Solomon and his bride, the fruit of her womb would have been welcomed by all. The baby in my belly has no chance. For Daniel and me, any plan I contemplate for the future comes complete with more sins heaped upon the ones in which we've enthusiastically participated."

"God creates the best plans. While your circumstances remain far from ideal, you and Daniel are married. I'm reminded of women bearing children of indiscretion who found their way into the genealogy of Jesus."

"Unless He is coming again as a baby…" Clara's face scrunched. "Should I laugh or cry?"

Rosa couldn't contain her smile. "I'm headed to the sewing room to redeem another dress. God redeems our lives and our choices for His glory. I pray for Him to reveal the purpose He has prepared for you and this little one."

Alone again, Clara traced the musical notes on the paper, inquisitive about the lyrics of Daniel's answer. He knew how to treat a lady, and he had said yes to her request. She had two more days to wait. Two more days until Thursday. Two more days she'd be away from him. Now Clara would need to find the words to tell him he'd soon be a Vater. She'd need to arrive at the cottage unseen and without sickness. She dared to believe for yet one more thrilling encounter.

Chapter Five

OLD ABANDONED COTTAGE, *Thursday, 22 December 1881*

DANIEL PLACED evergreens and berries in a pitcher on their little table. He had arrived at the cottage early to arrange an expression of his enduring love for his wife.

Clara's mouth opened wide in exclamation. "How thoughtful, Daniel! And beautiful!"

"Like you, my lovely lady. You're glowing. The winter air agrees with you." His kiss sunk deep into her rosy cheek. "Allow me to help you out of your cape."

As he laid it over a chair, he spun her into their familiar dance position. They rocked side to side as he held her tight and hummed *Deck the Hall*. His arms stretched a tad further than usual to encircle his love. "You have news for me? Your Vati knows we're married and he had no complaint?" He sat them on the edge of the bed and awaited her reply.

"If Vati knew he'd have many complaints."

A nudge from Daniel, and they tumbled onto the bed. She fell naturally at his side and the two were swept up in the pleasures of their love.

"Daniel," she whispered, "I'm expecting your child."

"She'll be beautiful like you."

"You don't seem surprised or even concerned?"

"Oh, my lovely lady, our very first time together a tiny voice whispered, *'Your seed has united with hers.'* Joy filled my heart. You're my everything. We must celebrate!"

Celebrate they did, until the sun began to set. "My lovely lady—my beautiful bride— your body's blooming. A flower in the winter." He allowed himself only the gentlest touches. "There's a little life inside you."

"Several have suggested I drink the tea, claiming it's not a living baby until I feel it move."

"Have you? Felt the baby move, I mean."

"I haven't yet. Only the sickness. Awful sickness. And the changes you've recognized. I've been in denial, but I've had every symptom. Only another living being inside me holds the power to undo me in the ways I've experienced. The sickness makes me question attempting to bring back my time."

"Please tell me you wouldn't."

"I won't. But many unmarried men abandon women when they learn news like this. As far as Vati and the church are concerned, we're unmarried—the very reason we've been so discreet. Vati will disown me, and you risk the loss of your position. How do you find delight in our predicament."

"The little one belongs to our flesh. I'm delighted she's a part of us. My lovely lady, leave with me now. We'll go to America and start our little family."

"Your optimism and sensitivity inspire me, but you don't have a job in America. And unless God worked a miracle for us, the total of the sunflower box's contents has yet to meet the needed Marks for two of us to travel to America and establish ourselves."

"We considered all this, and you said, "ja"."

Clara dipped her head in agreement. "But I never thought I'd become pregnant before we were able to leave."

"You love children."

Tears rolled down Clara's cheeks. "I do, but I hoped it wouldn't happen until we could truly live as husband and wife in America.

With a corner of the sheet, Daniel dried her eyes. "I'll tell you what I believe. I believe God is blessing us with this little one because He knows how much we'll love her." He grinned and wiggled his eyebrows. He's making up to us all the years we've waited. With Curt and your Onkel Martin's help, God made a way for us to realize our dreams. And now our first baby is on the way."

Clara's mahogany eyes lit up with joy. She gained strength snuggled to his chest.

"We'll make our plans to leave when the next ship sails. Write to Megs. She'll be eager for our arrival."

"I've been dreadfully sick a few hours every morning. I would be better off dead than traveling across wintry seas. How do we hide all this until we can both go? It wasn't supposed to be like this. Mutti is sending me with Tante Adeline after Christmas. I can return safely to Gut Apfelhof when I am far enough along.

"After I feel the quickening, it'll no longer be acceptable for Vati to make me force my body to spill its contents early like Georg forced Tilly to do. I saw every detail of the little person. I know a living baby already grows inside me. When I return, we'll decide what to do next. If I sound confused, it's because I am."

"How much longer until the quickening comes?"

"Maybe six weeks, two months. Your Mutter wore the dates off her calendar counting the weeks. I know the day. October sixth. I felt the connection, too, the first time we came together. The connection never became a baby in my mind until I could no longer deny the changes in my body. Thank you for still caring."

"I'll care forever. Night will be falling within the hour. Spend it in my arms."

"Will you be responsible for cleaning up the mess I make in the morning?"

"Happily!"

"Is my Vati at Gut Apfelhof tonight?"

"No worries. I'll be heading to Crailsheim to meet the morning train when he and Curt return from yet another trip. Your Tante and Onkel will be with them."

"Tante and Onkel may be our hope. Tante Adeline said you're welcome to stay with them too."

"Something we should consider."

"You concoct the plan, and perhaps we'll be on our way to America sooner than we imagine. But Daniel, for now, right here cradled in your arms makes my heart soar. Shall we make the most of this unexpected opportunity?"

Pounding at the door startled them from the wonderland of their escape. Clara grabbed her cape.

Daniel wrapped the quilt around him and stepped to the door. "Who goes there?"

"Oma. Open the door!"

"I can explain." Daniel stared at his bare feet.

Oma sighed and dropped her chin to her chest. "You've already explained about Onkel Martin Walther's favor to the two of you."

Before she said more, Daniel watched Oma scrutinize the room with her all-knowing look.

"Clara, you come with me. Daniel, get dressed. You're needed at the house. Mamsell fell while placing decorations. You may need to go for Dr. Pfeiffer."

CLARA GRABBED HER CLOTHES. Her cape would protect her from the chill in the air. She pushed her feet into her boots and followed Oma along the well-worn path to her cottage. She awaited Oma's reprimand. "Meine Kind, I acknowledge you and Daniel consider yourself married. But do you know what happens when you draw from this fountain over and over again?"

Clara pulled loose curls over her face. "Ja."

"How many more times before you're in a family way?"

"None."

Oma reached for Clara's arm. Her eyes widened, and the color drained from her face. "What are you saying?"

"I enjoy my husband. I'd joyfully come together with Daniel every day. The risk you refer to found me the very first time. All your warnings have been for naught, but you're going to be a great-grandmother." If only Clara felt as cheery as her words.

"You expect your admission to make me smile?"

"I hope it will."

Oma's obvious disappointment pained Clara. She gulped for breath before she spoke again. "Mutti knows about my marital status and the baby. She's sending me away with Tante Adeline after Christmas."

"Many women make the inconvenience disappear. I pray you haven't considered the option?"

"Every mention of the tea makes me more determined to carry my—our baby. I don't like the sickness, but I'm grateful not enduring the monthly time."

"You've become a bit sassy. Have some respect for your Oma, please. You've made the best decision. Don't drink the tea. Does Daniel know?"

"Ja. Seems everyone knows about the baby—everyone except Vati. Besides Curt and Onkel Martin, only you and Mutti know about our wedding. Oh, and I did let my sisters in on my secret. Curt helped me walk to the kitchen the first time I lost my breakfast, trusting Dora to tend to me. Unless he lacks good instincts, he knows. I pray he hasn't informed Vati.

Guess you're one of the last to learn of my condition and the one who first warned of consequences."

"I voiced my concerns too late."

"Even if it hadn't been too late, I would've ignored you. It was naive of me to believe pregnancy wouldn't happen to me so soon."

Oma's springy white curls bounced in her eyes as she shook her head. "Get dressed properly. Maybe with all the frenzy at home, you can sneak back to your room unnoticed. I'll see you on Christmas Eve. I'll never stop loving you."

"Are you planning to tell Vati?"

"Every bit of common sense this old lady possesses tells me I should. On the other hand, sounds like he's failed to figure it out on his own up to now. A hornet's nest I'm choosing not to overturn."

CLARA WELCOMED her sisters into her room and invited them to join her on her bed.

Hannah remained standing, once again wagging a finger toward her older sister. "We protected you on your way to the cottage. You promised to come home hours ago. We hoped Vati wouldn't ask us. He'd realize if we lied to him when pressed for knowledge of your whereabouts."

"And did he ask?

Pulling a cricket finger puppet from her pocket, Emmaline wiggled it by Clara's ear. "Vati came home early. He caught a ride with a neighbor headed this way. He mentioned Tante

Adeline and Onkel Martin will arrive in the morning. He made his displeasure at your absence at dinner known."

"Did you tell anyone where I was?" Her heart lodged in her ribs.

"We told Rosa because we trusted her." Emmaline said.

Hannah's hands rested on her hips, and her head shook. "We've seen what's come of your lies. We refused to add another one.

"Vati heard from Mamsell about you feeling under the weather. Her message may have served to excuse your absence tonight." Emmaline rubbed Clara's back.

"Is Mamsell okay? Oma said she was hurt, and Daniel may need to go for Dr. Pfeiffer."

"She's shaken up with a couple of bruises. Before Daniel arrived, she had busied herself again with her project." Hannah pulled Clara up from the bed and off to the side of the room. "Did you two enjoy each other's affections again?" she whispered. A smile teased the corners of her mouth. "I know you did, because your face gleams like crystals in fire-light. What was it like?"

"Heaven. Pure heaven, or at least as close as I imagine it on earth." Clara's heart nearly burst in her chest.

"What about heaven? Sisters don't keep secrets from one another," Emmaline said. "Tell me, too."

"I find it difficult to put the tingles of pleasure into words. You'll each learn for yourself in time. Be wise. Wait for the one who's your husband."

"But Vati will never view your marriage as binding. Would you do it with another?"

Hannah isn't about to give up. "Our hearts beating as one—completely magical." Radiant warmth quivered through her body, the brightest smile spreading quickly from blushing cheek to blushing cheek.

"You would!" Hannah's mouth twitched. "If Vati stops you and Daniel from being together when he learns of your marriage, will you do it with another man, too?"

"Not without marrying the man, but there isn't one other man on this whole earth I would marry or allow intimate touches. Only Daniel. I fear any other would be like Georg all over again." Clara wiped the sweat from her hands onto the back of her overskirt. *Now I've drawn my sisters into my lies. How many more will I need to repeat to cover for our impulsive decision?*

"What will Vati do when he learns you're having a baby? Will he send you away? Forever." Tears streaked down Hannah's face.

Chapter Six

CHRISTMAS EVE 1881

A HOLLY WREATH with a bright red bow had been affixed to each window of the Reinhold residence. Three carriages lined the cobbled circular path outside their gaily decorated half-timber home. The bright yellow Landau with the red Gut Apfelhof crest was positioned in the lead with Daniel driving. Kraig, Lydia, and their three daughters in the first one. Everyone, even the servants, attend the Christmas Eve service, and space was needed to keep from rumpling every-one's attire. Wilhelm and Curt rode in the next carriage with Tante Adeline and Onka Martin. Vati stood to the side as his driver helped each of the ladies embark. He took delight in observing them dressed fancily for any event—made him proud to be the head of this family and the Baron of Gut Apfelhof. The residents of his community would lavish compliments on his lovely daughters tonight.

Daniel caught Clara's hand in his. May I help you into the carriage? Noticing his daughter's balance slipping, Gut Herr Reinhold nodded to his driver and watched as Daniel guided her with extra care. He climbed up on the driver's seat and gave the signal for the horses to move. Ten minutes later he halted the carriage outside St. Luke's.

Girls from the Bible class stood in a circle outside the church. Their Mütter stood with them sharing Christmas wishes. The Mütter's friendly conversations turned to cold mutterings.

"What's stolen your joy this evening, ladies?" Kraig Reinhold asked.

The expressions on the women's faces froze.

"My daughters are their loveliest tonight. Wouldn't you agree?"

Smiles barely tugged at the corners of the women's lips. Their Gut Herr expected their compliments, but their widening eyes and the tsks they attempted to hide, made Kraig question what he'd missed. He felt a blush cover his cheeks and prick his conscience.

After gathering his daughters to himself, Kraig led them several steps away from the crowd assembling for the service. His head never moved, but his eyes traveled up and down the length of their flowing gowns. "This style you wear? Maybe those ladies are thinking it looks more like a nightgown?"

With eyes as warm and wide as a puppy dog, Emmaline gazed into Vati's and filled him in on the latest Paris fashions. "Oh, Vati! Soon all the ladies will be wearing the aesthetic style. We hate those tight-laced undergarments, and they're unnecessary when we wear dresses like these. Hurrah!"

"These gowns could hide much more." Kraig pressed a finger to his lips. "Please choose your words more carefully. We'll discuss this at home."

Kraig observed the other parishioners as they greeted one another with Christmas merriment. Not one eye missed his girls. None looked upon their faces. The whispering he heard coupled with fingers pointed at the young baronesses unnerved him.

He took his seat down front in the Reinhold pew between his Mutter and his wife. His daughters and Wilhelm just beyond their Mutti.

Gazing down the pew and back again, Kraig elbowed his Mutter in the side just before the service commenced. "I must visit you at your cottage tonight before dinner and festivities."

The organ bellowed the first chord of the processional and voices lifted in song. *Ihr Kinderlein Kommet. O Come Little Children*—the favorite of all.

Each of his women fidgeted throughout the service. Clara twisted her curl. Lydia worried her stiff fingers. Oma toyed with her lace handkerchief. Hannah and Emmaline sat on their hands and bit their lips. *What's this about?* When he took one more glance down the pew toward his daughters, what caught his eye raised more questions than those he already had for his Mutter. He prayed she had answers, and he prayed they weren't the answers he feared. For now, he returned his focus to the reading of the nativity story from Luke's gospel.

…And, lo, the angel of the Lord came upon them, and the glory of the Lord shone round about them: and they were sore afraid. And

the angel said unto them, Fear not: for, behold, I bring you good tidings of great joy, which shall be to all people. For unto you is born this day in the city of David a Saviour, which is Christ the Lord…

Following the reflective homily on the Savior's birth, acolytes helped the congregants light their candles.

"SILENT NIGHT. Holy night. All is calm. All is bright…" accompanied by guitar. Clara's joy echoed in her song. But would her reality snuff her joy?

OMA'S COTTAGE, *Christmas Eve 1881*

"WHAT DO you find so important, Kraig, to postpone our Christmas Eve festivities?"

"I'm a man, Mutter. I do not have the words to ask this."

She claimed her favorite rocker and pushed with her foot before pointing for him to sit in the chair next to hers. "Try."

"Something's different about Clara."

"She's your same beautiful daughter."

"Her face is puffier."

His Mutter chuckled. "Perhaps she ate too much Kuchen."

"You laugh. Are you mocking me, Mutter?"

She pulled her lips between her teeth. "I'm listening, son."

"The dress she wears. Is it really a new trend?"

"It is. All three of your lovely Frauleins show off the style tonight."

"They all wear it well. I prefer not to think like this, but I am a man. I notice things."

"What would those things be?"

"Not things I choose to discuss in mixed company. If you were not my Mutter…"

"But I am. What drew your attention and worries, son?"

"Maybe nothing at all. I do hope I've misjudged." Kraig rubbed his right earlobe and worried a spot on the back of his neck. "Clara's dress doesn't fall flat in the front. Her sisters' gowns do."

"Your face is as red as if you painted it to match one of those shiny apples you harvest." Oma smiled.

"You enjoy further embarrassing me, but one more question remains. I must ask. I'm not sure how?"

"Maybe just ask it." His Mutter shrugged her shoulders.

Kraig looked down at his knee and picked at an invisible stain. His head tilted toward his Mutter, and he blurted it out. "She filled the bodice of her gown far beyond what I've noticed before."

"Your little girl has grown up."

"New changes like this are unexpected ones at age twenty-six unless she hides something else. I told the girls I noticed their dresses could hide more than an unnecessary undergarment. What do you know Mutter?"

"Your daughter's leaving with Adeline and Martin on Monday. You need not worry about being embarrassed."

"Nein! Nein! A rock thudded to the pit of his stomach. With equal force, he pounded his fist on the table."

"Nein, what?"

"Who did this to her?"

"The little one's a child of love, Kraig, not of the force of a scoundrel."

"Either scenario is a disaster, but at least I could force Georg to marry her." Kraig scowled.

"He remains in prison for other discretions."

"Gratefully, but if not, it would require little persuasion to convince him to marry her. How did this happen?" Anger rose from his toes to the top of his head. He was certain the color of his face matched the apples more each moment.

"The method hasn't changed. Boy loves girl. Girl loves boy. Boy and girl play house."

"Danke, Mutter, for the lesson. I'm working hard to hide my agitation, while you find humor in the situation."

"Only in your question of how it happened. And you're welcome!"

"When did this happen? Is it too late for her to drink the tea?"

"She's frightened. Clara's been stricken with extreme illness and a body blossoming so quickly that her Vati has taken note. Several suggested the tea to her. She knows women have died from the drink."

"I need an answer. And this is really hard. When was her last time…"

"Right after the Paris trip, Kraig."

"The ladies traveled the middle of September. How've they done this? She knows she can't marry him?"

"Two young people in love will find a way. When it's forbidden them, the lure is sweeter still. Would you like me to go into detail for you?"

"Nein! But there is time to make it slip away?"

"There is not. *It* is a baby. Your grandchild."

"She hasn't felt movement, right?"

"Nothing but another living being could create the changes you see and the sickness she endures." Mutter chewed her lips. "There's one more thing you must know, Kraig."

"More? There's more? How much worse can this get?"

"They haven't played house as my words suggested. Martin married them at Erntedank. In the eyes of the state only, but a civil ceremony is the only requirement for it to be legal."

"Where is she? She's no longer my daughter. I'll disown her before I lose Gut Apfelhof, my title, and my fortune. The rules are clear. Nobility may not marry servants."

"Let her go with Adeline. She's chosen to carry the little one. I thank God she made the decision. And God loves everyone alike."

"My daughter willfully disobeyed me and the rules of nobility, church, and state. It's the same as if she were pregnant with an illegitimate child. Ignoring those rules, they've assured the child will have no future. She's embarrassed me and tarnished our family's name. How long have you known and not told me? All the gossiping and finger-pointing at the church. Everyone suspects. Am I the last to know?"

"I imagine you are. I learned of their marriage a few weeks after it took place. I told her I wouldn't tell you if they quit meeting."

"Did they?"

"Nein. I recognize the love in their eyes. Clara believes they're married—they both do—legally they are. They're adults who know their hearts and have followed them."

"Why didn't you tell me then? Mutter!"

"I warned them of consequences."

"But your warning wasn't sufficient incentive?"

"It was for a couple of weeks. Daniel asked you for time away."

"And I agreed. Well thank goodness, it was over then."

"Not quite. Thursday afternoon she went to tell him. They were still together toward evening? I asked her if she knew the risks they took.

"Did she?"

"Oh, ja, she did, but the consequence of their activities found her well before I discovered any of their rendezvous. I feel guilty for betraying her trust, but I believe you have the right to know the whole story. She and Daniel plan to leave. They're saving for ship fare to America in the Spring.

"She would do it the same if she had a hundred chances? I know they love each other. Always have. But this leaves me no choice except to disown her. We would lose Gut Apfelhof and all we've worked for and enjoyed for centuries if my daughter bears a bastard child. A child of a commoner."

"A harsh word especially coming from her Vati, and you've no need to disown her. She's leaving. You'll miss her."

"That's how I see it, Mutter." Kraig used his sleeve to blot the tears running down his face.

"And what will you do about Daniel?"

"He's the best carriage driver I have. He's like a son to me, but what son would do this to my daughter? Nevertheless, since she'll be gone. He can stay."

Reinhold's home, *Christmas Eve 1881*

At Tante Adelines' insistence, Clara stuck by her aunt's side all evening. Vati had never looked her way, but he had cut his eyes at Tante Adeline several times. Clara's sisters played the piano and led the after-dinner singing of the carols. Vati had not asked her to join them. Oma's eyes were red and filled with sadness. Vati knew.

"Clara, can you pack your things tonight?" Tante Adeline whispered.

Clara's chin dipped enough to convey her answer.

"Onkel Martin inquired before we left the station. A train leaves for Stuttgart tomorrow morning. The tension here strangles tighter than over-pulled corset strings."

"I'll pack now. If anyone asks, I'm taking care of personal needs. Alice will follow me to my room."

Tante patted her hand. Clara needed a hug, but hugs would have to wait.

Holding hands Clara and Alice stepped into Clara's room.

"Fritz brought your trunk up earlier. I packed all of your gowns and undergarments. Rosa completed an extra one, too. She styled it with smocking across the bodice, especially practical as the beautiful needlework will stretch with you."

Clara lifted the trunk's carved red lid and peered inside. "She's convinced I need more room on top? The tightness and tenderness I experience cause me pain. Will they grow larger?" Clara caressed the firmness in her expanding chest, holding back soreness even now.

"I asked Rosa the same question. She said some women's bosoms double or triple during their time with child. They enlarge again when your milk comes in. Be thankful. They'll be like large milk pails. Your baby will be well fed."

Clara laughed at the image she pictured but groaned at the thought of it. "I'll be back in a couple of months. She could wait and see if this is necessary."

"Your Vati knows, ja?"

"He hasn't said so, but he hasn't said anything at all since we left church. Oma's been crying. She must've told him."

"My heart's filled with sadness for you. I believe your Tante is leaving with you in the morning because she realizes your Vati knows, and she and your Onkel are protecting you."

"You don't believe Vati will allow me to come back, do you?"

Alice's head shook slowly. A somberness covered her like Clara had never seen. "He won't, Clara. Not unless you spill what grows inside you. He would lose Gut Apfelhof."

"His life here proves more important than the life of his child and grandchild? I always believed he loved me. Why am I telling you this? My maid shouldn't be worrying about my problems and my feelings."

"Before your Vati and Oma arrived back at the house, Daniel told me your Onkel Martin invited him to their home anytime. He said 'It may be difficult for me to get away, but let Clara know if it's at all possible, I'll be there.'"

"Do you know why would it be so difficult for him to visit at my Tante and Onkel's home? He's often in Stuttgart with Vati and Curt?" *After all, once he's there he could leave for America with me.*

"I'm not certain, but he left this for you." Alice handed her the neatly wrapped package.

Clara untied the string and pulled back the flowered fabric to find a tiny carved doll. The tag read, *For Our Beautiful Baby Girl.* Her eyes stung.

A note slipped from the doll's dress. She unfolded it and read the message. *My lovely lady, know I will come as soon as I am able. Extra responsibilities from the Baron are keeping me here for now. I'll see you in Stuttgart soon or send words of explanation with Curt. Please keep my Mutter in your prayers. As much as our situation has been difficult for us, it's affecting her, too.*

She shook her head and set the note in her lap. What's happened to Rosa? How many more people's lives have been impacted by our decision?

"I tucked your Bible and several of Daniel's little carvings including your favorite sunflowers in the trunk. A few more surprises are bundled in there, too. You'll find them when you unpack tomorrow."

Clara hugged her maid tightly for the last time.

"We all fear we'll never see you again." Alice sniffed.

"Nor I you. Another rotten consequence added to the mounting punishment for our decision. Still, I'd do it all over again just the same."

"Would your pleasure be as great knowing in advance what difficulties you would face?"

"From the most beautiful moments of my life have come the worst sorrow and heartbreak I have ever endured. But I am certain I'd do it all the same again. For more than ten years I have imagined no other man cherishing my heart the same as Daniel. His baby will help me to always remember the love we shared—the love stolen from us by the rules. I pray Daniel will overcome the obstacles and join me in America. I pray, too, that one day the rules will be erased."

First Light, *Christmas Day 1881*

She tapped on her parents' bedroom door hoping for one last hug from Vati or Mutti, or even better, a change of heart. Shuffling sounds. Her Vati cracked the door open.

"I came to say I'm sorry how I've hurt you and Mutti and the whole family. I'm about to be on my way. May I hug you and Mutti one last time?"

Vati gave her shoulder a quick squeeze. *Oh, how I want to just crumble into his chest and have him hold me and tell me everything will be alright again.*

Mutti stepped close and wrapped her arms around her daughter. "I can't imagine never seeing you again and never meeting my first grandchild. Oh, Clara…"

"You two, hurry your soppy goodbyes." Still in his robe and slippers, Vati padded off toward his office.

"Mutti, I'll be praying for the day you will visit me in America."

"Only God could change your Vati's heart for that to happen. I would like that very much. I'll pray for that too."

Both women wiped their eyes with their sleeves.

Mutti gave Clara a kiss on the cheek and nudged her on. "You best be going before Vati comes back and finds us still blubbering."

Clara walked toward the stairs and descended them slowly. She didn't worry one bit about missing the creaky places.

An unmarked carriage awaited Tante, Onkel, and Clara. No fancy Landau would carry the disowned daughter of the Gut Herr away from the place she had called home all her life.

"Clara, wait!" Emmaline called from the front door.

"We need another hug from our big sister," Hannah said.

"And I from you." She handed her reticule to Tante Adeline and grabbed her sisters hugging them both at once.

"We're never letting go." Emmaline laid her head on Clara's shoulder and sobbed. "I can't believe we'll never see you again."

"Or meet our niece or nephew." Hannah gripped Clara's hand. "Don't leave us."

"I'm so happy we had this last farewell. We're all struggling to let go, but I don't want you to be in trouble with Vati, too. It's probably best you return to your rooms before he spots you."

Tante Adeline gave them each a hug and led Clara to the waiting carriage. Jost, one of their coachmen, extended his hand to Clara and Adeline as they boarded. Onkel Martin, a highly-respected judge in Stuttgart, climbed in behind. Dressed in simple driver's attire, Jost led the horses pulling the conveyance down the drive.

Looking back Clara took in the last glimpses of her childhood and the place she and her family had made their memories. Those memories had been shattered now. Daniel was absent. The only remaining piece of their dream was tucked safely inside Clara's body. Oma had encouraged her to dream a new dream, but a future void of Clara's dream and her Daniel would be no dream at all. *I want to watch until it all disappears. I don't want to watch at all.* She wished Daniel would appear at her side and declare all would be okay. But he couldn't, at least for now. All wasn't okay. She wasn't okay.

Clara placed her shaking hand into her Tante's resting on the seat between them. "Tell me someone cares."

"Obviously, your sisters care. I care more than you know."

"Your sister, my Mutti, gave me a tearful goodbye hug, but she hates me for what I've done."

"Does she hate you? She's the one who suggested you write me. She's scared for you and for herself. She's losing her daughter. She'll not meet her grandchild. Maybe she saw a visit with Onkel Martin and me as a gift to you giving you time to pray and choose your next steps without interference."

"Danke." The words barely out of her mouth, she grabbed the bucket from the carriage floor. "The morning promises to be a long one on bumpy roads and clickety-clack tracks."

Onkel Martin signaled Jost to stop the carriage to clean up the mess. "Thank you, Onkel. Your kindness touches a tiny place in my hurting world."

With her head leaned against Tante's shoulder, Clara drifted to sleep to the rhythm of the horses' cadence. Screeching breaks and the whistle from a train pulling into the station aroused her from her slumber. "Where are we? Is this the train we'll board?"

"We await one headed in the opposite direction. This one just arrived from Stuttgart." Onkel jumped down from the carriage and looked around at the passengers exiting the train. "Wonder if anyone we know is among them?"

A young couple came running, hand-in-hand. Lacking even a hello, Curt shouted to the three. "We're engaged! She said, 'ja.'"

"Curt, Lillian, great news! The family eagerly awaits celebrating with you today." Onkel Martin shook his nephew's hand and kissed the back of Lillian's.

"Will you be married in the Spring?" Tante Adeline asked.

"At the Denzlers' estate—under trees instead of hidden behind one." He smiled at his sister.

"Congratulations. I'm happy for you both, but I'll not be at the wedding."

Curt pulled her into a full embrace. "Clara, you'll be there."

Clara was certain Curt knew, but she was grateful her red cape covered her well.

"Curt, you visit Stuttgart often. Sneak away from your Vati and visit us and Clara." Tante said. "Clara can tell you more then, but don't wait too long. Bring Daniel."

Curt's eyebrows drew together. Clara whispered, "Ask Oma."

"I'll visit you soon." He patted her bouncy red curls.

While the others chatted, Jost brought Clara and the Walthers' luggage to them. He retrieved Curt and Lillian's from the porter, carried it to the Reinhold carriage, and hefted it in. "Are you lovebirds ready to go? Christmas dinner awaits."

Through water-logged eyes and a stream of salty tears, Clara watched them leave. "Do you believe Curt will come, and will he bring Daniel?"

ON THE TRAIN *Crailsheim to Stuttgart*

"ARE we the only ones traveling today?" Clara rubbed her eyes as she glanced around the coach car they had boarded. Except for the three of them—empty.

"Settle in for the trip, Clara. I have women's magazines in my bag." Adeline handed one to her niece.

After stepping aboard the conductor checked their tickets. Onkel Martin thanked him for delivering the pillow he'd requested at the station, then snored before the train rolled down the tracks.

"An early morning for all of us." Tante Adeline flicked her wrist toward Onkel Martin. "We'll let him sleep. Let's claim seats out of earshot of his buzzing." And they did. Six rows away.

"Looking at the pages of these magazines while the train's moving makes me queasy." Clara set the publication aside and twisted the buttons at her cuffs instead.

Another quick survey of the rail car assured her no one would be listening in on their conversation. "You said my Mutter is scared for me and scared of losing her daughter. I saw a distant sadness in your eyes as you spoke those words. You agreed to take me in without question. Why?"

Adeline folded her hands. She studied the circles her thumb traced around the nail of her index finger. "Clara, sweet Kind, I've walked in your shoes."

Clara's hands came to her chin and then crept up to cover her mouth. She squinted her eyes tight. Her head moved slowly from side to side. "What?"

"I loved a commoner once, too. We never married even in secret like you and Daniel, but we enjoyed each other's company. I didn't expect it to happen to me."

"But you don't have children."

"Nein, but I've lived with the grief and regret of my decision every day."

"Does my Mutti know?"

"Ja, and the reason she sent you to me. It happened when she was in Paris. I'm a year younger than your Mutti. When she came home, I was spending much time in the room we shared and wouldn't join her for fun no matter how much she begged me. She asked about the young man—did I want to see him? She would help us meet."

"Did you?"

"Nein. He didn't care about me anymore."

Clara studied her Tante. "Why not?"

"To be honest, it was more my embarrassment than his reluctance."

"You knew by then?"

"I denied it. I reasoned my body was just behind schedule. Nothing made me think otherwise. But I knew it. I'd been so foolish. Your Mutti asked the dreaded question. 'How long since your time?' I remember curling my toes up in my shoes and feeling my heart thudding like a big drum. I didn't want to say. It would make it more real. She asked again. Four months," I squeaked out."

"Did you love him?" Clara asked.

"More than anyone could ever love another. I didn't want to tell him. Your Mutti brought me the tea. If drinking it would bring back my time, I decided it the best thing to do."

"The tea worked, then?"

"After five days I had the worst cramping. I experienced horrible things. I thought it'd just be like all the other times my monthly came. It wasn't."

Clara handed her handkerchief to her Tante. "You need this more than I do."

Adeline wiped her eyes. Clara watched the heaving in her Tante's chest slow, until the older woman regained her composure.

"I held a perfectly formed tiny person in my hand. I examined all his fingers and toes and his perfect little face and witnessed a couple kicks. His body went limp in the palm of my hand. I killed my child. I've never been able to scrub away the image from my broken heart."

"My Mutti has kept your secret all these years?"

"She has. She helped me clean up everything and bury the baby. She gave me the biggest lecture of my life, but our parents never learned of it."

"And when you married Onkel Martin, didn't he want children?"

"Oh, ja. Very much. We both did. It never happened for us. I'm left to wonder, what if? But we enjoy you and your siblings, and Martin's nieces and nephews. We love you all like you're our own offspring."

"Onkel Martin is a good man. I'm grateful you found happiness again, but I couldn't remarry like you did. I never want another man, but I do want Daniel's child. Even if Daniel's prevented from coming to America, I'll love her enough for both of us."

"It won't be easy. You'll need to leave Germany with or without Daniel at your side. Your child will never have a future here."

"Herr Worth invited me to sketch for Haus of Worth. The baby and I could live in Paris. It would be close for Daniel to come."

"And who would care for your baby while you work?"

Clara's shoulders sagged. "If I joined a commune, could

Daniel visit us? All the women work together to help each other rear the children."

Tante fanned the corners of the magazine's pages. "I don't have the answer, but would you be happy there?"

Eyes downcast, Clara sighed.

"How's your friend Megs faring in America? Chicago, is it?"

"Ja. She and Gus love their new home. The skills Rosa taught us allowed her to open a fine dressmaker shop on some fancy street in the city. Wealthy ladies discovered her talents. Her business thrives. She invited me to come. She'd make me a partner with her."

"An excellent new start for you."

"I'm no longer the same person she invited to share in her business. A baby, as you have pointed out, would make working any job difficult with no one to tend the child during the day. Where would I live? Chicago holds the same challenges as Paris but a giant ocean away."

"You're the same person—still her best friend. Paris may not be far enough to avoid the stares and the gossip when word gets around. Send Megs a letter. Let her reply. My answer surprised you. Maybe hers will, too."

Gently rubbing her hands across the bloom in her middle, Clara talked to the baby. "We're going to be just fine, my little one. Mama loves you, and your Vati will come. Should I tell Megs about you? Will she jump to the conclusion Georg's your Vater?" *I hope she knows me well enough to believe differently, but we both know her brother. Can an unaccompanied pregnant woman even gain entrance to America? My mind entertains a million questions and no answers.*"

Onkel Martin woke from his nap and ventured up the aisle to join them. "What are you two conferring about?"

"Just woman talk, Martin." Tante Adeline massaged her forehead. "I'm hungry as a bear waking from a long winter's nap. I left Cook a menu. The goose with all the trimmings—Apfel and sausage stuffing, red cabbage, and your favorite Kartoffeln."

Martin flipped open his watch. "Our train arrives in Stuttgart in ten minutes. Guten Appetit!"

Chapter Seven

MARTIN AND ADELINE WALTHER'S Home, *Stuttgart Germany, Christmas Day Evening 1881*

THE FAMILIAR WALLS surrounded her with the security for which she longed. Clara's favorite room in Tante and Onkel's home—the one she and her sisters shared whenever the family visited. With familiarity and respect, she caressed each doll resting in the pram. How many generations had played with these dolls before Clara and her sisters? They had belonged to Mutti and Tante Adeline.

Had they been new to them, or had they been gifts handed down from Clara's grandmother or even her Mutter before her? In her pocket, Clara carried the one Daniel had carved. Would their child hand this one down to her children and grandchildren, too? Thoughts of the doll prompted Clara to open the travel chest. The surprises Alice promised waited beneath its fancy red lid.

She removed her pillow and night clothes first. How thoughtful of Alice to place them on top. Underneath those— a full collection of Grimm's Fairytales with an inscription: *For my niece or nephew to be entertained by the stories of our childhood. Love, Tante Hannah.*

No signed note was required for the set of ten finger puppets. A gift from Emmaline, but a slip of paper fell from one of them. *Be sure she lives the adventures in the fairytales, too.*

Breathless at the sight of it, Clara pulled the familiar quilt from her childhood from the chest and brought it to her cheeks. An unfamiliar lump nestled inside. She carefully lifted the cross-stitched border of apples, then folded back more of the fabric until she set the blanket's captive free. A Steiff elephant! On their trip to Breuninger Department Store's grand opening this past March the Reinhold women fell in love with the recent newcomer to the toy world. Mutti's note was tied to its soft trunk. *I heard elephants have very long memories. Please remember your Mutti always, and remember me to your little one.* The signature was blurred, perhaps by a tear.

Lace hankies from Oma. *I can hear her say, "Every lady needs them."* White on white hand-stitched lettering danced across the linen. The beginning words to her favorite lullaby— *Lullaby and goodnight! With roses bedight.*

A few familiar gowns followed. Clara marveled at the details Rosa had added to camouflage every alteration. Among the treasures, not one, but two new gowns in the aesthetic style. A closer observation revealed hidden buttons and pleats, and ribbons woven through eyelets to allow further expansion. *For the short time in which she's created these, had Rosa begun them earlier anticipating my need?*

A tiny package poked from the pocket of the second one. Rosa included her message on the inside of the wrapping. *The gift to me from Daniel's Vater when Daniel was but a Kleinkind, I'm passing this cameo on to you and my granddaughter. Much love, Rosa.*

After removing it from its royal blue box, Clara held it up to admire the details. She rubbed her fingers across the woman's image just as she watched Rosa do so often—the very item that had been front and center in the debacle responsible for the whole Georg nightmare. Clara would choose to remember it, instead, as the prized possession of one of her dearest friends who is also her child's Oma. *I miss you, Rosa Becker. Thank you for entrusting your special treasure to me and my baby girl. She needs a brave name. Everyone believes the baby to be a girl. I could name her Emma. Emmaline would be pleased if I chose Emma, but I'll pray and ask God to reveal her name to me.*

When she heard footsteps in the hall, she removed the Bible and stationery she had placed among her things last night. Before the visitor reached her door, Clara returned the other items to her trunk. A small envelope fell at her feet, her name in Daniel's handwriting upon it. Impatient to open it, she tapped the envelope before quickly stuffing it under the cover of her Bible for now. "Please come in."

"Am I interrupting?" Tante Adeline stopped in the doorway.

"Not at all. Did you know about the gifts?"

"Some of them. I remember your Mutti purchased the elephant when you were here for the Breuninger grand opening. She wished for good marriages for her children and the promise of precious grandchildren. Her eyes danced with the familiar sparkle you inherited from her. Your Mutti cuddled the elephant and announced the soft stuffed toy as her down payment on the spoiling of her children's children. She told me she sent it with your things."

"Would you like to see the rest of the gifts?" At Tante's nod, Clara happily took each item from the trunk again and showed off the thoughtfully chosen items. She waved her crisp linen stationery with the deep lavender 'C' stamped at the top center. "Tomorrow I'll write to Megs."

"I see our Mamsell already provided you with a full water basin, a pan, and cloths to clean up. She'll care for all your needs while you're here. You need only ask. And, Clara..."

"Ja, Tante?"

"Sometimes God's answer is 'not yet' or 'no,' but I'll pray the sickness part of this is over for you." Tante placed a quick kiss on Clara's forehead. "Oh my." She reached for a cool cloth to stem the clamminess there. "See you in the morning."

Alone again, Clara retrieved Daniel's letter from her Bible. She would savor every word. Sunflower designs edged the stationery in the same pattern as those encircling the treasure box keeping watch over their savings for America.

My Lovely Lady,

I miss you already. If you're wondering when my Mutter, your precious Rosa, helped Alice pack your things she slipped this note between your gowns.

I have more orders for the sunflower boxes from Lillian's friends already. I'm working as quickly as possible to complete them. And when I do, I'll have enough for passage for us to America by Spring. When are you planning to sail? Curt has already secured permission from your Onkel Martin for me to join you on the trip. Curt and I plan for me to arrive at the perfect time. We'll make the trip together, Clara.

I need to ask, have you noticed my Mutter being clumsy or losing her balance? I've noted it more than a few times. She brushes off my inquiries, but I'm very concerned. I'm not writing this for you to worry, but to pray for her. Share any insights you have through Curt. He'll be certain I receive them—and any loving correspondence you include.

Take excellent care of our baby. We'll be in America together very soon.

All my love forever and always,

Daniel

∾

Monday, *26 December 1881*

Clara sat up in bed, swung her feet to the floor, and faced the day. The letter to Megs was fresh on her mind. She moved to the window and opened the golden velvet drapes. Sunshine swept over her along with another wave of nausea. *God answered prayers for this part of my condition, with the 'not yet' answer. The ginger and cold rags have minimal effect, but I'm thankful Tante supplied those, too.*

Nina, Tante Adeline's personal maid entered the room. "Why am I surprised to see you?" Clara hugged her long-time friend.

"Frau Adeline invited you because she loves you and cares about you. So do I, and I'm here to help you prepare for the day. When we finish may I hang your things in the wardrobe while you enjoy breakfast? Your Tante waited to eat with you."

"Ja. How thoughtful of you both." Clara opted for the turquoise gown. Nina spotted gold and turquoise ribbons poking from one of the dressing table's many tiny drawers. She tugged on the drawer's diamond-shaped knob and pulled the ribbon free. It pleased Clara when Nina wove it artfully into her curls.

"I haven't smiled much lately, Nina. Danke for the special touches."

Clara stepped over to her trunk. She lifted the lid and reached for the tiny package from Rosa. Why should she wait another day to wear this treasure? She sat again in front of the mirror on the dressing table, attached the cameo to the collar of her gown, and smiled at her reflection.

"You'll impress everyone you meet today. Your gown's beautiful, the cameo a lovely touch, and the ribbons a perfect match. All eyes greeting you will see only your beauty."

"Am I expecting to see others besides my Tante and Onkel?"

"Adeline will fill you in on the day's schedule. Go on to breakfast."

Dread welled up inside her. Clara grabbed her stomach. Another heave was imminent. *What exactly has Tante planned for me today?* Leaving Nina to settle her things into the wardrobe, Clara shuffled to breakfast.

Setting the Blue Onion cup and saucer before her, Trude asked, "Would you like sausage and fresh Himmel und Erde?"

"Be sure you serve it with a slice of Streusel Kuchen," Tante added.

"You both know me well. Heaven and earth. Potatoes and applesauce. The cinnamon you add to your Streusel, Trude, makes it taste heavenly. And sausage? I haven't handled this much breakfast in months."

Trude hurried off to fill Clara's plate.

"Maybe Trude's cooking will better agree with you than Dora's?" Tante's chest bounced to her giggling. "Oh no! My apologies. Dora's an excellent cook. There's no need for you to clean your plate, but I knew you would love it all."

"I'll be indebted to you forever for all the kindnesses you and Onkel Martin are extending to me."

"My lady friends come to play Hearts every Monday. Even with Christmas yesterday, we won't miss our weekly camaraderie. You do remember how to play the game?" She stirred her coffee with a dainty heart and floral embellished silver spoon.

"I do, but why do you ask?"

"You'll join us. One of the ladies fell ill, and you'll play in her place."

"My plan for today is to write to Megs."

"You have plenty of time." Tante waved her hand. "Write her after breakfast. Our Mamsell will post it today. The party begins at two. Tea time."

"I remember those. Are there still a dozen of you? Do they know?" Clara's heart hammered in her chest. Her legs wobbled—thankfully beneath the table where Tante wouldn't notice.

"They know my niece is spending time with me, and they're delighted to see you."

Clara squeezed her knees tightly together. She twisted the wayward curl. She prayed her insecurity wasn't too obvious.

"What if they ask?"

"Clara, my friends are ladies. It's not their habit to ask nosy questions or humiliate anyone."

But they'd be thinking it. Clara placed her folded napkin over her half-eaten breakfast and slid the plate a few inches forward. "May I be excused to write my letter to Megs?"

Tante nodded. "Afterwards, the game will be a perfect diversion."

Chapter Eight

GUT APFELHOF, *Thursday, 5 January 1882*

DANIEL STEPPED inside the Reinhold home and received the day's itinerary from Lottie. "What a perfectly sunny and warm winter day for delivering a huge load of Gut Apfelhof wine to the train station."

Most days the Mamsell's meticulous attention to detail kept the activities on the family's calendar free from conflict.

"Please pick up the desserts for the Twelfth Night party from Franken's Backhaus this morning, too. Frau Franken has everything ready for us." Lottie handed him a checklist for the order from the Frankens.

"But the wagons and carriages are already bulging with the big delivery."

"You can do both? Empty those wagons at the train, and help load the wine on the cars for transport. You'll have plenty of time to collect the baked goods before you return, ja?"

"I'll stop at the bakery." Daniel waved, but two steps toward the door he halted. He cupped his hand around his ear. "Do you hear someone crying, Mamsell?"

"The sound's coming from the stairway. Who? What's happened?"

Daniel spun out of the kitchen and toward the stairs.

"What time I am afraid, I will trust in thee. What time I am afraid, I will trust in thee. What time I am afraid, I will trust in thee." His mother lay in a heap near the top of the stairs—repeating the Bible verse.

He climbed the steps two at a time. Lottie followed at his heels.

"Are you hurt?" He knelt beside his Mutter.

"I was two steps from the landing. My legs began shaking. Then I couldn't feel them at all. Moments later I realized I was sprawled atop this bundle of fabric I was moving to the sewing room."

"Can we help you stand?" Lottie grasped one of Rosa's hands.

Daniel moved behind her supporting the tiny woman's frame. Together they helped her stand, but her legs gave out again. This time Daniel scooped her up in his arms. Lottie cleared the path. He carried her the rest of the way up the stairs and around the corner to the sewing room. He set her on the short sofa beneath the window.

Rosa rubbed her hands along the couch's royal blue and silver brocade stripes. "I'm sure I'll be better after I rest a few minutes."

"Lottie, please keep watch over her. I'm reluctant to leave, but the Gut Herr expects me to deliver the order and Twelfth Night desserts await."

"Perhaps you would inform the Gut Herin of your Mutter's needs before you leave. Together she and I will tend Rosa and finish up the special details for tomorrow's celebration dinner."

Dreikonigstag. Another of Clara's favorite festivals. Sadness from circumstances now affecting the two most special women in his life would dim the light of this Three Kings' Day celebration.

"What time I am afraid, I will trust in thee. What time I am afraid, I will trust…"

In spite of his mother's prayer—or admonition—or whatever her intention might be as she recited the verse again and again—worries, not trust, wrapped around him.

THE GUT HERIN assured him she and Lottie would take good care of his Mutter, and call for the Doktor. He'd informed the Gut Herr and Curt of the morning's incident while they attended to the winery's business. After helping load the Apfelhof Winery order onto the train, he collected the Backhaus treats. Curt and his Vati went straight back to Gut Apfelhof.

When Daniel returned, Lottie stacked the parcels in the kitchen and sent him to the sitting room. The Gut Herr and Herin, and Doktor Pfeifer were gathered around his Mutter. No one was smiling.

"The Doktor has serious concerns, Daniel. Please sit down." The Gut Herr pointed to the wood bench next to Rosa.

"I'd rather stand." He paced back and forth waiting for the news.

"I wouldn't know for sure without having a neurologist look at your Mutter."

"A neurologist?"

"A Doktor Charcot in France has identified a specific progressive disease with symptoms your Mutter exhibits. If the numbness in her legs and the trembling continue, I would like your Mutter to be seen by him."

"And where did you say this Doktor is located?"

"Paris."

"Paris might as well be China—a long way to visit a Doktor."

"Frau Reinhold and I will be responsible for the expenses."

"Very kind, but too much to ask of you, Gut Herr."

"And I'll be asking much of you as well. You'll make the trips to Paris with her. If Charcot determines this disease is what's causing Rosa's problems, you may be making monthly visits for a very long time."

"Problems? Wasn't this incident just today? What secrets are being kept from me?"

"Rosa, you should be the one to tell him." Frau Reinhold patted her hand.

"Mutter?" Daniel's shoulders tightened.

"This has been happening for the past six months. Only once in a while at first, and I could get back up again. No one saw me. In December, I fumbled with some dresses I carried into Clara's room. I got back up then, too—a bit more clumsily, I admit. She didn't say anything, but I'm sure she wondered. I haven't told anyone before today—only God. I asked God to heal me."

"But He hasn't?"

Rosa's head moved side to side. *"What time I am afraid, I will trust in thee.* God didn't fix me, but He's allowed this. Each time the struggle has been more difficult. Today I couldn't help myself at all. *What time I am afraid, I will trust in thee."*

"Doktor, does this disease only affect the legs and feet?"

Pfeifer's chest ballooned with his next breath. "Unfortunately, it often affects the whole body as time goes on." He turned to Rosa. "Frau Becker, have you encountered problems with other parts of your body, and you haven't told us?"

Her eyes turned red and teary. "My fingers." She rubbed them gently. "Right now, I barely feel one hand touching the other."

"Then you struggle to thread a needle and sew?"

Rosa nodded. "I'm so sorry."

"Doktor Pfeifer please wire the Doktor in Paris. I would like Rosa to see him next week."

"Daniel, you have leave to travel with her. Mamsell Lottie will request Tilly accompany the two of you. She can attend to your Mutter's personal needs."

∾

Monday, *9 January 1882*

While Clara and Tante awaited news from Megs or a visit from Curt or Daniel the two passed their time stitching a layette for the baby.

"This baby will be the best-dressed child in Stuttgart or Chicago, and you have created all these baby clothes in two short weeks." Onkel Martin whistled a happy tune.

"Short?" Clara groaned. "The past two weeks have felt like forever."

Onkel pulled a wire from his pocket. "I received this from Curt earlier today."

Coming to see your favorite niece. Visiting Lillian alone week after next. I will send word with my specific plans. I come with Vati's permission. Tell Kirsche she's my favorite twin.

"Like the colorful rainbow in the sky when sun and rain mix, your smile emerges through your tears. Another two weeks 'til Curt arrives, but a visit to look forward to, ja? Are you still a substitute for the Hearts parties?"

"Ja. Tante needs me every week. Still, time moves slowly. I'm grateful to be here, but my plight is no better than before."

"What might Tante and I do to help you more?"

"Begin checking ship schedules for passage to America. Zwischendeck, of course."

"Shall we wait to hear from Megs first?" Onkel rubbed her shoulders and brushed tears from her cheek. "Or perhaps your brother brings better news."

Chapter Nine

THE WALTHERS' Home, Monday, 23 January 1882

THERE WOULD BE no mistaking the meaning of *blossoming* any longer. Nina adjusted the buttons and tucks again for a better fit. "I'm so thankful for Rosa's ingenuity, but hiding the flower, as Daniel calls our baby, is no longer possible. All the Hearts ladies will know."

"I believe they will." Nina's eyes drooped and her lower lip protruded.

"Does every woman's tummy poke out so far so soon? My waistline expanded two inches the first three weeks – a fact I refused to acknowledge."

"All are different, Fraulein. Maybe your baby seeks attention." A smile replaced Nina's sympathetic expression.

"I'd rather no one noticed."

"But babies make their presence known." Nina turned the crystal doorknob to let herself out.

"Danke, Nina, for stating what's obvious to everyone."

Tante obviously considered the partially open door a sign it was safe to enter. "Clara, it's almost time for Hearts."

"Would you be disappointed if I stayed up here and sketched today?" As soon as the words left her lips, Clara knew she wounded Tante's feelings. "On second thought, I'll be there shortly."

"Good. Danke." Tante Adeline kissed Clara on the cheek, then headed downstairs.

A quarter-hour remained until two o'clock when the Hearts games would begin. Clara chose to arrive early. She'd seat herself without anyone noticing her middle. But Helene and Katrin, also early, jumped to greet her. Katrin expressed her pleasure in seeing Clara by wrapping measuring tape arms around her. When she finally released her, the short woman looked up at Clara with crossed eyes. Clara suspected Katrin would have preferred staring down her nose at her with the same demeanor.

"Tsk. Adeline and Martin are feeding you well."

"Trude's cooking is always delicious. We do eat three meals every day." Clara fidgeted with the deck of cards on the table.

Helene's approach proved much more direct. "Why, Clara, if I didn't know you to be a single woman, I'd say congratulations are in order. A little one on the way?"

Katrin blocked Clara's hasty exit from the room. "You're tired of our company, already?"

"Excuse me, please!" When the human wall didn't budge, Clara crumpled onto the floor.

"Is there a problem at my Hearts party? I won't have it." Adeline encountered the same blockade from the opposite side of Katrin.

Big words flew from the tiniest of the bunch. "A few of us wondered, Adeline. Is your niece staying in your home to hide something? She isn't concealing it very well. Does the Gut Herr of Apfelhof know how his unwed daughter has behaved?"

Adeline shoved Katrin aside and leaned down. She gathered the pile of humiliation—her niece—into her arms. "Excuse me. Clara and I need some fresh air. I'll be back."

"It's true, then."

Neither Clara nor Tante knew who the last voice belonged to. The ladies-turned-busybodies all talked at once.

"You promised the ladies don't gossip. They did, and my situation is the favorite topic of their day—probably their year. I need to leave now." Clara twisted free from Tante's loving embrace. "And where will you go?"

Her reply sounded like gibberish through her blubbering.

"You're not making sense, Clara. I'm sorry. I believed the ladies to be my friends and yours, too."

"I deserve their accusations. Will the consequences never end?" Her heart throbbed and her eyes burned. "A different decision on my part months ago and this wouldn't be happening. Or I could've partaken of the tea as some suggested."

"What I did prevented others from knowing, but I carry hidden pains that haunt me daily. Either of us could've chosen differently. We wouldn't bear the weight of those choices, but we would feel the pain of different wounds."

"My decision to carry Daniel and my baby is the right one, but I'm learning people are mean. I always believed we're to be kind and not point fingers at others." Clara tapped her foot. "Have some of these women shared our experience in their own life?"

"Perceptive of you perhaps?" The wisdom Tante found in those words oozed right out. "The ones quick to accuse you may be the very ones who have, but I don't know. I'll not be asking either. While they may have faced circumstances similar to mine, you're a married woman. Onkel Martin married you and Daniel legally. Maybe it's time to share the whole story. I'll demand the women leave my home immediately. They've over-extended their welcome here. Our home is a sanctuary, not a court of accusation and incrimination."

Clara tugged at her sleeves. "Danke." She raised her chin.

"Walk back to the carriage house where you can be out of sight and out of the cold until they're gone."

"They'll leave quickly? I've ruined yours and Onkel's reputations, too."

"Please don't fret. Do you believe we failed to consider this possibility when we invited you into our home? And by the way, I love your glowing and blossoming. I'm a bit jealous I never had another opportunity. Danke for making the better decision for your baby. Onkel Martin brought a record of your marriage certificate. He'll wave it in front of them if necessary."

CLATTERING sounds of commotion were heard behind Tante and Onkel's home. Clara scrambled toward the carriage house denying the ladies another chance to stare at her.

As the visitor drew closer, the voice sounded familiar. Her pace quickened. Inside the carriage house, Curt enveloped his sister into the tightest hug he dared. "I heard I'll be an Onkel soon?"

"To a baby you'll never see. Oh, Curt, I'm so sorry. Why did I do this to myself? To our family?"

"If I hedged bets, which I don't, I'd wager you didn't do this to yourself. I'd win. You did it legally and for love."

"Your jesting hints at the poker hands incriminating Georg. If your intention was to hear me laugh, you've succeeded."

"And lit up the sparkle in your eyes, too."

"But if Daniel and I had loved each other more, maybe we wouldn't have behaved so impulsively. We wouldn't have been so eager to allow Onkel Martin the honor."

"Belittling yourself and agonizing over what might've been doesn't change the present. Vati asked me to deliver this to you."

"But he's made it clear I no longer exist to him."

"He's hurting, too, Clara. You know he'll not say it, but his decision caused him grave anguish. Deep lines etch his face and the smile has disappeared from his eyes. He believes he had no other choice, but he'd also like you to have this." Curt placed the sheathed documents in her hand.

"I'm spending the night. Onkel's driver will take me to the train in the morning. I'm looking forward to a meal from Trude's kitchen this evening, and a long conversation with my sister."

The wings of the fireside chairs beckoned them to sit and warm themselves—Curt from the chilly trip from Lillian's home. The harsh cold of the Hearts ladies' words sank ever deeper into Clara's soul.

CLARA CHOSE a long narrow needle from Adeline's knitting basket resting on the hearth. After sliding it under the envelope flap of Vati's letter, she opened it with a clean slice. Her hands shook as she tugged the documents from their covering. *Are these another of Vati's unwelcome agreements like the one he had proposed binding me to Georg? I'd rather not look.* She addressed her brother. "Are these legal documents disowning me?"

Curt's eyes widened. "Oh, I pray he couldn't possibly!"

She unfolded the parchment smoothing the crease down its center. *One thousand gold marks, plus enough to cover your fare to America. Curt has the package in his care.*

Clara gulped down the thick knot in her throat. "He does wish me gone? He sent money to ease his guilty conscience?"

"Wishing you were gone? I doubt he does. Desiring to help you in the best way he knows how? Ja." Curt transferred the weighty package to his sister's trembling hands.

A healthy dose of pride shouted to her. *Don't take it. You can make it on your own.* But aware of her limited choices, Clara reached for the bundle. Rolling back the gift's cloth covering exposed the inlaid diamonds and triangles of the walnut trinket box from Vati's study. "One of his most prized possessions."

"He filled it with hope for your future. A future he wouldn't have chosen for you, but this is the only way he knows to be a part of it. Open it, Kirsche."

She'd opened this box hundreds of times before and skillfully maneuvered the hidden mechanism allowing the box to open freely. Firelight gleamed across five neat rows of ten gold coins–twenty Marks each. She saw them through a smoky haze of disbelief and wariness.

Curt reached for the folded handkerchief in his pocket. "Here are the additional thirty Marks for your passage."

When he placed it in Clara's hand, she flinched.

"Something I said or did?"

"The aroma of Vati's study clinging to the box has punched me in the nose. I replaced happy memories of the past with uncertainties of what the future will hold."

Curt was silent.

"You're about to cry, too. I'm grateful. I truly am. What is easy for Vati, lessens the burden of what's difficult for me. But he'll never come to America to meet his grandchild." Her lips quivered.

With his head lowered to his hands, Curt clasped his face tightly. "I cannot believe we'll never see each other again."

Images passed through her mind of play times and learning times, of family meals and friendships. Of Curt, Hannah,

Emmaline, and Wilhelm. The special friendship between Megs, Curt, Daniel, and herself took center stage. Her friendship with Daniel leading to love and a decision in the name of their love. Had Clara lost it all? She allowed the waterworks to run until she was too fatigued for either, but the images of all she'd miss and regret refused to leave.

Clara's hand rested alongside Curt's arm. "I've broken you, too. Broken us."

"By Vati's decree, everyone at home carries on as if nothing's changed, except a dark cloud hangs over the Gut. It promises to never leave. It threatens to unleash a full-blown storm every day. Wilhelm remembers games, hot cider, and stories with you around the fire on cold winter evenings. Brigitte barely eats. Your sisters–oh never mind. I'm making this so much worse for you." Two whole minutes ticked by on the mantle clock. "You've not asked about Daniel?"

The large knot occupying her throat earlier returned. It took three hard swallows to dislodge it. "How is he? Has Vati punished him, too?"

"He's as broken-hearted as you. Daniel's zest for life has vanished. Regrets abound."

"We both knew better, but news of the baby excited him. He asked me to leave for America with him. Start our little family in a whole new land of opportunities. Can you imagine Vati's reaction if we had? And now we're all miserable. Do you know how much money he has saved in the sunflower box? Maybe with this gift from Vati and the savings he and I could travel together to America."

"He's not punished Daniel, but Vati keeps him close—at his side except to sleep or tend to extra tasks."

"Daniel sent me a note before I left—something about Rosa not doing well. Are her problems part of the extra tasks? Whatever they are, Vati's ensuring Daniel has no opportunity to follow me.

"I'm certain he'll tell you himself in a letter or at least share the details. Rosa has begun having problems with her hands when she sews, and she often stumbles for seemingly no reason. Vati has Daniel accompanying her to Doktor visits to determine what might be helpful for her."

"How terrible for Rosa. And I'm embarrassed to say this, but what a perfect excuse for Vati to keep Daniel from leaving." Her elbow rested on the arm of the chair. She picked at a loose thread on the chair's dusky-blue upholstery. It matched her outlook perfectly.

"Or maybe Vati hopes others will believe you're the headstrong daughter who left because you couldn't have what you wanted. If Daniel's with him or helping Rosa, it helps squelch rumors. Folks have less reason to accuse Daniel for why you left. Vati's protecting your reputation."

"And his. Vati and I have given each other many reasons to be angry the last several months. The gift is surely a goodriddance one on his part. Nevertheless, thank him for me for what you say is the best way he knows to show me he still loves me. And thank Vati for keeping Daniel and Rosa in his care."

"He doesn't allow your name to be mentioned, but I'll take the chance your message will be an exception."

"Tell Daniel I love him. I don't blame him for my situation. I'll never love another man. His child will be well cared for. And be sure he knows I'm praying for his Mutter—dear precious Rosa."

Curt ground the toes of his shoes into the carpet and scratched his head. "There's one more thing, Clara."

"From the deep furrows in your brow, I trust this one more thing is almost too hard for you to say."

"Vati spent the morning meeting with the authorities to take steps to nullify your marriage."

"Be sure Daniel knows if he can't come with me, our baby and I will be waiting for him in America no matter what Vati does." The thirty Marks spilled from Vati's handkerchief as Clara grabbed it to blot another flood of tears.

"This means you'll never release Daniel to love another?"

"Is there someone else already?" She was certain her ears steamed.

"Nein. My courtship and engagement to Lillian convinced me man is made complete with a helpmate at his side. You both require time to heal, but I wish for another chance for both you and Daniel. Who knows who you'll meet in America."

"Not another man for me, but I'll pray I am able to release Daniel to pursue love with another if he chooses. It's unfair of me to hold his future hostage, to match the one I see for myself and our baby. But he did promise to come…"

"I pray he'll keep his promise."

"As much as it hurts me to acknowledge this, maybe Daniel will find another woman. But I won't even notice another man. Not ever." A yawn nearly swallowed her. "It's still early. I'd rather not miss one moment with you, but sleep overcomes me earlier each evening. Becoming a mother is tiring work. Give my love to everyone. Tell Lillian I had looked forward to getting to know my new sister. Maybe you'll both write or visit me in America one day?"

Curt hugged her. "Will I see you in the morning? I remember well what those looked like for you before you left."

"I'll see you off."

Chapter Ten

THE WALTHERS' Home, *Tuesday, 24 January 1882*

"YOUR BROTHER ALREADY LEFT." Tante rubbed Clara's shoulders. "Yesterday wore you out, and your Vati was expecting him by nine. Nina let us know you awoke late, not feeling well again. I'm so sorry."

"The women's ill-spoken words circled my head and poked my middle like bony fingers all through the night. I slept little." Clara stroked her hands over her belly. "If only I could erase the wounds their comments etched here and in my heart."

"I'm so sorry about the ladies' insensitive chatter. I wish the visible signs had appeared much later for you. But the time for wishes is past. Do you know your Mutti had a twin?"

"She never told me."

"He didn't live. My Oma told me about him when your Mutti was pregnant with you and Curt. She said my Mutter, your grandmother, ached with heaviness. Sickness stayed with her the whole time. Lydia came out first, healthy and squalling. Leonard was tiny and still. The midwife worked long and hard, but the little boy's body never took a breath. When your Mutti became ill early on, my Oma feared the same for her."

"But Curt and I are both healthy."

"Ja. A tough time for your Mutti, though. Followed by a long recovery."

"She feared for me?"

"So very much, Clara. I don't see the future or have a window into your womb, but your experience closely mimics theirs. You may also carry twins."

Her knuckles turned as white as snowcapped peaks as she gripped the edge of the breakfast table. Her voice low and shaky. "No, it cannot be. It can't." She crossed her arms over her bosom and looked down over her changing body. Beads of perspiration formed on her lips. "I ached clear into my underarms even before the sickness overcame me. I've been sick for weeks and weeks, and my belly doubles in size every few days." Oh, Tante. What do I do?"

"You wait. You'll know when the baby or babies are born."

"God has used you to get my attention. A new knowing has anchored itself in my soul. I'm certain God's sending me two babies. And your Mutter and my Mutti were both sick the whole time!" Clara's breakfast promptly landed on her plate and soiled the lace tablecloth beneath it.

"I've made a mess. Again." In the moment it took Tante to call for a cool cloth, Clara pushed her hair from her face and used her napkin to wipe her lips. "If only I could erase these last few months."

Along with the damp cloth, Trude offered a mug of ginger tea. "It often soothes the stomach, ja."

"Danke."

Edmund, the Walther's doorman, stood before the two women. "Great news! I deliver not one, but two telegrams for our guest." He extended the polished silver platter holding the messages. "Fraulein Clara, for you." Edmund bowed.

"One must be from Megs." Tante smiled. "Open it! I know it's the wonderful news you're waiting for."

Clara's fingers rattled the paper as she broke the seal. She read in silence.

"Oh, the suspense! Clara. Did she say ja?" Tante tapped her fingers on the table.

"I may come as soon as I've secured passage."

"She sent good news then, but you're hesitant?"

"There's nowhere for us to stay, and…"

"And what exactly?"

"She believes the us is Daniel and me. When we were in Paris, she urged me to leave Germany with Daniel and come to America where our class difference and the rules don't matter."

"Were you honest with her in your letter?"

"Nein, Tante. I wasn't. The baby will be a surprise. Babies, plural will be quite a shock. I feared she would assume her awful brother to be the Vater."

"Clara, your cauldron of partial truths bubbles over." Tante narrowed her eyes

"Like my tears and sickness, my life's filled with messiness." She tried to laugh, but mirth stuck in her throat. "I escaped marriage to Georg. I married Daniel. Curt brought the news Vati has been inquiring about having our marriage annulled."

Tante's face turned white as a ghost. "If he does, Onkel Martin will see the wrong is righted. Did Curt bring any other news?"

"He delivered a generous good-riddance gift from the man who has disowned me."

"That is some good news then. But if he truly disowns you, I'm tempted to hire someone to bring bodily harm on your Vati. I have another question instead. Tell me. Who's the second wire from?"

"The second one's a mystery to me. I've written to no one else." Clara unfolded the note and read this one aloud.

"This is your Great Tante Ingrid. Dorthea wrote on your behalf. You're in need of a room in Chicago? I have one for you. Also, I'm a doctor and midwife. When will you arrive in Chicago?"

"Your Oma went straight to the point telling her sister. The whole truth, too, and Ingrid welcomes you!" Adeline smiled and tapped her fist under Clara's chin. "Cheer up! Life's looking better for you. Father God looks out for his children. You're one of them."

"Or three of them." *Oh God, I am certainly testing Your patience and Your faithfulness.*

"We'll work together to ready you for travel. Don't make an impulsive decision to leave in a hurry."

"I could be gone before short February's over."

"Have you felt the quickening?"

"I don't know what I should feel. My stomach gurgles and churns, rocking my breakfast. Some days my lunch and dinner, too. Quickening would be difficult to discern."

"Our home's your refuge. We'll wait for you to feel the movement to ensure your pregnancy is well established before you set sail for a foreign land."

"No one has used *the p word* before. If my condition is not obvious enough, the word is full of reality. But no one says the pregnancy word until they feel movement, right?"

"Usually, true."

"Then I'm not–not yet. The word will apply soon enough, but not today."

Tante laughed. "Ok. For another few days or a week, you believe that you're not."

"You mentioned preparations? What more must be done?"

"I know Lehrer Frederick included some English in your studies, but learning more English words will serve you well. And Clara, sweet Kind, you'll need some additional clothes before these babies come. Rosa did beautiful work, but already the seams are strained. Nina mentioned only two more adjustments remained to expand the bodice."

"And no end in sight to these ever-broadening changes. Rosa's not here to create more. She'd sew more gowns if she could. What I have will suffice."

"For modesty's sake, you would need to cover yourself with a cape all the time."

"Purchase some fabric with a portion of the money Vati sent. I'll sew another gown myself—be certain I'll have enough yardage to cover all of this?" She patted her tummy. "It grows larger every day."

"I have fabric. I've asked my seamstress to create garments for you. She'll be here in a few weeks."

"Danke!" Clara paused and pressed her hand to her forehead. "I do hope she's kinder than the Hearts ladies who've shown little heart."

"Ahh. She is, but Onkel concerns himself about you traveling alone. He'd like you to wait to leave with a couple from our circles. They board a ship on April twelfth, leaving from Bremen."

"Which couple from your circles?"

"Vera and her husband." The name hung in the air.

"She only said I was glowing until Katrin cut her off with her measuring tape arms. But Vera won't be content to travel in the Zwishendeck."

"You're correct. They have first-class passage to visit their family who immigrated to New York City last year, but they happily agreed to escort you to the ship and see you through the entry process."

"They're not leaving until April? Vati made it clear for me to leave as soon as possible, and he's paying the fare."

"I believe April is the next sailing with tickets still available. Waiting for Spring is excellent advice. The weather will still be chilly, but crossing the cold Atlantic less unpleasant, I've heard, after the air warms a bit."

"Is Onkel's plan confirmed, because I'm still praying Daniel will travel with me?"

"He intended to purchase passage for you this morning. The Norddeutscher-Lloyd company has representatives in Stuttgart today. It's a great convenience to purchase your fare in advance. Otherwise, you may have to wait in long lines at the shipyard for a ticket. The boats fill quickly. There may not be any left by the time you get to the front of the line. I'm certain he'll have your ticket with him when he returns home this evening."

"You and Onkel look after me well, but I admit I am not excited about traveling with Vera and her husband onboard. First Class passengers wouldn't visit the lowly steerage passengers, would they?"

"True, but if you go alone, how will you explain why you're traveling unaccompanied, especially in your condition?"

"Maybe Daniel will come."

"For everything to work out for him to come? I'd not count on it. I'm sorry."

Clara wore the cameo every day reminding her of one true friend back home. She rubbed it now, just like Rosa had so often. "I've not mentioned it, but Daniel carved a tiny doll for the child. I believe his Mutter made the doll's dress. He slipped a ring around its waist to hold the hand-stitched garment in place. It fits my ring finger perfectly. Wearing it will make it appear I'm a married woman."

"How thoughtful of him." Tante stood, grasped Clara's hand, and pulled her to her feet. "Let's direct your thoughts to other things, shall we? It's an unusually warm day for January. Would you like to stroll through the shops in the Marktplatz? By afternoon you often feel much better than in the mornings. You'll enjoy the outing."

"I'd love an adventure as long as we don't encounter the busybody Hearts ladies. Perhaps I'll find a new piece of sheet music. A lullaby."

"Perfect. I'm so happy you're playing our piano while you're here. You inspire me to play again myself. I'm sure the carriage is ready. Let's be on our way."

Martin and Adeline Walthers' driver reined in the horses in the center of the Marktplatz. With his assistance, Clara stepped carefully from the carriage. Definitely a warm day for January, but Clara appreciated her red wool cape. It warded off any chill and, with a prayer, any undesired stares as well. She wished the cape fell from the top of her head rather than her shoulders when she spotted Helene and Katrin across the square. "Tante!" Clara pointed at the two women.

Adeline spied them at the same moment. "Wait right here!"

Strolling at an unladylike pace Tante marched straight toward the duo. Clara followed her despite instructions. She kept a modest distance, then ducked behind a statue where she witnessed the exchange. A flashback to hiding behind the horse statue in the Tuileries in Paris to avoid Georg flew through her mind. *I've had too much practice at this maneuver.*

Before Adeline uttered a word, Katrin opened her mouth. "You bring the strumpet out in public? Have you no respect for yourself or your friends?"

"You're making strong accusations, ladies." Adeline rubbed under her nose. "Clara asked a thought-provoking question yesterday, and I believe it has merit. Do you point fingers to appease your own guilt? Have you faced a similar predicament?"

"Women like her must be hidden. It's just what's done."

"Avoiding my question? My niece is the same lovely woman she's always been and a married one. Please keep your distance from us today, and I promise I'll start no ugly rumors of your past."

Helene kicked at the cobblestones and shook her fist as a crimson rash raged up her neck. She opened her mouth to speak, but the long blast of expletives Clara anticipated never came. The two turned and stomped away. Tante had embarrassed them.

"Where to, Fraulein? This adventure is for you."

"You'll choose the best shops. I'm following you."

The afternoon flew by quickly. Pretty undergarments, hair ribbons, fresh pastels, and music to *Weisst du, wie viel Sternlein stehen—Do You Know How Many Stars There Are?* were all nestled in the packages they carried. Clara popped a lemon drop in her mouth. "You always spoil me. Danke!"

Evening

"Himmel und Erde. Maybe I'll keep the potatoes and apple sauce down better at the evening meal."

"And sausages, too," Onkel said. "Adeline asked Trude to cook one of your favorite meals. Heaven and Earth—a sort of celebration."

"I have so little to celebrate these days," but yum—I do enjoy this Kartoffel dish."

Martin retrieved the document from his vest pocket and placed it in front of Clara. "Passage to America."

"April twelfth." She twisted her curl around and around. "Just over two months.

Martin winked toward his wife before producing more documents from his vest pocket. "Tante Adeline and I will accompany you to the ship. He waved the train tickets for fare from Stuttgart to Bremen. A one-way for you, and two round-trip for us."

"Tante told me Vera and her husband are escorting me to the ship?" Clara stirred her fork around in the food still on her plate.

"You'd prefer to go with them?" With his head cocked he wiggled a smile.

"Nein, nein. I'm a grown woman. I'd be fine alone, but the two of you accompanying me would truly ease my fears."

"I don't approve of any woman traveling alone, especially one of my favorite ladies. And no matter what he said about disowning you, Kraig Reinhold knows the risks and appreciates this plan."

"Besides my obvious condition, do you have other concerns about my safety?"

"You'll need to be accompanied on the ship."

Chapter Eleven

THE WALTHERS' Home, 15 *February 1882*

Clara chose three from among the many bolts of fabric available at Tante's home. After she had selected her favorites, Tante held another up to Clara's face.

"This one brings out the fire in your locks and the sparkle in your eyes." She added trims and accent fabric.

Clara snuggled the fine coral silk and matching sheer. Beads and braids in ivory, turquoise, and copper added to the enchantment. "What a dazzling ensemble these will make, but I have nowhere to flaunt the extravagance."

"Shall we tuck it in your luggage? You and Megs design a special gown later. Your body will shrink again."

"I can't believe my body will ever be small again." She hugged Tante. "Danke!"

"Gut Apfelhof with so many women residing there, has its own seamstress. Sandra, my dressmaker, has had a very full schedule. Because I'm the only Frau here, we schedule the sewing lady's time. I expect her later today. With her skills and creativity, you'll arrive in Chicago with gowns matching your noble upbringing."

"Which no longer counts for anything. Your lavish generosity is wasted on me." Clara groaned. "I might mess up these fine fabrics in her presence, making a not-so-fine-at-all mess all over your seamstress."

"You always feel better in the afternoons." Tante rubbed Clara's back.

"I do, but that was before I began experiencing flutters. Fish blowing bubbles a few seconds at a time in my tummy adds to the plague of nausea and a weak stomach."

"What wonderful news!"

"Wonderful? How do more waves, gurgles, flutters, and heaves sound wonderful to you?"

"I have no first-hand experience, because—well, you know why. But you describe what everyone speaks of when their baby moves! Those fluttery fish bubbles are the quickening! We can use *the word* now."

"Really?"

"Most women enjoy these internal tickles during pregnancy. The baby's movements do intensify. Be ready for little elbows, knees, and toes to poke around in your belly soup."

"I should take the word of a woman without the experience to believe more turmoil in my insides is a good thing?" Clara laughed out loud. "We've veered way off the subject of sewing gowns. The ones I have will be adequate as maternity wear. Do you need things made for yourself first? A traveling ensemble for the trip to Bremen?"

"I have many to choose from. Sandra will come for you this week and the next Wednesdays until the gowns are completed. She has helped many ladies navigate this time and prepare for after the baby, too. I trust she'll have wonderful ideas."

"But I'd rather keep these fabrics for after the babies arrive. I sketched a design, too. I would love for her to create my vision."

WITH THE CONSULTATION and necessary measurements completed, Sandra suggested designs that would be perfect compliments to the fabrics Clara had chosen—one an iris and yellow tiny print from Liberty of London and the other a sapphire and charcoal windowpane plaid wool. I believe there's lace among your Tante's stash to add a touch of femininity to the plaid?"

"I cannot imagine my body being small again, but I would love some new things after the baby comes. Tante Adeline assured me you would imagine wonderful ideas, and you have. Thank you! As I told her, I look forward to new gowns after the baby or babies arrive."

"You need at least one new travel dress, Clara." Tante picked up the blue windowpane check. "I love what Sandra's envisioned for this one. Let's have her create it now."

Clara nodded and chewed a corner of her lip. Fearful touching it with her sweaty palms would blur the image, she crisscrossed her arms clutching the sketch close to her heart. "Sandra, are you familiar with the Aesthetic fashion trend?"

"I've seen drawings in the women's magazines. I'd enjoy stitching one." Her eyes twinkled. "May I see?"

"I sketched this one with ideas from Aesthetic style gowns I saw in Paris last year. Do you think this wispy fluff of grape fabric would be a good choice? Its soft gentle flow makes me smile."

"It is lovely!" Sandra pressed her hands to her heart. "I'd be delighted to accept your challenge."

Clara's eyes met Sandra's blue ones. They held as much tenderness as Rosa's. *I hope Sandra sees a sparkle of gratitude in mine.* "I would love for you to, but could it be made so that I could still wear the gown later? I adore the fabric, and the aesthetic style is very forgiving."

"Give me time to ponder your question. I must be on my way today. Danke, Frau Walther, Frau Becker. Shall we schedule a first fitting in three weeks for the blue one? March eighth by my calendar."

"We'll be ready for you." Adeline handed Sandra an envelope. "A deposit on your work."

Sandra gathered the fabrics and was on her way.

Clara remained standing in front of the Venetian mirror of Tante Adeline's wardrobe. "Danke. You told Sandra I'm a married woman. I'm grateful for the respect it garnered." While playing with her curls, she turned completely around viewing herself from every angle. "We left so quickly Christmas Day I have no idea what I forgot to pack. I could hide under a hat. Do I have a hat becoming of the lovely clothes I'll wear? Do women headed to the Zwischendeck wear hats at all?"

Adeline scratched her head. "A hat indeed! You would be the most charming woman in steerage. I imagine it more likely the ladies in the lower quarters wear babushkas."

"Tell me more about the Zwischendeck."

"I've heard it isn't an easy passage."

"What should I be most concerned about?"

"I pray my worries are for naught. You'll travel on the S.S. Elbe, the first express steamer. The ship made its maiden sailing about a year ago, and the Norddeutscher-Lloyd line brags of its improved conditions over previous models of Transatlantic ships."

"What are you saying? The voyage still promises to be difficult? Crowded? How many do not make it to America at all?"

"The April sailing should be perfectly timed. A late winter chill may still hang in the air, but the days are moving further into Spring. Your pregnancy will be well-established, but you'll still have a few months until you deliver. If you were to birth the babies on the ship, you'd be obliged to name them Elbe and Willigerod."

"Why ever would I name them Elbe and Willi-who?"

Tante giggled. "Tradition. Babies born on board are named for the ship and for the Master of the ship."

"Those names are enough incentive to hold them inside until I arrive in America and prayerfully, well beyond." She patted her belly and instructed its residents. "I remind you, meine kinder, this is where you belong until July. Please, no untimely surprises."

"We'll ask around among the passengers waiting to board with you. Onkel Martin and I pray for a kind couple who will agree to watch over you on the journey."

"What could happen on the ship? You never answered my question about how many never make it to America."

Adeline looked Clara in the eye. "You're strong. You'll do fine, but it would be nice to make a new friend, ja?"

"Gossip aplenty has reached my ears about Zwischendeck conditions, but I believe you're refusing me dismal details of my voyage ahead."

8 March 1882

With Nina's help, Clara fastened her new undergarments. She and Tante waited in Clara's room for the first fitting with Sandra. "I expected her arrival before now, Tante."

An hour later than scheduled, Sandra carried the carefully bundled gowns into Clara's room. Her nose and eyelids scrunched and a grimace pulled at her mouth when she plunked the muslin-wrapped parcel on the bed.

"I don't know you well, Sandra, but you're shaking all over. Shall we call the Doktor to come?" Clara's eyebrows inched up.

"I've no need for a Doktor." She sniffled wiping her already soaked handkerchief over her eyes. "I received the worst news, and I may have ruined your gown."

"Please have a seat." Adeline pointed to the needlepoint cushion on the bench next to her. "Tell us what has you flummoxed."

Sandra withdrew the telegram from her pocket and handed it to Frau Walther. "Read it yourself. I can hardly speak through my weeping."

Samuel died pneumonia on ship. Buried at sea. Hilda and I in Chicago alone. Pray. Come. I love you. Belinda.

"My heart breaks in a thousand pieces for you, Belinda, and Hilda." Tante Adeline's hands rested on Sandra's arms. The two wept together. "I remember your anxiousness when they left. She had asked you to travel with them."

"And I couldn't do it. A big boat in the middle of a never-ending sea scares me. See what happened. Samuel became ill and died. Poor Belinda. And sweet Hilda with no Vater." Sandra's chest heaved with each sob.

"We could travel together, Sandra."

Tante Adeline nodded her approval. "What a splendid idea, Clara! We'll have Onkel Martin secure another ticket.

"Say, 'ja,' please," Clara begged. "Unless God sends a miracle for my husband to travel with me, I'll be all alone, too."

"I'm too scared." Sandra shook her head. "I'm set in my ways, and I find it too difficult to face change. Another thing. Frau Walther, who would sew my clients' gowns and cloaks?"

"I understand your reasons, but you're all alone here—widowed five years already. You sympathize with Belinda's despair. She is your only child, and she and Hilda need you," Tante Adeline's chin quivered.

"I predict my friend, Megs, would welcome your skills and provide you with a position. She owns a dressmaker's shop along one of those fancy streets in Chicago. A few months ago, she and I visited Paris to be inspired by the newest styles from House of Worth and others. She purchased beautiful fabrics and trims from Sajou. Her clients are excited, and have given her more business than she can handle alone." Clara smiled. "What's even better, we would be working together."

"What you're suggesting would be a lovely opportunity, but have you asked her?"

"When we were in Paris, she promised we would be equal partners if I came to Chicago. With her pledge, I feel free to make the offer. Megs will be pleased."

"Allow me time to pray about this. Remind me when you'll be leaving." She dabbed her nose with her soaked handkerchief, then stuffed it inside her reticule.

"Here." Tante Adeline offered her own newly embroidered one in its place. "Martin purchased train tickets for April 10, for the three of us to travel to Bremen. We'll see Clara to the ship. We've been praying for someone to watch out for her on the ship. God answered our prayer. The circumstances make me sad. All the details of this upcoming journey are sad, but I believe God has His own plans for both of you."

"Just say, 'ja,'" Clara lifted a page and pointed to a date circled on the wall calendar. "The ship sails on April twelfth. We'll be in Chicago before the end of next month."

"Pray about it, but we will count on God to lead you to join your daughter and granddaughter," Tante Adeline pointed to the muslin package on the bed. "Shall we unveil the dress?"

Sandra's fingers shook as she fiddled to undo the strings tied about the bundle. "I fear my tears stained the grape fabric for the one you designed, Clara. It lay in my lap when I opened and read the wire."

Tante Adeline examined the gown in question.

When Tante held it up, Clara oohed and aahed. "What a perfect rendering of my sketch."

"This is splendid!" Tante Adeline's mouth gaped open. "Megs will welcome the combined creativity of you both. Clara, try it on, please."

"But the tear stains," Sandra pointed toward the skirt of the gown.

"These at the hemline?" Clara gathered the lower edge of the dress in her hand. "You haven't hemmed it yet. The stains will disappear when you do. Voilà!"

"There's still a problem. I haven't agreed to go."

"You will." Clara steepled her hands

Somberness mingled with expectation throughout the remainder of the fitting.

"A few minor adjustments are necessary. I'll have them completed before you leave."

"Allow me to say, God has a way of turning our sadness into great joy." Tante Adeline rubbed Sandra's back and hugged her again.

Clara twisted an ever-errant curl., and rubbed the cameo at her neck. "Rosa would say: 'Isaiah 61:3… *to give unto them beauty for ashes, the oil of joy for mourning, the garment of praise for the spirit of heaviness; that they might be called trees of right-eousness, the planting of the Lord, that he might be glorified."*

"A perfect word for both of you," Adeline said.

"I need a tent-size garment to cover all of this?" Clara's arms swung wide to encompass her expanding waist. "One big enough to cover both my poor choices and these promises for me and for my children. *Lord, help me trust You."*

Chapter Twelve

WALTHERS' Home, *Monday, 10 April 1882*

CLARA SQUINTED at the sunbeams filtering through the rose-lace curtains. Reminiscent of Goethe's words in *Osterspaziergang*. The bright dawn of this Easter Monday delivered a bit of the hope he had penned in the Easter Walk poem—more hope than her heart dared believe. Resurrection hope—the pastor spoke of it in yesterday's sermon, too. Easter—a day more gloriously celebrated at Gut Apfelhof than even Erntedank.

The message I most loved to share with my Bible class ladies, but His hope isn't penetrating my heart today. The story of Mary Magdalene meeting Jesus early Easter morning has always been one of my favorites. He cared about her. She was privileged to be the first to see Him, and the first to share the good news that He's alive!

The coins from Vati were sewn into pockets she had added to her underskirts. Her trunk was packed. Besides the sheet music lining the bottom, it contained a few gowns and necessities. The special gifts from her family and her Bible rested in the basket she'd carry over her arm.

Daniel promised to sneak in a visit if he could. He never came. I'm so alone. Will he really follow me to Chicago? Will Megs retract her offer when she realizes 'we' doesn't include Daniel, but me and a baby—or babies? The sickness has tapered off a bit, but boats must rock on the big waves. More nausea. Will I make sour messes every day? Oh God, I am scared.

A knock at the door. She opened it just a crack.

"Fraulein, I have come to collect your trunk and load it in the carriage."

Clara lowered the lid, locked the latch, and withdrew the key. "Danke, Edmund."

His head was cocked to one side. His eyebrows arched and his nostrils flared. "Are you ready?"

"Are my misgivings obvious?"

"Would it help you to know your Daniel will drive you to the train station?"

Her eyes rounded and her hands framed her cheeks. "Do you mean it?"

"He rode into the drive minutes ago—on horseback. I heard him have a few words with Herr Walther. He'll be driving your party to the train."

She buttoned the trunk's key into a tiny envelope attached to the inside of her reticule and rushed for the door.

"Are you forgetting your basket?"

One frazzled step backward, Clara grabbed it and headed to the stairs on her way to the waiting carriage.

DANIEL LOOKED DOWN from the driver's seat and soaked in the sight of his beloved as Tante Adeline, Onkel Martin, and Sandra stepped up to the carriage.

He hoped his smile matched hers—the one shining at him like the noonday sun. Jumping down and skipping the formality of a kiss to the hand, he embraced his lovely lady. He whispered in her ear. "Your Onkel Martin gave me permission to kiss you, too."

"Oh, did he?"

"Ja, he did." Daniel desired more but kept it respectable. His hands lingered on her shoulders. He held Clara arms-length away and rubbed her tummy.

"Daniel! People are watching."

"But this is the closest I'll come to holding my child before she's grown."

"Your children."

"I'm confused. What are you saying?"

"Daniel, I believe our baby is two babies. Tante Adeline can tell you about it next time you're in Stuttgart."

"I'm going to miss everything. I'll find a way to join you and the baby or babies before the year is out."

"How I want to believe you will, Daniel."

"I haven't visited while you've been here for a most important reason. Wait for me in America. I will come."

"Curt told me about your Mutter, but he didn't share any details. How is Rosa doing? Can you tell me more?"

"Your Vati made me promise not to burden *anyone* about it. I don't want to put a damper on our short time together either, but her condition may be one that afflicts her for her entire life"

"Does that mean you'll be taking care of her for the rest of your life, too? I want to trust you will come."

"Doktor Pfeiffer connected us with a Doktor in Paris. When we find out more, I'll write with details. I'm praying he can help her. And I will see you in America as soon as I am able."

"I'm holding fast to your word, Daniel. Please don't disappoint us." Clara rested her free hand on her tummy.

"I will honor your trust."

"Who gave permission for you to drive us to the train? Not Vati?"

"Your family and the Gut Apfelhof staff have been in Stuttgart celebrating Easter at your Tante Caroline and Onkel Knut's home. Curt arranged for Onkel Martin to join them yesterday evening. He assured your Vati of your travel plans. The Gut Herr of Gut Apfelhof doesn't want you to know, but he does care—very much. Curt convinced him to allow me the short time this morning to drive the four of you to the train station. I think he allowed it only because he expects this will be the last time I'll see you."

"I'm grateful you're here. If Vati allows the opportunity to mention my name, please thank him for me."

Daniel helped Tante Adeline into the carriage. He lingered a few moments more assisting Clara. "Pregnancy looks beautiful on you, my Lovely Lady." He brushed stray red curls from her face. Taking her in his arms he pressed his lips to hers, and they melted together. The flutters of her heart beat against his chest. He deepened the kiss memorizing everything about this moment She wrapped herself more tightly to him. Her lips blossomed, and he tasted a remnant of peppermint igniting the growing fire of the passion they shared. Oh, how he desired more…

Onkel Martin cleared his throat. "We'll be late for the train."

Daniel slowly released his wife. "I'm not sure how this one kiss will hold me—hold us until I get to America."

"Oh Daniel, me either. Is that another promise you will come?"

"It is." He extended his hand to help her into the carriage. He climbed aboard the driver's seat and led the horses and conveyance onto the street. Herr Walther's coachmen followed behind in another carriage with the luggage.

Fifteen minutes later they arrived at the train station. After summoning a porter to carry their bags to the train, Onkel Martin took Clara's hand in his own and nudged her closer to Daniel. "You two say your *goodbyes*—again." He pointed to the coach car they would be occupying. "Clara, be on board when the whistle blows."

"Danke, Onkel."

"We have only a moment, and a train platform is too public for what I'd love to do right now," Daniel's lower lip protruded. "Please tell me what you meant by babies. You and Curt are twins. Is there reason to believe we made two babies?"

"Daniel, my dear husband, my middle expanded so quickly, and I've stayed miserably sick since the beginning. I'm better than I was, but I understand this is how Mutti fared when pregnant with Curt and me. I also learned from Tante Adeline that Mutti had a twin brother. My Oma was sick the whole time with them, too. The little boy never took a breath."

"Oh, Clara, how this must worry you."

"I don't want to believe there are two in here." She pointed to the extra-large hump in her middle. If your Mutter is correct, I still have about three months before they arrive. I have bloomed, as you say, so quickly. And my expansion never slowed down. I have poked out well beyond what's expected every moment of this pregnancy. The garments your Mutter made for me are snug already. You remember when you told me how sure you were that you knew the moment it happened?"

He nodded and squeezed her shoulders. "You're that certain?"

"When Tante told me about Mutti and about their Mutter, her words sank into my spirit with deepest knowing."

"I want to be there for you—all of you."

"Like we've planned all along, but it's important for you to help your Mutter right now. God tells me to be courageous. He'll be with me. Oh, how I want to trust Him. And you. I'll write. Please write back." Her eyes welled up.

Daniel stood tall. He forced a smile on his face and led her to the train car. "Maybe it wasn't the best idea for me to come?"

"I'll treasure the memory of this moment. I needed to know you care. I love you forever, Daniel Becker. Let me gaze on every detail of your face, your sky-blue eyes, your wavy golden hair, your single dimple, and your broad shoulders, remembering every inch of you for always, my handsome prince."

Daniel laughed. "You still believe frogs turn into princes, do you?" He brushed his hands over her cheeks. "I love you with all my heart, and I always will, Clara Becker. I'm so thankful for your Mutti's paintings, many with your image, hung with care all over the Gut Apfelhof home—many reminders of my lovely lady." He gripped her hand while she stepped into the train car, then handed her the basket. She rubbed the cameo, as he released his hold.

A long blow of the whistle roared above the noise of people like him still on the platform, waving farewell to friends and family. Pungent gray puffs of smoke billowed from the engine's stack.

He blew a kiss. She blew one back. Their arms reached toward one another until the train and his lovely lady rolled toward Bremen and the ship—the one transporting his wife far away from him and their dreams.

TOMORROW SHE WOULD BE in Bremen. Memories filled Clara's head, as the travelers settled in for the long journey. *My babies will never know the place from which they came.* Will they know their Vati? Daniel's promise to come to America loomed like an improbable dream. Her eyes stung. She quietly hummed the tune of *Weißt du, wie viel Sternlein stehe? —Do you know*

how many stars there are? The words and tune quieted her aching heart.

CAN *you count the stars that brightly twinkle in the midnight sky?*

Can you count the clouds, so lightly o'er the meadows floating by?

God, the Lord, doth mark their number, with His eyes that never slumber;

He hath made them every one.

∾

BREMEN, Germany, *Tuesday, 11 April 1882*

CLARA RUBBED her swollen eyes before reaching to gently squeeze Sandra's hand.

"Wake up, Ladies!" Onkel Martin nudged his wife and whistled a happy tune. "We'll arrive in Bremen within the hour."

Clara stretched her arms and twisted in her seat. She pointed at her Onkel. "I pray your jolly attitude predicts a joy-filled future ahead. I can't imagine one at all."

"Clara, precious one, trust God for His plan." Onkel Martin smiled. "The one He worked out behind the scenes long ago. Remember the Psalmist's words.

Thou art my hiding place; thou shalt preserve me from trouble; thou shalt compass me about with songs of deliverance. Selah.

"I know He cradles you securely in His hands. If I didn't, I couldn't deliver you to the ship tomorrow. We'll enjoy our time together today and trust all our tomorrows—yours and the baby or babies', Tante Adeline's and mine, Sandra's, too—to God."

"You speak God's truth, but you're not the one sailing into an unknown future. Forgive me for any disrespect. You've been nothing but good to me."

"We're pleased to be of help." Martin motioned to a porter to deliver their luggage to the hotel, then turned back to the ladies. "We'll head to the Ratskeller—the best food in Bremen."

"You mean the four-hundred-and-something-year-old restaurant?" Clara swung her arms wide.

"Ja, the very same. They prepare delicious fare." Onkel waggled his eyebrows. "I have attended many business meetings in their magnificent dining rooms."

Sandra tucked a loose hair into her bonnet and surveyed their surroundings. "Herr Walther, you're generous to suggest such a fine establishment. From what I see, and acknowledging my lowly station, I'd be an embarrassment to you in such a place."

Looking straight into Sandra's cornflower blue eyes, Clara winked. "No more than their unaccompanied niece, full with child." Laughter lightened the moment.

"My treat." Onkel handed a tip to the porter attending their bags and pointed the group in the direction of the Ratskeller.

The cathedral-like domed sections clustered together provided an intriguing setting. Wine barrels in each one stood twice the height of a man. Clara studied the fine artwork decorating them. She noted the familiar crest of the Gut Apfelhof Winery. They serve Vati's wines.

Following their hearty meal in the Old Market Plaza's Ratskellar they made the short walk to the neoclassical Stadthaus. Onkel Martin gazed up at the building's façade. "I've been privileged to attend many meetings in the city hall. Originally built in the Romanesque style during the thirteenth century, it's been through a few renovations."

They wandered through the narrow streets of the old city passing inns, shops, Rococo-style homes, and the once-opulent, but now-crumbling St. Peter's Cathedral. Onkel pointed to Muhle am Wall. "This windmill was built in 1699 —not nearly as many centuries old as the others, but an interesting reminder of Bremen's early fortifications. Clara, you would love all the flowers blooming around it in the Summer."

"Belinda sent a letter describing Chicago. We'll miss many things about this old world, Clara."

"Ja, much more than centuries-old buildings"

THE ROMANTISCHES HAUS' opulence more than compensated for its dwarfed size. *I have stayed in many lovely buildings, but Onkel's treating me to amazing luxury today.* Clara pirouetted like a clumsy roly-poly. Lavish bouquets of fresh flowers. The fragrance of scented soaps. Original artwork. Finest antique furnishings.

Waiting to be directed to their rooms Clara's gaze landed on a vaguely familiar pair of eyes. Onkel shook the man's hand. "Max, my friend, what a surprise to meet you here."

Max? Gold-glinted turquoise eyes and wavy chestnut hair. The man who intervened in Paris. Please, God, don't let him recognize me.

Too late. "Max, let me introduce my wife, Adeline, and our niece, Clara. This is our friend Sandra."

"The pleasure is mine, Ladies. Max Engel. Herr Walther and I have known each other for many years."

Clara felt his eyes lock on hers. "We've met before, Fraulein. Refresh my memory."

Feeling heat and fire blaze from her neck to the top of her head, Clara averted her eyes to a lavish color palate of wild-flowers blooming in a painting behind her.

"I don't forget beautiful faces. Paris, I believe. You and your friends assisted me in choosing fabric for my client."

Clara lowered her eyes. "I do remember, and you returned the favor. Danke again."

"You married the fellow?"

Excruciatingly aware of appearances, she chose honesty. "Nein, Herr Engel." She was thankful he refrained from asking more questions.

"My niece and our friend, Sandra, board the S. S. Elbe in the morning. Clara's Tante Ingrid will meet them in Chicago. They'll also be joining Clara's best friend and Sandra's daughter and granddaughter."

"The best friend who was with you in Paris? She purchased many items for her dressmaker shop."

"Ja, my friend, Megs," Clara said. "You have a great memory."

"An asset in my profession. Protecting my client's interests puts me on the same ship tomorrow, Martin. It would be wise for the ladies to have a man to protect them. I'm available."

"These ladies travel Zwischendeck accommodations. Quite a lot to ask of you, Max."

"Not at all. The change in plans will get me away from some of the dull folks occupying the upper cabins."

Oh, Dear God, he was most kind to us in Paris, but I'd rather not give him the wrong impression. He has to be blind to not realize my predicament. I'm not at all interested in any man but Daniel in any romantic way.

A small voice in her head—*ah, but love is so much more than romance. Trust him. Trust Me.*

Shivers slithered up and down her spine. *Ingrid, Megs and Gus, Sandra, Belinda, Hilda, and these tiny ones on the way. Enough to worry about. Scary thought adding this man to the list.*

When Onkel Martin and Max stepped aside to discuss the arrangements, Clara noticed Sandra's expression. Lines in her forehead disappeared for the first time since they learned of Samuel's death.

"You look unsure about this, Clara," Sandra said. "I believe God sent Max. I've heard the stories of women traveling alone. If this young man is with us, I'll feel safer and rest easier."

The two men rejoined the ladies. "Max is one of the finest men I know, and he'll be joining the two of you. I, for one, am grateful. We'll meet here in the morning, find breakfast at a Backhaus, and hire a ride to the harbor. You'll be on your way to America."

Chapter Thirteen

A BACKHAUS IN BREMEN, *Wednesday, 12 April 1882*

WITH THE RISING of the sun, a rerun of Kartoffeln and carrots from last night's dinner greeted Clara.

The acrid smells stirred Sandra from sleep. "You poor thing." She grabbed a cloth from the table between their beds and wiped Clara's face and neck.

"Danke, Sandra. You'll wish you stayed in Germany when I'm sick on the boat every day. You have a poor travel companion."

"As long as you're well now, only your nightgown is soiled. We'll rinse it well, and wrap it until we're on the ship and can hang it to dry. I'm praying God will grant you a reprieve from the sickness."

"Danke. I'm happy to have you with me, and grateful we'll travel together. I'm a strong woman, but when I'm honest, I am petrified."

At a cozy Backhaus an hour later, they joined the others for Apfel pancakes and coffee. When the time came to make their way to the boat, another grip of fear anchored Clara to her seat. She would have preferred her Onkel's help to get up. Anxiousness paralyzed her, and she accepted Max' offer of assistance instead. Her fingers trembled as he took her hand.

"THIS BOAT IS ENORMOUS!" Clara gripped her Onkel's hand and feared she would crush it.

Max grinned. "Over 400 feet long. Boasting four masts and two funnels, this impressive express steamer travels fast."

"It took little convincing to persuade Charlie to swap his steerage ticket for first-class passage." Max introduced the young man at his side. Charlie stood tall, tipped his hat to Max, and proudly joined the 150 or so privileged guests boarding the S. S. Elbe.

When the call came for the third-class passengers to board, everyone's eyes misted.

"I hope I can send you a photo of the babies." Clara sobbed on Tante Adeline's shoulder.

"Ja, A tintype or one of those fancy new cabinet cards would be lovely. I'll be certain your Mutti sees it, too."

Following one more round of hugs and kisses on the cheeks, the trio made their way down the planked companionway, merging with the nearly 800 men, women, and children headed to the belly of the ship—their quarters for the next ten days.

All Sandra's belongings fit in an oversized duffel bag she easily handled on her own. Clara's load proved more challenging. Her favorite red cape flapping about her and her basket hooked over one arm, Clara drug her modest-sized trunk behind her with the other. She tripped on her skirts. The masses pressed into her, but she dismissed Max' offer to help.

A boy waved his stick, rolling his hoop through the passengers. Clara's basket tangled in the hoop and set her already off-balance body in a twist, tossing her to her knees. *I'm not even aboard the ship yet and humiliated by what I can't accomplish.* But no child should be allowed to freely run through a crowd. She patted her tummy. *My children will be better behaved.*

Max stood to the side with an eyebrow raised and jingling coins in his pocket. She succumbed to the gold glints in his eyes inviting her to ask for his assistance.

"Will they allow you to bring my trunk into the women's area?"

"I'll make sure they do."

His broad smile almost disarmed her. "I'm not interested in a man, Herr Engel."

"Fraulein. May I call you Clara, and you call me Max?"

"Perhaps you missed what I said."

"I heard you, but friends address each other by their given names. So—friends?"

She tipped her head. "Friends. Until we get to New York."

"As you wish." He placed the trunk by the bunk she and Sandra would share. They had been assigned to the top spot along with another woman traveling alone.

"I'll return to escort you both to dinner."

"I believe we can make it to the table." Clara faced the stacked beds until he left. *Why is he being kind and helpful to me —just like in Paris?*

Chapter Fourteen

STRASBOURG TO PARIS, *Wednesday, 12 April 1882*

JUST AS HE had carried her down the steps and off the train from Crailsheim, Daniel lifted his Mutter's petite frame and followed Tilly onto the one taking them to Paris.

"These larger seats will be more comfortable for the three of us with our belongings." Tilly placed Rosa's and her bags on one seat.

Daniel allowed his Mutter to stand and seat herself next to the bags, then took the seat across from them. Tilly settled in next to Daniel. Rosa leaned her head on the stacked bags and soon drifted off.

"I'm so thankful you're with us, Tilly. It's difficult to watch Mutter struggle with walking and tasks she accomplished with ease just months ago."

"I hope the special Doktor can help her."

"He will interview her tomorrow about her symptoms while he lectures his students about the disease. I question how lecturing about it while people stare at her helps. How long do you think my Mutter has been experiencing symptoms?"

"Do you think she's suffered much longer than she's told us, but hid much of it?"

He massaged his chin. Daniel's jaw bobbed open and closed. Once, and again. "Maybe Clara would be the better one to ask."

"And the better one to be with you now." Tilly allowed her hand to come to rest on Daniel's forearm. "You miss her."

"Ja, more every day while our dreams and our promises drift further across the widening sea of impossibility."

Memories of all the joy and all the pain their love had endured clunked through his chest like a rusty old bell, all broken down and wasting away. Should he admit to Tilly, that he and Clara are no longer married? The wound so fresh, and he had yet to write Clara the truth of her Vati's action. But she carried his baby or babies, and his letter would assure her he'd still come, but then if he couldn't... *O God, I admit I've prayed less and less when You're the only One who can truly help. I'm asking now. Will You fix what Clara and I have broken?*

"I'm your friend through it all whatever the outcome." Tilly's thumb made circles where her hand rested on his arm.

"Danke, Freund."

Tilly's head tilted toward Daniel. He watched her doze off and nudged a stray hair from her cheek as he pulled her head onto his shoulder. Warm feelings for this woman beside him arose. But she wasn't Clara. Who would care for his children

—their children? He drummed a jittery rhythm on the armrest and stared out the window while Tilly slept.

"Daniel."

Mutter's wide eyes met his as she awoke. She fumbled with the clasp of her reticule. "Your predicament is my fault, son. If I hadn't become ill, you would already be on your way to America."

"Mutter, you would be the first to remind me God's plans don't always agree with ours, and He knows the end from the beginning of a matter. I cannot fathom any beautiful end from this beginning, though."

Tilly stirred, stretched one arm, and covered a yawn with the other hand. "Are we there yet?"

Chapter Fifteen

ON THE SHIP, *Wednesday, 12 April 1882*

When Louise entered their dark cramped quarters, Clara immediately recognized the airs of nobility. *A female Georg.*

"Ew!" Louise pinched her upturned nose. There has been a mistake. I'm certain my fiancé secured a first-class ticket for me. I don't intend to travel in this stench and with commoners."

"My name's Clara. This is my *Freund*, Sandra. Are you Louise?"

"How did you know?"

"Your name is here with ours. You'll be sleeping in the top bunk with the two of us."

"Two?" She studied Clara's extended mid-section. "Looks like you're carrying extra baggage. Where's your husband? You'll never be able to climb up there, and *four* of us will not fit at all. I demand to see the Master of the ship."

Clara bit her tongue holding back the venom forming and turned away. Sandra reached out for Louise's hand. "I don't believe your request will be granted. Welcoming the first-class cabin passengers and his many tasks onboard the ship take the Master's time. We'll be together for at least ten days. Can we agree to get along?"

"This is not what I expected!" She dropped her bag and plopped on the nearest straw mattress.

"There is more to your story than the first-class ticket you believe you're entitled to. Would you like to share?" Sandra asked.

Louise chewed on her fingernails and bounced her knees. "If I tell you, you'll hate me. Everyone does."

"Everyone has a story." Sandra touched her heart. "I'll share mine if you tell us yours."

They hadn't left port, and the rocking of the boat already disturbed Clara's stomach. She was grateful Sandra engaged Louise in conversation.

She gripped the door frame with one hand and clutched her stomach with the other as dry heaves rolled again. Remembering Trude had sent ginger pieces, Clara poked through her basket until she located them on the bottom. Of course.

"The fever took him. Albert died in my arms two days before our wedding. I learned then his family had lost their fortune gambling. He promised me he had first-class tickets to take us to America where we would begin a new life in New York City. It appears he fooled me about that, too. I was so gullible."

Hearing her story Clara's heart began to soften toward the girl. "Men can't be trusted. None, save one. I am sorry for your loss, Louise. Who's meeting you in New York?"

"My brother and his wife have made their new home in New York City." She brushed her skirts and pushed some stray hairs under her charming purple hat. "I'd place a bet the fellow who placed your trunk is the one man who can be trusted."

"I apologize if I gave you the wrong impression. The man is merely an acquaintance."

"But you blush."

"It's not a blush, but it's too warm down here already."

Louise cocked her head. One eye squinted shut. "Alright, as you say."

The occupants of the bottom bunk arrived. A woman with two children.

"Hello. I'm Bertha. This is four-year-old Eliza and three-year-old Freddy."

"Pleased to meet you, Bertha, Freddy, and Eliza. I'm Clara. This is my Freund, Sandra." She pointed to the third woman. "Our new friend, Louise, is assigned to these quarters with us."

"We're meeting my Vater in New York," Freddy said.

"I have a doll, and Freddy has a spinning top. Do you want to play, Clara?" Eliza twirled around with a shout of glee as her skirt lifted from the floor. She placed the doll in Clara's hands.

"Call her Fraulein Clara, please, children," Bertha corrected.

"What a beautiful doll. I love her long blonde locks. They're in a braid, just like yours." Clara patted the child's head and wiggled the end of the plaited hair. "Do you like fairy tales?"

"I like your red curls, Fraulein Clara. I like fairy tales, too. Do you know *Little Red Riding Hood*? Your cape is red like hers."

Clara slipped the cape from her arms and laid it on the bunk. "I do know about Red Riding Hood and the big bad wolf, but your doll reminds me of *Rapunzel*."

"A pretzel. I want a pretzel," Freddy chimed in.

"I don't have pretzels, but I brought a book of fairy tales. If your Mutter approves, I'll read you a story before we all go to sleep."

"Ja! Ja! Ja!" the children chanted together.

"We love stories." Eliza grabbed Clara's arm and hugged it tight.

"Danke, Clara. Their Vater always reads to them, and he's been in America six months already. So many things I had wished we could bring. Alas, we left our books behind."

Lord, I love children, and I thank You I have met these two already. Are Freddy and Eliza too small to sleep on the top bunk? Help me ask Bertha if we might switch places.

Taking her children's hands Bertha stepped out of their quarters. Clara realized she whispered to them, but could not make out the words. *Is she warning them about me?*

A few minutes later they returned to the tiny space the six of them would share. "Clara, Sandra, Louise, we would gladly swap bunks with you."

"Danke! Climbing was a concern." Sandra smiled.

"My concern is sharing with the two of them at all." Louise widened her eyes staring at Clara's middle. "I suppose the bottom bunk will ease the discomfort a bit."

Before Louise could complain more, a knock interrupted them.

"Herr Engel—Max. Dinner time already?" Sandra asked.

"Not yet, but only one more hour until we leave the dock. Then they'll send our dinner down. I brought some rope."

"Not much room in here for jumping games?" Clara shrugged.

Max busied himself adeptly tying the rope to the framework of the bunk right next to the ladder steps. "There. Use it to steady yourself and pull up and onto the top bunk. Coming down should be easier."

"Easier for Bertha and her children. They have agreed to swap places with us. Do you notice everything?"

"I make it a point to be observant. Besides, I made a promise to your Onkel to make your passage as comfortable as possible."

"Without consulting me?"

"Was it just an act in Paris, or were you genuinely grateful I took care of the scoundrel who caused you so much trouble? I assure you there will be more like him with less integrity than he, prying into your business while we're on board."

"My thanks again for your trouble to intervene many times in Paris. My Vati and his barrister removed the sloppy braggart from my life for good a short time later."

"Max, I'm thankful for your presence now." Sandra spoke up. "You've eased my worries."

Their Mutter hushed the children while Max attached the rope.

As soon as he finished, Freddy tugged on Max's pants leg. "Herr Max, look at my top. It spins like this." The child leaned over and turned the wooden toy with his thumb and forefinger. It lost its balance immediately.

Max set it back up and set it spinning around the tiny space.

"You're really good at it!" Freddy bounced in place on the floor of their cramped quarters.

"Hold it just like this. Then spin like this." Max taught the little fella, repeating the lesson over and over.

Freddy tried again and again. Finally. Freddy shouted, "I did it!" The top took off on a wild ride.

"Congratulations!" Max held out his hand to Freddy. "You did do it! Tomorrow I'll show you some coin tricks."

"Will you show them to Eliza and Fraulein Clara, too? Please?"

"What a grand idea, Freddy." He winked at Clara. "Will you join us?"

His reaction to the child was so unlike the scene with Georg in the park in Paris. She smoothed her fingers over the cameo and allowed her thoughts to travel back to the good and the bad she'd left behind. *Will Daniel come? What lies ahead? Does Max hope I'm interested? I'm not, but I do need a Freunde.* She blinked from her reverie to a little man and a grown one staring at her, awaiting her answer.

"I'd be happy to."

"Dinner awaits. Shall we?" Max pointed toward the makeshift tables.

The children scrambled to Max's side and grabbed for his hands. Bertha, Sandra, Louise, and Clara smoothed their garments and tucked a few wisps or curls into place, then followed behind Max and the children.

"We're one happy family for at least ten days." Max grinned.

"Your voice is loud enough for everyone to hear," Clara protested. She lowered hers to a whisper. "Remember we're just Freunde."

"Excuse me a moment, children." He tugged on Clara's hand, then reached up and pulled her cheek toward his mouth. "Family is precisely what I want them to think." He whispered in her ear. "Some of these men have undignified thoughts toward women. If they even slightly believe we're a family, they'll hesitate before acting like stinkers."

Even as Max spoke the words, she felt a poke to her chest. "What large jugs you have, my Lady. May I have a swig?" The brute cackled.

Max grabbed the man's fingers and twisted his arm behind his back. "You won't speak to a lady rudely—at least not in my presence."

"Danke." Clara stared at the floor.

"He'll be nursing those bruises until we reach America!"

She picked through the few things in the reticule she carried until she found her paper fan and waved it before her face.

Kitchen staff stationed buckets of smoked bacon, sauerkraut, and Kartoffeln around the deck. Tin plates clanked as the passengers gathered their share and crammed themselves elbow-to-elbow onto the benches provided.

"Your cooking is much better," Eliza said to her Mutter.

"We'll survive on this until we reach New York. We'll sleep nine times before then. For children time stretches out forever, doesn't it? But the days will pass quickly. We'll see your Vater soon."

"STORIES SHOULD HAVE HAPPY ENDINGS," Clara said.

"But Dame Gothel is a mean old woman!" Eliza proclaimed at the end of the story. "I'm happy the prince found Rapunzel and her babies, and they lived happily ever after. Are you having a baby, Fraulein Clara? Is Max your prince?" Eliza asked.

"Why do you ask, precious Kinder?"

"Your tummy is really big, and I heard Herr Max say you are a happy little family."

"Ah, he did. He's not my prince, though." Clara pressed her palms together and placed them next to her ear like a pillow. "You sleep soundly and dream about your prince. Every little girl should dream of the one who will come for her one day."

"Fraulein Clara." Eliza squeezed her arm. "Are we going to say our bedtime prayers together?"

Clara's inquiring eyes searched out Bertha's. The woman nodded her permission.

"Do you have a special prayer, Kinder?"

"Do yours, do yours, Fraulein Clara," Eliza insisted.

"When I was your age, my Mutti and I prayed this little prayer together — *Ich bin klein; Mein Herz ist rein; Darf niemand drin wohnen als Jesus allein.*"

"We say the same one—*My heart is small. My heart is pure. No one may live there but Jesus alone.*"

"Amen." Freddy was all smiles. "Max said he'd show me a coin trick tomorrow. What's a coin trick?"

"A surprise for tomorrow." Clara kissed her fingers and touched them to the children's foreheads.

"If we sleep fast, Fraulein Clara, will the surprise come faster?"

"I believe it will."

When they laid their heads on the pillow later in the evening, Sandra whispered in Clara's ear. "Eliza is the same age as my Hilda. Makes my heart smile knowing we'll be in Chicago soon."

148

Chapter Sixteen

ONBOARD THE S.S. ELBE, *13 April 1881*

CLARA POKED her head out of their quarters and pointed to a crowd gathering in the common area. "Looks like Max has a way with children and adults. He entertains them all."

"You should consider Eliza's words." Louise cut her eyes as sharply toward Clara as the biting tone of her words. "A *prince* for you and your baby. He'd make a fine one."

Hairs on the back of her neck stood on end as Clara moved away from Louise. She kept as much distance between them as possible in the crowded quarters while still standing where she could observe the children.

"I saw you move the coin to this hand. It has to be there," Freddy pointed to Max's right hand.

Max opened his palm. The coin wasn't there.

"Again, Herr Engel." Eliza clasped her hands to her chest.

Max repeated the trick over and over, each time the children were convinced he had moved the golden Mark from his right hand to his left. Each time it was gone. Moving it from the left to the right. No matter which one they guessed, still gone.

"Again. Again. Again." The children shouted.

Max gazed Clara's direction. She covered her eyes but peeked just a bit. His smile spread wider than the ocean they were crossing.

"You decided to join us." Max motioned her toward them.

The crowd he attracted looked back and forth between the two. "You'll be a fine Vater to the little one, Max." The man commenting shook Max's hand. "Looks like congratulations to you and your wife are in order."

Max stepped toward Clara taking her by the hand. His arm stretched around her waist. "Danke, sir. We are one happy little family." He leaned down and lightly brushed a kiss on her cheek.

Clara's chest tightened. Her heart beat faster. *I promised Daniel I'd wait for him, and I will. But I can't deny Eliza's observation. He would be a fine prince if ever I needed one. I don't need one.*

"Looks like you could use some fresh air, darling. Shall we stroll up on deck?" Max kept up the pretense.

In the open air, Clara nudged him toward a quiet spot. "Why did you make him think we're a family? I'm not your wife, and calling me *darling*."

"Don't get ahead of yourself, Clara. I only said we're a happy little family."

"An illusion then, like the magic of your coin tricks?"

"Family means many things to many people. I haven't asked, but I am puzzled. Whose wife are you? I pray he left earlier to prepare a place in Chicago for you and the baby. You're meeting him there?"

She tugged a wayward curl down over her face, but it did little to hide her embarrassment. "You've been too kind. If you knew the truth, you'd end your valiant knight role."

"I've been told I'm easy to talk to."

Clara stared down at her palms counting eenie meenie minee moe on her fingers. *Do I tell him or not?*

Elbows pulled tight to her body, she shrunk her bulging self into a tight ball and whispered her answer. "As for the scoundrel in Paris, my Vati finally realized how Georg and several other people had used him. Vati broke his promise of my hand in marriage. He and I made peace. I told you the truth. I didn't marry the contemptible fool. The life I carry isn't his, but I am married."

Dead silence. *I wonder if he'll ever speak to me again. He's regretting his choice to travel with us.* Head hung low, Clara twisted the dangly curl and chewed the fingernails on her other hand.

"I consider myself an excellent judge of character. Your story must be a sad one, but one you face with determination and courage."

"Danke." She swallowed hard. "Rules. It is all about rules, and my heart ruled my head. I made irresponsible choices."

"What rules? You are Martin's niece. You have a noble title, if I guess correctly. Rules of nobility?"

"I had a noble title. Reconciliation with Vati evaporated in a few short months when he learned of my condition."

The gold glints in Max's eyes fizzled. "Your Vati is Martin's brother-in-law, the esteemed Baron of Gut Apfelhof?"

Clara nodded.

"I know your Vati."

Clara's jaw dropped. "What? How? He'll hate you after Onkel Martin tells him."

"Slow down, Clara. Martin has assured me under the circumstances, he'd never tell your Vati I'm traveling with you."

"But how do you know Kraig Reinhold?"

"In my business, I escort goods safely to America. He arranged with me to accompany his wines to customers in the United States. Chicago in particular. Multiple cases of his fine vintages are on this ship."

Clara clamped her lower jaw back in place. "It's almost like he planned to make sure someone watched me leave and be sure I stayed gone. He's finished with me."

"Clara, he never mentioned you when he and your brother made the business arrangement. He didn't know we'd be on the same ship. You haven't told me the rest of your story, though. The Vati of your baby must be a fine man to have won your heart."

"He is." Clara found herself twisting up one of her grandmother's lace hankies while she dabbed it at her eyes. *This is way too personal to share with a man, especially one I have only recently met.*

"Would you like to tell me about him?"

Her voice quivered, but she took the risk. "Daniel is Gut Apfelhof's carriage driver. He and his Mutter came to live with our family when he was two years old. Curt, my twin brother, and I were babies. I have loved him my whole life. He's the best man I've ever known. I thought Vati was, too, but the rules.

"Daniel and I side-stepped the *commandments* of nobility. We married legally, but secretly. We're not married in the eyes of the church. You see the obvious consequence. I brought shame on myself and the family. Gut Herr Kraig Reinhold disowned me."

"In whatever role you'll accept, please be a part of my family, Clara."

"But why would you invite someone like me into your family? What about your family, Max? Tell me about them. There must be a reason you're so good with children."

"I come from a large family. I'm the oldest of twelve. Our Mutter died giving birth to our baby sister, Mila. She's ten now. I do love children. My wife and I helped my Vater raise them until businessmen asked me to escort their finished products to markets in America. The position likens me to a member of the historic Hanseatic League, which disbanded many years ago. The group followed strict requirements of honor, character, and behavior from their members.

"My Vater's pride swelled for me. He said, 'The organization chose only the best men, son. If these businessmen seek associates with those same qualities and are asking you to be an integral part of their companies, they offer you their highest respect and trust. Join them.'"

Clara studied her rounded middle. Barely lifting her eyes toward him she asked, "You're married? Who cares for your brothers and sisters now? Your wife?"

"My brother, Ike, is two years younger than me. He took on the responsibility. And my sister, Anna, does the cooking and household needs. She and the little ones are closely knit together. I'm grateful for both of them."

Clara twisted the ever-wayward curl. The wheels in her brain turned like the gears of a fine-tuned timepiece. "You mentioned your wife, and then you stopped speaking of her?"

Max's broad shoulders slumped. He stared down at his empty hands, tapping his fingertips together. "She's gone."

Adjusting her hands on the rail, Clara turned away and stared at the vast expanse of the sea. Hesitation laced her next question. "Gone?"

"How do I tell you this without causing you great fear?" He chewed his lower lip and tapped his heel. With the back of his hand, he swiped tears from his eyes. "Emelia died giving birth to our first child. The little girl lived only a few hours. I named her Emelia, too."

Max slumped forward and rested his face in his hands.

The gesture poorly disguised his grief. *Is a hug too forward? Would I send an unintended message?* She chanced it because it was the only thing she thought to do. She leaned into his shoulders for a side hug. "I am so sorry."

He accepted a few moments of her sympathy before he straightened. "Life is hard, Clara. God gives us Freunde for times like these."

"Your family is the perfect picture of contentment and joy. They don't need any additions, but I like being Freunde. I glimpsed qualities of your honorable character in Paris. You've saved me from difficulties here already, and this is only our second day on the ship. I'm uncertain what family would look like."

"Do you pray for Daniel to join you in Chicago?"

She nodded. "He promised to come by the end of the year. Twins run in our family, and I imagine Daniel and me and our babies together in America."

"A double blessing for you and your husband. Trust your hopes and dreams. We'll be family long enough to see you safely to Chicago—our mutual destination." He squeezed her hand. His fingers lingered a few moments. "Agreed?"

"Agreed." She daydreamed of Daniel while her insides danced to Max's touch once again. *Oh God, Show me Your plan in all of this. Will You bring Daniel to America? I keep telling You he's the only man I desire. Why does my flesh keep reacting to this man before me? Besides, he sure does not need a woman expecting twins with the grief he has faced.*

"One more thing before we go back to the Zwischendeck. I love children, too. I've taught Sunday school at home—what was home—since I was fourteen. I'd like to have a story circle for the children each day we travel. We would act the stories out with several storybook character finger puppets my sister knitted as a gift for the baby. Could we do it together for the children? It would be like we're doing it for your brothers and sisters."

"And my little Emelia. What a fine idea!"

~

16 April 1882

. . .

THREE DAYS out from the Southampton port, clear weather allowed for time on deck. A steady stream of third-class passengers passed up and down the companionway between the Zwishchendeck and the lowest open-air deck. Clara's sickness came in dry form only the last couple of days. She regretted giving Max so many details a few nights ago. But the idea of the story circle proved a hit. The children loved the coin tricks he shared with them, too.

Breathing the fresh air rejuvenated her. Just past dinner today storm clouds rolled in. Hatches normally opened for light and air were battened down. While that kept the rainwater out, it left the travelers in total darkness.

Parents confined their children to their bunks to avoid losing them in the blackness. No story time or coin tricks tonight. Clara's stomach protested the storm. Every turbulent rock of the boat threatened to return the meal of salt meat and prunes.

Soothing notes of a violin wafted through the fear-filled atmosphere. Clara's ears perked to the notes of a flute and an oboe sounding a familiar hymn. Clara added her voice:

FAIREST LORD JESUS, Ruler of all nature,

O Thou of God and man the Son,

Thee will I cherish, Thee will I honor,

Thou, my soul's glory, joy and crown

BEAUTIFUL SAVIOR! Lord of all the nations!

Son of God and Son of Man!

Glory and honor, praise, adoration,

Now and forever more be Thine.

A VIOLIN. A concertina. A harmonica. Triangles. A Harp. All joined the unusual orchestra. Then more voices. The space became uncomfortably warm. No one cared. *What a Friend We Have in Jesus, Nearer My God to Thee, Savior Like a Shepherd Lead Us,* and more. They sang the storm away, worshipping until the hatches lifted, and air moved again in the wee hours of Monday morning—still a few hours until sunrise.

Clara lay in their bunk with her arms curled around the ball in her belly. She rehearsed every thoughtless word she'd spoken to Max. She shouldn't care, but what a foolishly loose woman Max must consider her. *I do need his help even if I prefer not to admit it out loud.*

MONDAY, *17 April 1882*

LIGHT FILTERED INTO THE BUNKS. Instead of rising to greet the day, Clara buried her face deeper in the pillow Alice had sent from home. If she inhaled just right, a whiff of her sisters' sweet perfumes greeted her. She had recounted her dreadful conversation with Max over and over again the last few days.

A lady doesn't tell those things to a man. By now it's obvious I'm no lady. Does it even matter? Why would he want a disrespectful girl like me in his family? And my condition adds a reminder of his loss. At least six more days on this boat. Why did I suggest we host story time together? I can't look him in the eyes again. Choking on her tears brought on more dry heaves.

"Cry baby." Louise stuck her tongue out at her. "I'm going to find Max, and have breakfast with him."

Sandra stayed by Clara's side. Louise dressed, grabbed her tin plate, and sashayed to the food buckets.

"Can you give me a clue what's upsetting you this morning?" Sandra rubbed Clara's back and waited.

"Everything." She blubbered her answer toward the makeshift wall. "I smell my sisters' fragrance. Max embarrassed me again. He got the story out of me. And his wife died."

"Whoa. You're not making sense. Start again from the beginning."

"It began the second day on the ship. I can't believe those men congratulated us on the baby, and he took it in stride, acting like I was his wife. Sandra, I don't want another man. I want Daniel. I believe I've stated my wishes emphatically."

"You've said so many times, ja."

"Why would an upstanding member of some business guild want to be seen with a pregnant woman who's not his wife? He gently pried the whole story out of me. He told me to wait for Daniel, but until then, I'm part of his family."

"If his family's anything like him, then what an honor, my friend."

"Do you know he's escorting a shipment of Kraig Reinhold's wine to Chicago on this very ship? He knows my Vati and my brother!"

Sandra laughed, then patted Clara on the arm. "Such irony. Your Vati can't lose you no matter how hard he tries."

"I don't see the humor. I can't look Max in the eye again after telling him everything."

"I'm sure you told it graciously."

"After the way I dumped the story on you in the wee hours of the morning, you believe I could tell it graciously?" Clara's eyes widened.

"Your parents brought you up to handle every situation with the tact and reserve expected of nobility. Those manners didn't disappear when you left home. Max shared some of his story, too? You mentioned his wife died?"

"In childbirth. The baby lived only two hours."

"Such sadness for him, yet he sows seeds of kindness and joy everywhere he goes."

Clara scrunched her face. "Ja, but I'm embarrassed. Time to see what slop those breakfast buckets hold today. Sausage and Kartoffeln, I'm hoping? Despite the rocking boat, my dinner stayed down last night. I hope breakfast will today, too."

Up ahead Clara witnessed Louise clutching Max's arm and batting her long lashes at him. "You don't need a woman in her condition. I'm available. Shall we stroll up the companionway—together?" Louise tugged on his arm encouraging him along. The gesture appeared unnecessary as they strolled away from the table.

"Does your unease this morning stem more from jealousy than pregnancy? Moments ago, you said you couldn't look him in the eye again. By the expression on your face, you're aggravated because another gives him attention."

"You know Daniel's the only man for me."

Sandra raised her eyebrows. "From my perspective, you have a keen interest in another, and you fear you spoiled your chances last night."

"Nein. I love Daniel. Ten years ago, so many times in between, and again last week, I promised Daniel I'd wait. I will." *So, why do I encounter giddy twinges and flutters near Max?* Clara clutched her throat, laid a hand on her tummy, and crumbled to the floor.

THE COMMOTION DREW Max's attention even from a distance. He pushed Louise's hand loose from his arm. "Excuse me, please."

"You're going to help *her*?"

"It's who I am to offer help when able."

Loud enough to be heard by the gathering crowd Louise called out. "Hurry back, sweetheart."

"Sweetheart? Nein." Pulling himself away from the pushy tart, he made his way to discover Clara doubled over on the floor. He studied Sandra's face for even a hint.

"She turned green before she plopped down on the floor. Might have been something she witnessed rather than her morning ritual."

Max grimaced. "Have you created a riddle, Sandra?" When

he reached down to help Clara up, she placed both hands on the back of her head.

"Family helps family, remember? May I?"

"I'll stand when I'm ready." She shoved at his leg.

He feared insulting her, but he said it anyway. "It would be difficult, I imagine, to get back up alone."

"I am alone. Just go back to Louise."

Max froze in place. *The crowd is really quiet—staring at us.* The same voice congratulating them a few days ago spoke up again. "Problems in Paradise, Max? You have her in a family way, and you cheated on the little woman?"

What had Clara said about lying? And what did I say about character and integrity? Max's mind reeled faster than a racing carriage pulled by a dozen horses. *Should I betray her confidence? Would anyone believe me if I told the real story? It would surely earn black marks on my character and hers.* If only Louise minded her own business. A strong voice jolted him from his deliberations.

"Ladies and gentlemen, all of you should be ashamed of yourselves right now!" Sandra's tone commanded their attention. "You gossip and accuse where you have no knowledge."

Surprise registered on many faces. The group remained still.

"Clara and I both travel because of extremely difficult circumstances in our lives. This man knows Clara's Onkel, the man who saw the two of us to the ship. Max offered to escort Clara and me to America to keep us safe from the foolishness of the masses on this ship. You have provided ample evidence we need him!

"He traded his first-class ticket to accompany us in the Zwischendeck. Now I cannot imagine a man having any reason to step down for an old lady and a pregnant woman, neither of whom he knows. The fact he does care attests to his character and kindness.

"You should know Clara is married. Her husband is unable to travel with her. Beyond that, the details of our struggles are mine and Clara's to bear. To have Max travel with us eases our worries and grief on this journey. Kindly disperse yourselves. Maybe Clara and Max will be over the embarrassment you've subjected them to soon enough to entertain you and your children again with their stories and coin tricks. Be grateful for them."

Max knelt beside her. With his arms on Clara's shoulders, he risked asking again. "May I help you up?"

Clara lifted her head just enough to mouth her agreement. "Ja."

"You're already on your knees. If I lift you from the back, can you push with your feet?"

Once on their feet, Max stroked his fingers across her cheeks wiping away the stray tears and tucking a few wayward strands behind her ears. He peered into her dark orbs. "Clara, you'll always be a part of my family. Whatever lies ahead for you, you can trust me—until you tell me to go away—and at least until we reach Chicago."

"What happened with Louise?"

"She's lonely. I'm not responsible for what you observed. Just as our fellow passengers jumped to conclusions the other day, I believe they allowed their imaginations to host another party this morning. Sandra made them understand their opinions aren't appreciated!" A wide grin spread across Max, face. "They'll ignore us for now."

"Come back to our bunk with me for a few minutes before we grab breakfast, please," Sandra tugged on Clara's arm.

CLARA FOLLOWED Sandra back to their cramped space.

"What's wrong with me? I have no interest in any man except my Daniel. Why did the scene with Louise stir jealousy in me? And why, oh why do my insides fill with sparks like meteor showers every time Max touches me? His fingers on my cheeks just now—what shade of red did I turn?" Instead of twisting the loose curl, she gave it a ferocious jerk, then stomped her foot. "I'm so angry with myself!"

Sandra stroked Clara's hair. "A verse from Proverbs comes to mind: *A man's heart deviseth his way: but the Lord directeth his steps.* You and Daniel made big plans, but God has directed your steps along a quite different path. As much as you wish for it to be so, will Daniel be able to follow you?"

"He promised—to try."

"The word try often hints at failure to come. What you really hoped is for the rules to disappear. You hoped your parents, the church, or any person or entity with the power to change things for you would make an exception. You and Daniel would marry and live happily ever after in Germany—at Gut Apfelhof."

"I never believed anything would change. We believed our prayers were answered, though, when Onkel Martin officiated our secret wedding."

"Many decisions and choices we make bring pain into our lives. This one brings joy, too. God is preparing a sweet child —or maybe two—to meet you soon."

"And I'll love them very much. They're Daniel's and mine, but I don't need anybody else to go through this horrible story with me. If I can't have Daniel, I don't want anyone." Her breath caught in her chest, making her already snug gown even more uncomfortable.

"Are you certain?" Sandra's hand rested on Clara's.

"You haven't explained how I could be so under Max's spell every time I'm in his presence and totally undone with his slightest touch."

"God has a plan to use your situation for His good and His glory. He hasn't answered your prayers the way you asked, but maybe Max is a God-has-a-different-plan-answer. You're an attractive woman with emotional needs. Daniel may not be ready yet, but he could take another wife one day."

"My head and my heart are pounding. I barely recognize myself. I'm certain I couldn't hurt Daniel more, or love another. Nothing makes sense."

"When the rules didn't change in your favor, you and Daniel made plans. You married in secret and you didn't believe *this* would happen to you. Keeping your little secret provided time for you and Daniel to save the money to travel to America. All the while you snuck away to enjoy the pleasures of married life while you waited to leave."

"The rules are so unfair. We're all the same in God's eyes. We believed God would recognize our love for each other and excuse our foolish decision because He understood our predicament."

"You speak truth about all being equal in God's eyes. He does understand, but He doesn't necessarily just allow our choices to go without consequences. Would it have been wiser for you and Daniel to wait until you saved the money to travel, then married, and immediately left for America?"

"I've thought about that more than once. If we hadn't been so sneaky, we would have avoided so many lies and so much pain. I hear Rosa's voice in my ears. *'Lying lips are abomination to the Lord: but they that deal truly are his delight.'*"

"Once you stepped into your private world, you found yourself drawn back again and again. God already knew the end from the beginning. Should He have overlooked your deceitfulness?"

"I wanted to believe He loved us enough to allow us the pleasure our class differences denied us, and without consequences—especially since we were married."

"Truth is, He did allow you the pleasure. You knew your Vati would have the marriage annulled or you wouldn't have hidden your actions. God held you accountable because He loves you."

"And I broke His heart. And my parents' hearts. And my Oma's. She forgave us time and again. We didn't fool her. She asked if we realized the risks and urged us to stop. I shared our secret with her, and she promised not to tell. What an enormous burden I placed on her shoulders."

"The risks your Oma spoke of—a baby—a beautiful blessing. I can imagine everyone's excitement over the news had the circumstances been different."

"The end from the beginning thing. I was so sick from the start. I lived in denial for weeks. Alice, my personal maid, pointed out the extended absence of my menses. Truthfully, I would happily do it all over again to be with the man I love."

"Give your past to God. Allow Him to redeem your mistakes. Ask His guidance for your future. Wait for the man God chooses for you. He may be Daniel, or he may be another if your Vater has had your marriage annulled."

"I no longer believe for God's best for me and the babies inside me. And Louise still sleeps in our bunk for at least six more nights." Clara wiped her brow with her sleeve.

"I'll be the buffer between you. She's lonesome and confused. You may have more in common than you believe. Her fiancé duped her. She deflects her grief with spitefulness toward others.

"Allow the Good Lord to work on your behalf. Maybe He'll lead Daniel back to you. Or maybe He has another. Max has a heart of gold and loves children. You told me his story last night. Have you considered he overlooks your past and would like you to be a part of his future? *The Lord directeth your steps*—and Daniel's and Max's steps."

MAX AND FREDDY sat on the floor of the ship. Freddy squealed in delight as Max spun his top through the feet of the other passengers and regaled the boy with stories of the toy's adventures. "Now it is a frog hopping its way to the pond."

"There's no pond, Herr Engel!"

"Sure, there is. See the hollow spot right there. Froggy hopes someone fills it with tea so he can enjoy a swim."

"You're funny!" Eliza pushed Freddy away and hugged Max's neck. You're like my Vater."

"Fraulein Clara! You're here. We can eat breakfast now. I'm hungry," Freddy said.

"You waited for us? Danke."

Max jumped up to grab Clara's hand and lead her to the breakfast buckets. "We have our plates. Time for us to grab the morning grub before it's devoured."

Clara pulled away. Max mouth gaped. "Something I said or did, ma'am?"

She shook her head while staring off to their right. Max turned in that direction.

If looks could kill, Louise shot stinging darts straight at his face. "You're worthless. I leave you for two minutes and you're back with the tramp."

"You humbled yourself to take a ride in the Zwischendeck, Max." Sandra sighed. "For this drama? My confidence in your role is slipping."

"You told me you don't want him and you don't trust him." Louise cozied up to Max. "He is a fine prince. Keep your eyes and hands off."

Bertha took her children's hands and led them away from the unfolding scuffle.

Max stared at Clara. "Please, ladies. I'll decide who unhands me."

Sputters without words came from Clara's mouth. Her hand clasped the neckline of her gown. A yelp followed. "My cameo. It's gone!"

"It looked like a cheap one. It's probably a faded-out conch shell." Louise shrugged.

When Clara reached to search the woman's pocket, Louise slapped her hand causing whelps to rise.

"I believe we'll find it among your things!" Clara shouted at her.

"What are you going to do about it if you do? Huh? Who will you tattle to?"

"I punched a man once. Don't think I won't do it to you. I'll scratch your face, too."

"I wouldn't be surprised coming from a hussy like you." Louise jammed her fists to her hips.

Sandra stepped between the two directing a question to Louise. "Did your parents raise you to be a bratty child without manners—one who turned into a mean-spirited woman?"

With a frustrated stamp of her foot, Clara stalked away.

Max followed Clara far enough to see her head for her bunk. "Would you like to talk about it, Clara?"

"Nein. The cameo is gone. One more broken piece of my heart."

"I'm going to join a card game." He waved to her. "We can talk later."

"Wait! Nein! No card games!"

Max disappeared among the crowd, his mind took sharp turns to the left and the right and upside down and inside out. What in the world was her last outburst about? No card games? One woman clearly pregnant, and by a man she is supposed to be married to, but her Vati wants to make sure she's not. A crazy widow—oh, but they never quite made it to the altar, and she's been duped.

I'm caught in the middle of these women fighting like cats. Lord, I never talked to You about escorting Clara and Sandra on this trip. And now there's Louise. Guess it's about time You and I discussed this. What did I get myself into? I'm not looking for a replacement for Emelia. Speak, Lord, I'm listening.

A still small voice. *Help her find the cameo.*

CLARA, Sandra, and Bertha searched their cubby-sized space from top to bottom. Sandra stood behind the others making a shield from any prying eyes while Bertha and Clara carefully went through every piece of Louise's belongings. Max conveniently drew Louise's attention away from them.

"I still believe it's in her pocket." Clara nervously bounced one heel and twisted her curl around and around her finger. The cameo was not to be found.

Sandra moved sideways. Louise returned and forced her way into the space.

"You didn't find it, did you? I told you I didn't take it. I knew you would go through my things. If I did take it, do you think for one minute I would leave it in here?"

Clara nudged Sandra and Bertha into a huddle. With heads close together she whispered. "If we keep constant vigil over her, she'll tell on herself. I'm praying about it until it is found. You both have your own worries and concerns, but will you both pray? Lately, God hasn't answered my prayers the way I want. Will He help locate the cameo, or will He consider it a silly request?"

Sandra whispered back, "Luke 12:7."

But even the very hairs of your head are all numbered. Fear not therefore: ye are of more value than many sparrows.

Just like Rosa, the gifter of the cameo, Sandra imparted Bible verses often. Clara almost heard them in Rosa's voice.

A FEW PASSENGERS played their instruments and others danced. Clara joined them almost forgetting the condition making it impossible for her to waltz around as freely and easily as she once had.

Waltz around? Memories of waltzing in the cottage with Daniel thrilled her. Thoughts of the lost cameo needled her. *I think it best if I put my attention elsewhere.* Clara returned to the bunk, opened her basket, and removed a drawing pad and pastels. *Is there enough privacy in here on the bunk to do some daydreaming? It's doubtful, but time alone sketching always lifts my spirit.* Until weariness claimed her, images flowed from the color sticks in her fingers gliding in their own symphony across the textured paper.

Voices and laughter from her bunkmates returning from the frolicking fun awakened Clara. *I just had the best sleep I've experienced since I left Tante Adeline and Onkel Martin's home — maybe the best since I left my home where I'll never be welcomed again.*

Max caught Sandra's attention before she entered the women's room. "Will you let Clara know I'd like to speak with her?"

"Of course."

Yawning and pushing back her wild curls, Clara stood in the doorway.

"I pray you've rested well. Will you do story time with us? The children have asked for you."

"What story do you wish to tell today?"

"Brier Rose. Her prince rescues the sleeping princess and her babies."

On cue, Clara's babies jammed her ribcage. She held her side, massaging the spot. "Excellent choice. I imagine it further inciting our fellow passengers' vivid imaginations."

"So, you agree? I'll gather the children. I plan to show them the trick where I slip my thumb off and on, too."

"Alright, entertain them with your detachable thumb. I'll freshen myself and join you shortly."

Clara chose the princess and the prince from among the puppets and added a needle to represent the pretend piece of straw. As she looked through the figures Emmaline created, she noticed one she hadn't been aware of before. Where did this set of twin babies come from? *We hadn't even discussed twins before I left Apfelhof. And this prince looks a whole lot like Max, not Daniel.*

Glancing down at the drawing pad, another prince smiled up at her. Even without a face, his appearance closely resembled the puppet. Clara flipped through the pages of her sketch-book. Panic swept through her. The older drawings of the man with no face stared back. The same wavy chestnut hair and the golden glints where eyes should have been. *Nein. Nein! I want Daniel. Only Daniel.*

Now, I wish I hadn't promised Max that I would join him. She took a deep breath, then picked up the puppets. "You're the only princess in here. You will be Briar Rose, but you sure do look like me." She held the prince too, but wouldn't say his name. With one puppet on her thumb and one on her index finger, she pinched the babies between them. *Like hiding them will change the story?* "It is time to join the children." She patted the twin puppet's head.

"You sketched Max?"

Clara had not heard Sandra return.

"If I didn't know how much you believe you and Daniel will be reunited, I'd say for sure you have set your sites on Max. Look at those likenesses you've drawn."

"The puppets and I are headed to story time with Max. Don't mention the similarities, please. They are more than obvious. Besides one of these drawings was done when I contended with Georg. I hadn't even met Max." She shoved the hanky to her eyes and blotted away tears. "I don't want anyone asking questions."

"I promise to not ask any out there." Sandra pretended to button her lip. "But I do have several for you when we're alone again." They walked to where Max had the children seated around one of the tables. The group had grown to at least twenty now. Freddy pointed to the two women. "Do you know Herr Max can make his thumb come off, Fraulein Clara?"

The corners of her mouth turned up at the display of the boy's energy and enthusiasm. Clara hoped it would ease the distress she felt. "Really? Do you think he'll show me?"

"Have a seat, Fraulein, and prepare to be amazed." Max motioned to the empty spot on the bench in front of him.

Clara tried to repeat his moves, but her thumb didn't cooperate—maybe because puppets covered her fingers.

"You brought the puppets." Eliza clapped. "What story will you tell us today?"

"Do you know the story of Briar Rose?" Max asked the boys and girls.

All their heads bobbed up and down. Nothing got past Eliza, one sharp-eyed little girl. "Herr Max look at Fraulein Clara's puppets. They look like you and her."

The golden glints in those turquoise eyes of his lit up like mini-lightning bolts in every direction.

"Let me see what you have there." Max lifted Clara's hand to study the little dolls more closely. A broad smile stretched across his face. "Why I believe they do, Eliza." Max moved Clara's fingers around having the little people speak to one another, telling the tale of the sleeping beauty. He held onto the babies until the right part of the story.

Uneasiness coupled with bliss. They mingled through her flesh. *He's holding my hands again. I'd welcome the uncomfortable mix of tossing breakfast and tumbling babies to this other fluttering.*

When Max leaned in having the prince puppet tenderly kiss the princess to awaken her, every nerve in Clara's body went to dancing with a quickness compelling her body to a whole new level of elation. *I like this feeling, but I would prefer it with Daniel. This can't be happening. Oh, why am I so conflicted?*

"Princess, look, you had twins while you slept." Max placed

the two little baby puppets in Clara's palm and rocked it ever so gently.

"And they lived happily ever after," Eliza said. "Fraulein Clara, will you and Herr Max live happily ever after, too?"

Bertha instructed her Kinder. "Thank Herr Max and Fräulein Clara. Wash your hands before lunch."

When Bertha and the children walked off, all other eyes were fixed on the couple.

"Well, you two, is there something we should know?" The man's jowls jiggled as he joked and laughed.

Clara's stomach lurched again. Dizziness when she stood hampered her speedy exit.

A woman nearby removed her apron, cleared the mess, and offered her a damp cloth. Clara thanked her and silently prayed Max wouldn't touch her again—today. Before the thought took hold, he laid a hand on her forearm and planted a kiss on the top of her head.

The nerve of him!

"You could use the fresh air. Come for a stroll up on the deck." Max spoke softly. His words tickled her ears, and the kiss spread goose pimples down her arms. She hesitated, but followed.

The same spot from a few nights ago provided privacy. Barrels in the corner sufficed as seating. Max motioned Clara to sit first. He lowered himself to one across from her and sat tall. His arms folded across his chest emphasized his broad shoulders. He tapped his fingers on his upper arms and chewed his lower lip.

What unnerves this otherwise confident man? Clara waited quietly. Her hands tucked under her hips kept them from shaking. *Why am I scared of what stirs in Max's head? My babies stir too. Are you two in there playing giddy-up on a merry-go-round?*

"Clara, has God ever spoken to you?"

Her eyebrows lifted skyward and she pressed two fingers to her lips. A few moments passed. "He has used other people to speak His truths into my life. I'm not always a good listener."

"But have you heard His voice?"

"You mean sometimes Bible verses jump off the page and come to life in a special way at the moment?"

"I don't know what I mean exactly. I have always believed in God. My family attends church together. Since I began my current position, I'm often away from home and not attending at all. I find myself forgetting to pray. I do what seems right at the moment, but I don't ask God first if it's the best thing or even the right thing."

"Guilty. Daniel and I didn't care if it was the best thing or the right thing, it just felt so right at the moment. For certain, we didn't ask if our secret marriage was His best for us. It was an impulsive decision. Why do you ask?"

"After meeting you in Paris, I never forgot your face. I didn't desire to forget. Laying eyes on you again in Bremen, my heart took over. When Martin asked me to escort you and Sandra, I'm not sure if my heart or my head made the decision. I know I didn't pray about it.

"And now you regret your decision."

"Not at all." Max's eyes lit up with his smile. "But I am regretting not asking God what I was getting myself into. You say you only want Daniel, but you blush at my slightest attentions. Jealous green fails to flatter you, but when Louise is near me your dark brown eyes begin to fill with a verdant haze. I'd rather avoid a squabble between two women dueling because of their personal problems. Do you really believe she stole the cameo?"

"I know the cameo is gone. I could release you from the deal to protect Sandra and me. You'd be free to go after Louise. I expect Daniel's coming by the end of the year. He's the only man I want. And what does all of this have to do with God's voice?"

"I'm confused. I talked to God last night. The unexpected situation I invited when I agreed to protect you and Sandra— I never asked God if I should. Last night I asked Him what He wanted me to do about these women—you, Sandra, and Louise."

"Did God confirm you erred in helping us?" Clara looked down at her hands and picked at her cuticles.

Max's hand settled on hers. "Look at me, Clara."

She lifted her head to face his.

"I heard *a voice* say, *'Help her find the cameo.'*"

"Whose voice?" Clara gasped. "It's important to me to find the brooch. I'm praying and I asked Sandra and Bertha to pray, too. I'm not very hopeful. God hasn't answered many of my prayers the way I'd like in months."

"Could we purchase another cameo in Chicago?"

She hung her head. "The cameo is irreplaceable."

"There's more to your story, but you don't have to explain. The brooch means much to you, and I have my answer. I did hear God speak. There's one problem. I have no idea where to look. I could hang around some card games. It might show up as payment for a gambling debt."

The hairs stood up on Clara's arms, and not from the kind of tingles she had recently experienced in Max's presence. "Gambling was not listed among the character traits you said would land someone in your fancy *club*."

"I would only watch them play." He squeezed her hand that still rested in his. "Your teeth are chattering. You seem edgy, and not from a chill."

"Not in the air, but still a chill—another kind. I'm reminded of a Bible verse about associating with the wrong people ruining good character."

"A bad experience from your past perhaps? I'll not pry."

"Danke."

"If Louise stole it from you, she seems to want to hurt someone because someone hurt her—the old *miserable people enjoy making others miserable* adage. Could she have known it would take a card game to win it back, and my involvement in the pursuit would offend you?"

"She was betrayed by a gambler. So was my family. Georg's troubles and his family's troubles all began in Baden-Baden at the Kurhaus. Everyone knows what activities went on inside its walls. When the spa closed, they relocated their activities to Monte Carlo in Monaco. The saga of my troubles became very complicated, but I never told anyone on the ship. She couldn't have overheard. When she told Sandra and me her

story, I responded by telling her no men could be trusted—
none save my Daniel."

"My turn to be hurt. You don't trust me?"

"I told her I didn't. I wanted and trusted only my Daniel."
She tugged on the bodice of her gown to let the sudden wave
of heat escape. "Then she moved in on you. As you say, her
actions have turned me greener than I can explain. She's
resorted to calling me ugly names."

"Many challenges face us down here in the Zwischendeck.
Louise added an extra trial for you."

"We all have troubles. Louise enjoys sharing hers with others.
How many more days?"

"This crossing has been better than some. On many a voyage,
dozens succumb to pneumonia."

"Sandra's son-in-law died of pneumonia on a ship and was
buried at sea. She's traveling to America to be with her
daughter and granddaughter."

"And she's encouraging you. She deserves time to grieve, but
she keeps us all uplifted instead."

"She's very observant of what folks say and what they don't.
Her words have calmed a few threatening tempests. People
are people and we are cramped together down here. You'd
hope we would all get along for the good, but tensions esca-
late instead, and she's always willing to step in to ease the
situation. I'm so thankful for the comfort she offers me."
Muscles in Clara's face began to relax.

Looking the other way, Max shook his head and ran his hand
through his hair. "There are always men who take advantage
of women. And there's always someone cheating others in a

card game, another is a sore loser, and the reactions become ugly."

"Ja, and gambling woes began the blackmail nearly destroying my family." Clara cleared her throat hoping to moisten her dry mouth. "Is there another way to find the cameo?"

"I can't say." Max shrugged. "Pray with me God will show me where to look."

"I will, and I'll listen for His answer. I do trust you." Clara squeezed his hand.

"I'm honored. I'll do my best to maintain your trust."

"I'm still waiting for Daniel." A hint of a laugh escaped. *Should I laugh or cry? Will Daniel come at all?*

"And I'm still grieving Emelia. We make a pair, Clara Becker."

They made their way back down the companionway to their gloomy quarters. "We'll find the cameo, Clara."

Chapter Seventeen

LATE EVENING, *Tuesday, 18 April 1882*

OTHER THAN THE storm a few days ago, weather had been clear. Passengers in the Zwischendeck had moved freely up and down the companionway to breathe fresh air and gather a few rays of sunshine. But today had been rainy and the hatches secured. Nearly unbearable stuffiness filled the lowest deck. Clara wiggled on her tiny patch of the mattress.

Her mind traversed all the corners of her muddled situation. Sleep alluded her.

While I lay awake, O Lord, I'll talk to You. Would You agree to keep us all alive until we reach America? I hear a few folks coughing. I pray you won't allow anyone else to become ill. We have only a few more days. You know how important the cameo is to me. Prove to Max, it was You who impressed the cameo message upon his heart, by showing him where to look. Then let him find my treasure, please.

I haven't prayed much lately, God. I'm more inclined to complain about how You haven't answered my past prayers my way. Truth is, I am grateful—grateful for friends on this ship, for Sandra who brightens the day for all of us while she grieves her own losses, and for Bertha and her sweet children. I'm not so sure I can thank You for Louise. Maybe You could show me a reason.

I'm grateful for Max who chooses to protect us while he grieves silently, and for Daniel who will come to America for the babies and for me. For the puppets from Emmaline and the book of fairy tales from Hannah. Those have helped to pass the time and delighted the children. How did Emmaline create a puppet so close to Max's likeness?

And before she knew it Clara's prayers wandered into fantasies of Max's attentions leading her to a land of sweet dreams.

∾

Wednesday Morning, *19 April 1882*

Aromas of peppermint and eucalyptus filtered through the accumulated stench of body odors and roused Clara from slumber. *Peppermint tea for breakfast? Really, the cook's menu has changed significantly.* She poked an elbow to nudge Sandra but found she and Louise had both abandoned the bunk and were standing by the bed.

"Freddy began to cough early this morning," Sandra said. "I had packed dried herbs and spices in my bag. Mixing peppermint and eucalyptus leaves may help alleviate his cough and any fever."

"Your friend's amazing, Clara. If she had been with her daughter's family, I believe she would have saved Samuel's life." Bertha stroked her son's head while Sandra rubbed the mixture on his chest.

"And little Freddy will get well," Clara answered. "Last night I prayed for all of us to arrive in America healthy."

Louise scratched her arms and legs. "Sandra, do you have any special leaves in your bag for the itching?"

It would be a just punishment for her if Sandra had no remedy. Wishing evil is not exactly a thought to give me good reason to be thankful for Louise, is it God?

"Your skin may be sensitive to the straw we're sleeping on. I pray it's not from fleas. Clara, reach in my duffel for the little paper wrapper marked rosemary. We'll crush it with some of the eucalyptus and sprinkle it on our mattresses just in case. We need to pray the rash is not from fleas, though. Our remedy would only send the critters scurrying to another part of the ship."

"What about my itching?" Louise scratched at the bumps on her arm.

"I brought baking soda, Louise. Rub some on your forearms where the rash is the worst. Then wrap the area with a cool damp cloth. Clara, find the soda and help her, please."

Clara gathered the items. "I prayed we'd make it to America without incidents like this. Was it too much to hope our trip would be different than other third-class passages we've heard about?"

Louise rubbed her itchy arms. "I wouldn't have a rash on my arms if my fiancé had purchased the tickets he promised. With my family's station, I deserve better than this."

Would sharing my family's noble status and where I am now, add to her disdain for me? Best I keep quiet, and let her rant about how unfair life has treated her. I prayed for a reason to be thankful for Louise. Then this. Is God listening to my petitions?

A tiny voice. *Has life been any more unfair to either of you, Clara? Did you both make choices with consequences you'd have preferred to avoid? Maybe you could change things. Become friends. Maybe then you'll find something about her to be thankful for.*

Clara rubbed her curls. *Am I hearing God after I accused Him of not answering my prayers, and how do I respond? Maybe we both made unwise decisions, but God, is that a good reason to be her friend?*

Clara stomped the three steps over to Sandra's bag. She gave her loose curl a tight twist and took her time digging around for the baking soda. *God, I need the right words and a pinch of Your love sprinkled in my heart if this is what You want me to do.*

"Let Freddy stay here in his bunk and rest. Bring him a little tea to sip." Clara encouraged Sandra and Bertha to take Eliza and join the other passengers for breakfast.

When they were on their way, Clara wrapped the cloths for Louise. *I'm grateful Rosa packed strips of fabric in her trunk for any necessary adjustments in my clothing.* She retrieved them. After rubbing the baking soda on Louise's arms, she wet the strips and wound them over the rash.

"Thank you, Clara." Louise's words didn't sound entirely genuine, but it was a start.

"It must be difficult for you to allow me to touch you and care for you in this way?"

"Why would you make such an accusation?" Louise huffed.

"You believe in social status and all the rules attached to it. You come from a privileged family. You'd prefer a commoner not tend to you. You're too good for any of us down here—save Max."

"Especially a trollop!"

"We're all created equal in God's eyes. My Vati is a well-known and well-loved Baron in a Württemberg community."

Louise's jaw went slack, then clamped back in place. "I didn't know."

"Vati and I were both betrayed by a worthless man I never trusted. My Vati promised him my hand in marriage. I understand your circumstances more than you can imagine. I sympathize."

"You're pregnant by the jerk?"

"No, Vati realized in time. He voided the agreement, and he and I reconciled before I would've been forced to marry the fiend."

Louise raised the hand of the wrapped arm to her chest. "Who? Why?"

"You made a poor choice to trust Albert. Did you love him?"

"Ja—at least I love the memory of him I have from before I learned the truth."

Clara began wrapping Louise's other arm. "I love Daniel. He's our family's carriage driver. He loves me too. We made a poor decision. The Bible says we're all equal in God's eyes. We cast aside the class rules claiming otherwise. We married secretly without our parents' permission. Then we kept our secret from everyone.

"You see the consequences. Even after the peace Vati and I made, I disrespected his rules. He disowned me—my title thrown away with our shameless choice."

Both arms now securely wrapped in the fabric, Louise tugged on her dress just below the bodice. Eyes cast downward she nervously twisted the fabric one way and another. She slowly lifted her quivering chin. "I thought Albert loved me as much as I loved him. I allowed him to have a man's way with me."

"And you fear…

"Ja. I'm most thankful to not have my time while on this boat, but I haven't had it for nearly four months. My dress pulls taut over my belly."

"Four months, and you've been unwilling to admit it. I understand. I denied it to everyone who asked."

"I told myself that we were getting married in a few weeks. No one would know, and it wouldn't happen to us if we did it just once. Then he became ill and died. The wedding was to take place on February 4, and we had planned this trip to join my brother and sister-in-law in New York.

"Our stories are much the same. However, Daniel and I were married. For weeks Daniel and I continued secretly enjoying each other as the husband and wife we are. Weeks became a few months. He admitted to me that in his spirit he knew beyond a doubt from the moment of our first beautiful coming together, his seed was planted. We were saving money to travel to America. We worried everyone would find out before we could leave. Vati did learn the truth, and here I am."

"When I insulted you, my worries were easier to bear."

"When people are broken, it becomes convenient to make others miserable too, but their pain remains. I'm quite jealous of you. You've not been sick at all! You laugh at my easily upset stomach. I'm happy it has eased up for me while we've been on the ship. I expected all the ship's rolling on the waves would make it worse. Before we left Bremen, I was sick every morning since late October."

"Life isn't easy for any of us, is it?"

"We're all sinners in need of His grace."

"And I'm in need of some certain tea. Does Sandra have any in her bag?"

"Please don't, Louise." Clara shared the story of her friend Tilly's baby.

"She buried it herself?" Louise pulled her collar up to cover her mouth.

"*It* was a baby. Ja, she did. My brother, Curt, and I found the makeshift grave."

"Enough! If I didn't have a nauseous stomach before, I do now."

Clara continued anyway. "We had no idea who the Mutter was, but because of the location where the baby was buried, we recognized the end of life was deliberate. We gave the baby boy a more proper burial. We learned later he belonged to Tilly. Deep pain haunts her as my friend grieves her loss."

"You knew it was a boy? Please don't tell me anymore. You shared too many details already. I need to do this."

Clara shook her head. "No, you don't. Several people suggested I drink the tea. I considered it, but the memory of what I saw in that grave convinced me there was a living baby in my belly long before I felt the quickening. I couldn't do it. Tilly realized the fact too late for her perfectly formed little boy. She had missed three monthly times. A tiny human life grows inside you, too, Louise. Cherish your baby."

"Tilly's story is a sad one, but my family may disown me like yours did. I must take care of this while I can."

"While you can? You've missed four times. Have you felt the bubbles—the quickening?"

Color flooded Louise's cheeks.

"You have!" Everything in Clara wanted to shake Louise. She twisted the curl around and around instead. "Promise me you'll pray first, and listen for God's answer. I'm weak in the listening department, but I'll ask Him to help us both pay better attention to God's answers."

"I promise to pray, but I won't promise to not go through with my plan."

"Promise you will listen for God's answer."

Louise gave her a weak smile. "Will you forgive me for treating you poorly?"

"*Seventy times seven.* I may not forgive you for taking my cameo, though. Where have you hidden it?"

With a chuckle, Louise said, "Max snatched it and made it disappear like a vanishing coin trick. You told me no man can be trusted."

BERTHA AND SANDRA RETURNED. Louise escaped quickly. Bertha stayed with her boy. Sandra and Clara went in search of fresh air. Finding an unoccupied corner, the women leaned against the deck rail. Breezes, sunshine, and silence surrounded them.

"I brought you up here." Clara cleared her throat. "To tell you the man we trusted stole the cameo for one of his silly magic tricks. Louise told me."

"Louise said so, and you believe her?" Sandra scratched her forehead.

"We forgave each other. Then she divulged the information about the brooch. She even chuckled as she said it."

Sandra swept wind-blown tresses back from her face. "Back up. Tell me about the forgiveness part."

"Expect her to ask you for some special tea. I hope you don't have any."

Sandra shifted her weight. Lines deepened in her forehead. "I don't." She sucked on her lip and stared out to sea. "Did she tell you they never married?" Sandra whispered. "He died in her arms two days before their planned wedding day."

Clara pressed her lips together and offered Sandra her hand-kerchief to dry her tears. "While we're still alone in this corner, I'll tell you the rest—the part Louise kept secret. We shared our stories. She loved him, and believed it wouldn't happen if they did it just once before the wedding."

"A common lie of the enemy—an easy enough one to believe in the moment of desire I suggested you and Louise may be more the same than you realized. I never considered this common ground. Oh, the burdens we bear. He wronged her in so many ways, but in this, Louise engaged willingly. Now she's asking assistance to pile one poor choice atop another."

Her handkerchief already soaked, Sandra wiped more tears with the back of her hand.

"Blessed be God, even the Father of our Lord Jesus Christ, the Father of mercies, and the God of all comfort; Who comforteth us in all our tribulation, that we may be able to comfort them which are in any trouble, by the comfort wherewith we ourselves are comforted of God."

"Beautiful words from Second Corinthians. Why are you sharing them now?" Clara took Sandra's soggy hand and looked into her eyes.

"God brought you and Louise together on this journey. Your decision required much courage. As the verse says, I pray you allow Him to use your struggle to bring comfort and hope to others—yes, even Louise."

"Georg's first wife died from the tea. And Tante Adeline…" Clara pinched her lips. "Perhaps I shouldn't divulge her secrets. I've said too much already."

Sandra's eyes widened, but she asked no details. "Pray Louise chooses the high road, and allows her little one to live."

"And on the chance God is waiting to answer our prayers with *yes*, pray her brother and his family accept her and give her a home. It's unlikely she'll be allowed to return to her family in Germany if she's carrying the child of a man she never married. I can't return home even though Daniel and I are legally husband and wife. She's from a privileged family as well."

With their eyes closed and heads bowed, they each prayed silently until Sandra said, "Amen."

"She's not been sick at all. Louise, I mean. If I wasn't already jealous, she dangled another reason in front of me. By next week she'll have missed her monthly visitation four times. I understand her denial. But she knew, and she thought it would make her feel better to humiliate me."

"Those who are miserable enjoy making others miserable with them. She learned too late the man she loved couldn't be trusted even if he had lived. I believe the revelation created bitterness in her heart. She thought she could easily snub you —a perceived commoner."

"She did judge without the facts, just as I judged her. I lost my noble title with my impulsive decision. When her family learns of her foolish one, will she lose hers, too?" Clara fidgeted in her pockets. Her fingers locked on a pair of lemon drops. She held one out to Sandra. "Sweetness and sourness together—too often a picture of my life." Clara laughed.

Sandra shrugged and turned her palms up. "What does any of this have to do with Max and the cameo?"

"Louise asked my forgiveness. I forgave all, save her stealing the brooch. She snapped at me." Clara shared Louise's revelation.

"I don't believe Max took the cameo. She made a sarcastic comment for sure, but I'm not sure she's not covering for what she knows about your cameo's disappearance."

"I opened up to her. She told me more of her story. I thought we were headed toward reconciliation. But she is unhappy because I didn't rush to you for the tea she hoped would end her plight. She stirred up my anger toward Max—the one person who is helping us. The situation became more difficult, not less."

"Allow her more time. Her pride took a pounding long before she discovered her fiancé relegated her to travel in the Zwishendeck. She continues to feel sorry for herself."

"Do you think she believes in Jesus?"

"I don't know, but we'll shower her with an abundance of His love these last few days on the ship." Sandra's arms stretched wide wrapping Clara and her babies in a warm-hearted embrace.

"Your hug reminds me of my Oma's and my Mutti's hugs. Rosa's too. Thank you! I have missed them."

"My pleasure, precious Fraulein. Find Max. Hear his side of the story."

MAX PACED three steps forward and three back in the limited space by the dining tables. *I'm going to thump on their door.*

"Ladies, breakfast is almost over." Max inhaled deeply as he approached their bunk area. "Am I smelling peppermint and rosemary? And a touch of eucalyptus? I know herbs when I sniff them. Sandra mentioned Freddy is ill. Are you two healthy?" Since he first delivered Clara's trunk and attached the rope the first day, he knew the rules better than to stick his nose all the way inside.

Bertha stepped to the entrance of their small space. "I'm watching over Freddy. The others left."

Max scratched his temple. "They couldn't have gone far." Before he made his retreat, Clara and Sandra sauntered up. Louise followed them. When she caught up, Louise whispered to Clara.

With her eyebrows pinched together, Clara cringed back from the woman.

Max waited.

Palm up, Clara extended her hand toward him. "Don't come closer, please."

"Has Freddy taken a turn for the worse?"

"Nein. But he's my boy and my responsibility." With hands in prayer position, Bertha nodded toward Clara and Sandra. "Danke to both of you for your kindness in helping me care for him. You too, Max. Freddy will be asking for you again soon."

"I'll pray your itching stops, Louise." Clara smiled.

A vice-like pressure squeezed Max's chest. "Um. What are you not telling us, Clara?"

She moved her head from side to side. "Keeping our conversation private for now. I wish I hadn't told you yesterday I trust you. Today waves of distrust swell."

"Please don't speak to me in riddles." He pegged his fists to his hips and stared.

"After telling me God spoke to you about helping find my cameo, I learned you snatched it like a coin in one of your tricks. I'm certain God can help you find something already in your possession. What impression have you made? A dark mark on your reputation, Max Engel."

Every eye intent on him, Max's fists slipped into his pockets. Heat singed his ears. "I would have preferred privacy, but you blurted out your accusation in front of the whole gallery."

Chapter Eighteen

OUTSIDE DECK, 20 April 1881

CLARA CLUTCHED her art supplies to her heart and made her way back outside. She sketched the billowing sails and the colorful stacks of the S. S. Elbe before they reached New York harbor—three or four more days.

"Have your pad and pencils ready when we approach New York. Capture your first impression of the harbor welcoming you to America."

Her fingers squiggled through her messy curls. "Max, you startled me."

"Are you afraid I'll steal your drawings, too?" Sarcasm edged his voice.

"You did take the cameo then." She kept her voice flat.

"Do you really believe I did?" He stared at the sea.

"I don't know what I believe. Others I've trusted disap-pointed me."

"Louise has intimidated you since we boarded the ship. What makes her attempt to trap you this time any different?"

"We chatted this morning. We learned more about each other. I forgave her for most of the ugliness she aimed my direction."

"Most of it? Did you open a door for her retort? Sandra told me what she said to you. I came to find you."

"Sandra told me to hear your side of the story. Will it make a difference if I do?"

"I know you remain uninterested in men except Daniel, but you show a jealous streak about the attention I receive from Louise. I have no romantic interest in the woman. I'm unaf-fected by her overly-dramatized attentions. We spend time together—as friends. If she finds offense in my lack of inter-est, she'd desire revenge on both of us."

"I want to believe you don't have the cameo and didn't substitute it for coins in any of your tricks."

"Then believe it. I've asked others on the ship for clues. Something so small could be hiding anywhere among a crowd on this dingy ship."

"Rosa. The babies' grandmother—Daniel's Mutter—and one of my dearest friends in the world. She wore the cameo every day. She rubbed it often when she was nervous or deep in thought."

"Like I've seen you do."

"Ja. It's a small token, but one I treasure. And if cameos could talk, this one has quite the story to tell." Her eyes stung as she blinked back tears.

"I've prayed more. I still consider myself inadequate, but could I pray with you for the cameo to be found before we arrive in America?"

More passengers had joined them on the deck. No matter, Max took her hands in his and spoke aloud. *"Vater Gott, I remember this verse from Sunday school. 'If ye then, being evil, know how to give good gifts unto your children, how much more shall your Father which is in heaven give good things to them that ask him?' We do not consider our earthly Vaters to be evil, and they do give good gifts. Clara and I ask You to help us find the cameo. You know its importance to her. We pray You see it as a good gift to restore it to her. In Jesus' name. Amen."*

"You prayed Matthew 7:11. A difficult verse for me since Vati and I had our first disagreements over Georg. Maybe I should remember earlier times, to all the wonderful gifts Vati did give me."

"You may not think this way right now, but your Vati gave you the opportunity to build a new life in America. That is a gift, too."

"Maybe. It grieves me how he and I wounded each other by the choices we made. The rules applied to him as well and in an even more important way. Vati's position depends on all of his family following them. He provided adequate means for me to have a start on a new life in America. Still, he chose his noble status over his oldest daughter and his future grand-children. I embarrassed him and tarnished his image. Many suffer."

"I probably know the answer, but I'll ask anyway. Have you talked to God about the problems with your Vati?"

"Many, many times. He did answer me when Georg's evil intentions were revealed, and Vati reversed the marriage arrangement. Then Daniel and I moved forward without respect for Vati's rules—nobility's rules. I hear Rosa's voice even now. 'Psalm 66:18.'" Clara doodled in her sketchbook. "You know what it says, too."

"Even the verses I memorized as a child, I don't know where to find them in the Bible. Please tell me."

"'If I regard iniquity in my heart, the Lord will not hear me.' God may not answer our prayer for the cameo, because of me."

Max stroked her back.

As if she could force all the bad out of her by doing it, Clara squeezed the sides of her head and shook it side to side. "I have poured out more personal things than anyone should tell a stranger—especially a male one."

Max rested his hands on Clara's shoulders. He looked her in the eyes and said, "Life came at you hard and fast the last several months. God's very patient. I know, because He has waited a long time for me to seek Him again. I stopped praying when Emelia died five years ago, but today I'm praying again. I pray He leads us to the cameo."

"Danke."

"May I see?"

Clara handed her pad to him. Max studied sketches. "You're an excellent artist. Would you draw the story for the children today?"

"Which story?"

"Is Hansel and Gretel too scary?"

"No more than others we've read to them. My imagination is dreaming up a slurry of confections to build the gingerbread house."

"Gretel is smart like you. She outwits the mean old lady."

"Had they not trusted the stranger, they wouldn't have fallen into her greedy clutches. Wonder how many strangers with less than honorable intentions we encounter when we get off the ship?" Her body wriggled at the potential troubles ahead.

"The story will warn the children. Parents will thank us for reminding them." Max handed the sketchpad back.

"Hansel and Gretel make it back home with the woman's treasures." Clara winked. "Who will make it home with my cameo?"

Enthusiastic children grabbed their hands as they returned to the common area. "Yippee! Storytime!" Eliza shouted.

"Do you have another story?" A little red-haired girl with big green eyes bounced on her toes. "My name is Edith. Mutter says I can come today."

"Edith, welcome. We have a special surprise for story time today." Max picked Edith up and spun her around. Her giggles encouraged all the children to beg for the same.

"Me, Herr Engel. Me. Me." Freckle-faced Finn's arms stretched toward him.

Eliza pulled on Fraulein Clara's sleeve. "Will you ask Herr Engle if I can be next?"

Max whirled them each about.

Clara reflected on their time at sea. Freddy, Eliza, Paul. Stefan. Mia. Ella… We know them all by name. Life among the crowd on the ship presents challenges, but the children's smiles and energy help to pass the time. *I'll miss them when we arrive in New York.*

"Did you forget me, Herr Max?"

"Eliza has been waiting patiently," Clara said.

"Nein, sweet girl." He picked her up and whirled at least three times around. "Where's your brother? Is Freddy still ill?"

"Frau Sandra's medicine made him better, but Mutter wants him to rest another day."

"Freddy's improved condition is good news indeed!" Max rubbed Eliza's shoulder. "I hope Sandra has extra herbs in case others need it?"

Clara entered their berth. "Freddy, you're sitting up!"

Morning chores complete, Bertha sat by Freddy on the bed keeping him still a while longer. She mended a hole in his knee-breeches.

"I took my thumb off. Wanna see, Fraulein Clara?"

"Can you put it back on again?"

The little fella nodded enthusiastically.

"You've mastered the stunt. Herr Max will enjoy seeing what you've learned."

Clara glanced up at the top bunk. "Bertha, where's Sandra?"

"She made more of the herb medicine. She keeps tending to passengers, sick like Freddy was. Sandra's so kind."

"Shivers just ran up my arms. I do hope they recover quickly and the others remain healthy. We must be very close to America now."

~

20 April 1882

Word circulated among the Zwischendeck passengers. The ship is on course to arrive in New York City in two days. Coughing could be heard around the ship. Sandra made her rounds with the herbs. Those receiving the concoction were recovering quickly. *O Lord, please let there be enough herbs, and persuade these people fresh air and sunshine would help restore their health. Some of them haven't left the stuffy space down here even once.*

Sandra clapped as she returned to their shared quarters. "Good news! Some passengers have recovered as Freddy has. Keep praying for the others."

"Look what I can do!" Freddy removed his thumb for Sandra.

"Are you excited to show your Vater your new trick?" Sandra tousled Freddy's hair. "I know you miss him. I'll miss all of you when we leave the ship. And I missed your help today, Louise. You lay in bed while the rest of us rose early. You neglected your part of the chores."

"Please, Sandra, I'm exhausted all the time. I'm certain some special tea would restore my strength."

"We'll not find out." Sandra clenched her jaw. "My stern look is your answer, especially in front of children, ja? I thanked God at least a dozen times already, I don't have any."

"Someone on this ship brought some. Lina—the one who almost died from the coughing. I'll check on her and inquire if she has some." Louise smirked.

"Please don't do this." Sandra's plea fell on deaf ears as Louise went visiting.

DURING THE LONG days onboard Clara had been consumed by thoughts of the missing cameo. She touched the place where it should be attached to her gown. Each of her dresses included a special spot to pin it. *Will it show up before we disembark? Will there be more music and dancing tonight and we'll spy some other lady wearing it?*

A man's hands covered her eyes from behind. Reaching up to pull them away, she immediately recognized whose they were. "Max, you—you made me jump—again!" *And not only with surprise but spiking tingles again. This needs to stop.*

"While I have your attention…"

Clara cut him off. "It appears you have mine and everyone else's in close proximity. Since you're here, keep a close eye on Louise's behavior."

Feigning interest in the ladies' crochet circle at the next table, Louise sashayed back and forth from one woman to the next.

Clara backtracked far enough to invite Sandra to join her. "Wait until you see this."

As she approached the table where Louise flattered all the women stitchers, Sandra wagged a finger toward their bunk mate's nose. "Thank goodness I'm old enough to be your mother! Your Mutter ought to be filled with gratitude I'm here to set your misguided steps on a better path. Please leave these women to their handiwork. They might enjoy your compliments while failing to recognize your manipulative intentions." Sandra laid a hand on Louise's back to direct her toward their bunk.

"A tattling little tart!" Louise squished up her face and pointed at Clara.

"Be mindful who you call by what names." Ignoring her manners, Clara's tongue plunged from her mouth like a long sharp dagger. "The same title fits you all too well."

With hands planted on her hips, Louise threw her head back and cackled. "I thought you forgave me?"

Max gripped Clara's hand. "Ignore her."

Waving a plain paper wrapper in Sandra's face, Louise boasted her success. "You can't stop me. Clara can't either."

"You're correct, Louise, we can't." Sandra's mouth snapped shut.

A FEW HOURS later Clara and Sandra returned to their bunk area. Louise huddled in a corner toying with the paper wrapper.

Sandra took several deep breaths and seized the moment. "Louise, does your family attend church?"

"Ja, but don't give me a Sunday school lecture."

"A Sunday school lesson is exactly what you need, young lady, but I don't carry lectures around in my bag or my head. I prefer to share the wisdom I've gleaned from living life for a

LYNN U. WATSON

lot of years. Sometimes I've lived God's way. Sometimes my way. I've learned much from life's struggles."

"And you plan to share God's way with me." Louise's sharp tongue snapped like a whip.

"Are you familiar with this verse from Proverbs, chapter one? *'A wise man will hear, and will increase learning; and a man of understanding shall attain unto wise counsels:'"*

"I'm not a man, and you imply I have no understanding." Louise blew a breath through her pinched lips.

"The verse applies to all of us the same, whether man or woman. Will you at least hear what I have to say before you split open the paper and spill its contents into your tea and your body?" *O Lord, please give me Your words, and prepare Louise's heart to receive them.*

"Clara's behavior merits no spiritual reward. Her path is no better than mine. Besides Albert and I were about to marry. What happened to make you so wise?"

"Wisdom grows with years of life lived. I've learned those who make the decision you contemplate do it out of fear, because of the inconvenience, or in the hope of avoiding judgment from others. One friend confided she has had nightmares for years after of the grim reaper coming for her baby."

"And you're judging me now." Louise glared at Sandra.

Sandra studied Louise's hands curling in tight balls against her stomach, her elbows pulled tightly into her sides. Her cheeks took on the bright pink hue of her dress.

"I'm not judging you. Clara convinced herself God would make an exception for her when she disrespected her Vati's rules. When she became pregnant, hiding her marriage from her family became impossible. It would have been convenient for her to do what you're about to do. I'm so thankful she didn't choose that plan in spite of the hardships she now faces, but I wouldn't have judged her for making a different decision. I would have been sad for her, but God's our only judge."

When tears filled Louise's eyes, Sandra reached with her handkerchief to wipe them away. She gently loosened the young woman's clenched fists and set aside the paper wrapper. "But...

"But what?"

"God has a plan for your little one, Louise. Will you trust Him?"

"How would you know that?"

"When my daughter was six months old, my husband—her Vater—was trampled by a horse at Marbach where he trained and bred the magnificent animals."

Louise gasped and slapped a hand to her chest. "That's terrible. How hard it must have been for you."

"It was a very difficult time in my life. My brother and his wife took us in. They were very gracious. After a year of wallowing in my grief and caring for my baby, I began feeling like we were a burden.

"Thankfully, a kind woman from the church we attended had experienced similar troubles in her life. She took me under her wing, leading me through God's word and how I could trust Him for Belinda's and my future. She introduced me to a fine gentleman. We fell in love. We married. He was a wonderful husband and became a doting Vater for Belinda— the only one she ever knew."

"So where is he now? You're traveling alone."

"I've been widowed twice, Louise. I'm immigrating to help Belinda and my granddaughter. My son-in-law lost his life on the ship on their own journey to embrace the promises of a new life in America. Now they're alone, too, but I trust God has a plan for their lives."

"My child's Vater is already gone. I might as well drink this tea and not have to worry about a situation like yours or your daughter's."

Sandra clasped Louise's hands between hers.

Hands trembling now but nestled between Sandra's more weathered ones, Louise asked, "But doesn't God forgive all our sins? I'll tell Him I'm sorry after I drink the herbs. He'll forgive me like he did the thief on the cross, right?"

"What you're asking is 'Will God forgive me, even though I know what I'm choosing goes against His will?'"

"Won't He?"

"Of course, He will. God allows us to make our own choices. When we repent, He forgives us, but He also allows consequences for our actions. I wouldn't want to put Him to the test with such a willful wrongdoing."

"This is sounding like a Sunday school lecture. And Clara? She really messed up! God's holding her to account for the lives of two babies. And her Vati doesn't want her. Disowned her. I'll opt for the nightmares. Only I'll see those."

"Please stop your judgment of Clara. Carefully consider your own life. If you make this choice, you might live through the first nightmare—the one induced by your selfish flesh and those potent leaves, but you'll never escape the pain of your decision."

"I haven't experienced the quickening yet. I'll finish this job before something alive stirs in there. Everyone would know and call me horrible names."

"How many times have you missed?" Louise's body collapsed into Sandra's arms. Silence impregnated the grief-laden air around them.

"It's almost story time," Bertha's children called to them.

Sandra withdrew from the embrace and whispered. "Allow God's grace to empower you to make the right choice."

Louise murmured while she wiped her tears with her sleeve.

"You both did wrong, but Clara made the better decision. Think how cute and full of life her little ones will be. They'll gather attention and provide an opportunity to encourage others to make wise decisions. Your baby could too. It is a baby, and it isn't too late. I believe you have felt the movement."

Louise lifted the lid of her trunk and removed a small item. An intricately carved alabaster rose poked up from the cover of an inlaid wood box. Louise placed the paper wrapper inside and turned the key.

Sandra watched as she retrieved a safety pin from her pocket and secured the key in the folds of her skirt. *Where was this box when we searched for the cameo?*

LADIES KNITTING, taking care of laundry, tidying the beds. Men playing checkers, wiping their brows, polishing their dusty boots. Freddy spinning his top. Eliza and her dolly. Grief. Joy. Pain. And more joy. Clara thumbed through the pages of her sketchbook. *Memories to share one day with my babies, crossing this ocean I never believed could be so wide. I must include the music makers and the dancers tonight. And Max's encouragement not to miss the arrival in New York City.*

Max. I must warn him again, this family thing is only for the ship. I'd rather not be indebted to him when our feet touch land again. I have enough sketches among these to haunt me with an everlasting reminder of his kindness. From their poking and bouncing, these babies play tag inside me.

Clara smiled as if she could see them, certain her eyes sparkled when she rubbed her tummy. "Your Vater will come."

"I hope he does." Max startled her for the second time today. "But we can still be family."

"Tante Ingrid awaits my arrival in America. We'll be fine." She rubbed more circles on her tummy and reached to massage her lower back. A deep groan.

"She awaits your arrival in America—in Chicago. New York is a long way from Chicago—also my destination."

"I remember. With my Vati's wine."

"I would shirk my responsibility to your Onkel if I did not see you safely to your final destination."

"Sandra and I are resourceful. We'll find our way. Onkel asked you to protect us on the ship. You've done that well. Danke. When we're off the ship, I need to focus on my babies and my work for Megs. My time will pass quickly until Daniel arrives. What a wonderful surprise if he comes early."

"You're a stubborn woman, Frau Becker. As you say, then. But you'll dance with me tonight when the musicians tune up their instruments? Only tonight and tomorrow evenings are left. My friend, Master Wilhelm Willigerod, assured me we'll arrive in the harbor on Saturday."

"I do love a good twirl on the dance floor. It would look more like a waddle than a waltz." She pointed to her inflated mid-section.

"Maybe they'll play a duck march."

Laughter bubbled up. "Most apropos!"

Max kissed his finger and planted the gesture on the tip of her nose. She giggled this time, while flutters of delight returned and life inside her danced.

"You sure you can make it without me?" Max teased.

Shoving her sleeves up to her elbows, she said, "I can and I will." *Daniel's coming.*

Pipes, fiddles, and flutes reeled out an Irish tune. Crescendos of music stirred passengers to dance with extra merriment. *Tonight, and tomorrow evening, the final nights of our journey. Saturday we'll arrive in New York. A giant milestone for celebration.*

Her fingers glided across the page. Clara admired her work. She had captured the quickly moving feet of the Irish dance, and a jolly fiddler leading the song.

Woodwinds and horns followed drums beating out a march. Max pulled her to her feet as the men and women, boys and girls began circling to the tune. "A duck march. I told you! Set your sketches aside. Dance with me."

Clara moved with the others. Awkwardly. Round and round. "We heard this same song as we boarded the ship. Probably coming from the fancy area of the steamer."

"The piece is the S. S. Elbe March. I asked Master Wilhelm for the music. He kindly provided a copy for our little Zwischendeck band."

"Maybe no one notices my web-footed moves."

"Just enjoy the merriment."

Music swirled long past the sun's setting. Excitement grew. Only two more nights until we reach America. *Only two more nights to find the cameo.*

Long after the music was silenced, one vision for the future argued with another, back and forth, round and round, stealing Clara's sleep for the night. *Could Megs' offer come true?* MEGS & CLARA—FASHION & DESIGN FOR THE MOST DISCRIMINATING. *Will my babies be healthy? Will Megs still welcome me when she learns 'we' includes me and two babies and no Daniel? Will Daniel come? Will Max try to follow me? Do I want him to?*

Will Tante Ingrid be the kind lady who lives in my sixteen-year-old memories? Each scene plays out as good versus evil. Which one is the perfect one I should be praying for?

By the wee hours of Friday morning, her mind calmed.

She heard a still small voice. *I saved you by grace. I have created you for a purpose. And your babies—one little life at a time.*

Chapter Nineteen

ONBOARD THE SHIP, Friday, *21 April 1882*

CLARA RUBBED her eyes erasing the bleariness of a sleepless night. "Good morning." She stretched and yawned.

The other women hustled about tucking each belonging in their bags and trunks. Tomorrow they would arrive in New York City.

"Sleepyhead." Sandra tossed a pillow at her.

"Because she partied too much last night." The sarcastic edge of Louise's voice burned Clara's ears.

"Everyone enjoyed themselves last night, including you." Sandra pointed at Louise and then grinned in Clara's direction. "And you, Clara, replayed jigs and waltzes several times during the night. Did you get any sleep at all?"

"Very little. Max said we'll be entering the lower harbor before the sun sets tonight. I fancied sketching the scene before we move into the Narrows and anchor at the Battery Saturday morning."

Sandra scoffed. "You expect us to believe visions of sketching the harbor kept you awake all night?"

Bertha and Louise laughed.

Grateful the rosemary and eucalyptus had kept their bedding free of dreaded fleas, Clara sprinkled them one more time before straightening the covers.

She folded the few undergarments she laundered the day before, and set things in her trunk for tomorrow's big day. She kept out the drawing tablet and pencils. "I do plan to sketch the city as we approach."

"You don't have your colors, Frau Clara?" Eliza pouted.

"I'll remember them in my mind and add the colors later. I'd rather capture all the details of the scene."

"Can I draw with you?"

Clara dug down in her trunk where she remembered seeing some loose sheets of paper. "Of course." She slipped the pieces inside her sketchpad and patted the book. "I'll tuck extra paper right here for you." She laid her tools on the bed to grab when the time was right.

A MAJOR TOPIC of conversation all week, but now the day had arrived. Practice interviews for the immigration officials continued again this morning.

Clara heard someone sitting down the breakfast table from them say, "I heard they put letters on your shoulder if they suspect you're a health risk. You can't even have a limp or be pregnant or anything out of the ordinary. There's a dreaded eye disease, too." Fear struck its chord! *What about me? What about Louise? Will she lie?*

"Do they single anyone out when the person has someone meeting them, who'll be responsible for them?" A deep voice chimed in. "Or if someone escorts them?"

"Who will you be covering for, Max?" One of the same men always jeering him chuckled.

Max and I had this conversation. I don't need his services after we leave the boat. Clara fanned the heat rising in her neck and face when all eyes shifted between her and Max.

From behind her, Max rested a hand on Clara's shoulder. "I promised a good friend I would see his niece safely to America, and on to Chicago."

Her resolve melted beneath his touch.

Max grinned. "Much excitement awaits on the outside deck all day today as we approach New York City."

He extended a hand to Sandra and Clara. "Ladies, shall we get some air? Maybe we can catch a glimpse of the city."

Sandra pointed to the fairytale book and puppets. "Clara, why not share one more story with Eliza and Freddy?"

"Would you enjoy that, children?" Clara sat on the bunk and gathered one of them on either side of her.

Sandra stepped outside their tiny quarters. "The very person I'm looking for. I'd be most thankful for a few moments alone with you, Max." Sandra scanned the area for eavesdroppers. She kept her voice low.

Max led them to as empty a corner as available on a packed ship.

"Yesterday I watched Louise hide something in a wooden box she took from her trunk. She locked it and pinned the key to a fold in her skirt, then stashed it under her pillow. I found her behavior curious."

"Your suspicions are?"

"She locked away a personal item. I'll keep its identity secret, but the box was not there when Clara and I searched for the cameo. We know she didn't purchase it on the ship."

"Unless some individual sold it to her?"

"Hmm?" Sandra chewed her lower lip. "Maybe. I'm not sure how you could help, but if Louise has hidden the cameo in her box, we need to retrieve it."

"I prayed for help to find the cameo. If it is indeed among Louise's personal items and she's tucked it under her pillow, I'll need many more prayers than mine to put my hands on it. Only a sleazy fellow would dare to go there."

THE SUN HAD a few more hours to shine this late Friday afternoon. The S. S. Elbe anchored in the lower New York Harbor for the night. "What a spectacular sight!" Clara's eyes savored it all. Her fingers rushed ahead. She recorded every detail in the sketchbook.

Eliza stood at her side with her own paper and pencil. "Do you think I'll see my Vater from the boat?"

"I'm certain he'll be waiting for you! He may be looking this way, asking himself which of these ships his family is aboard."

"There are a lot of boats, Fraulein Clara." Then Eliza tugged on Max's sleeve. "Are there always this many boats?"

"Ja. Sometimes more." He patted her head.

Clara set the sketchbook aside. She reached below her rounded belly lifting the load she carried. "Thousands of people from all these ships to pass the interview and be on their way to their new homes. This could take a very long time tomorrow."

"No reason to worry. I venture we're the first ship docked in the morning."

"What makes you so certain, Herr Engel?"

Max rubbed his chin and frowned. "Back to proper names again are we, Frau Becker?"

Clara jutted her head at a sharp angle toward Max. "We are. I answered your question. Now answer mine."

"Port authorities admire and respect Master Willigerod. My friend has his manifest ready. I believe they'll guide us in quite early. Before daybreak tomorrow the ship will make her way through the Narrows, arriving at Castle Garden on the south end of the Battery in lower Manhattan."

"I'll be on deck to see the sunrise."

"And I will be up and ready to assist you in carrying your trunk." He winked and flashed half a smile.

"I can handle it…" The ice in her voice shaved her vocal cords.

"Like you did when we boarded?" Max shook his head. "I made a promise, friend." A broad smile accompanied his words and set her all aflutter again.

"Have you found my cameo?" The question gave her a moment to regain her composure.

"Nein. Still missing?" He swallowed hard.

"Then you failed me. Daniel would've found it."

"And I'm not Daniel."

"Danke for your acknowledgment and for caring for us on the ship. Sandra and I will be on our own from here."

"As you please."

Chapter Twenty

WEE HOURS OF THE MORNING, *Saturday, 22 April 1882*

HER BACK ACHED. Her feet swelled. The babies' jumping game created an urgent nature call. Sandra and Louise groaned, but both moved to give her space to abandon the bunk. She grabbed her pillow as she sat up. After tending to business, she sobbed into the bag of feathers. Geese lost their life for this pillow? *What an odd thought I ponder before the sun even rises.*

Sandra knelt beside her. "We're here, Clara. We made it to America. Why all the sobbing?"

Silence. The older woman stroked the younger's wild auburn curls and waited.

"Come outside the bunk area with me." Sandra helped her up. "If we keep our voices low, we can talk without disturbing the others. Bring your pillow."

The two women huddled together. "My dreams are broken." Clara spoke slowly through her tears. "The cameo's gone. I'm certain I have two babies in my tummy. I want to love them because they're all I have left of Daniel, but I don't know how to care for them. I never told Megs of my condition. The babies will be a disturbance in the shop. No way she'll still wish for me to be a partner.

"Last night on the deck the person speaking didn't realize I could hear him. He announced the medical personnel at Castle Garden would send me back because I'm with child and without a husband. You know my family won't take me back. What if Tante Ingrid doesn't meet me? What if she refuses to take me in? I was disowned. Sent away. I no longer have a family. And I told Max we no longer needed his help. You and I are on our own from here."

Worry lines furrowed Sandra's forehead the way Clara remembered back in Bremen before Max offered to be their protector.

"What a long list of worries. Life is never easy. It's full of challenges. Being alone and a mother, I imagine, will be one of the most difficult of all."

"But I'm a married woman."

"Ja, but will Daniel come? When will he come?"

"Lots of babies have lost their lives to the pennyroyal tea. Maybe I should have made the same choice. Maybe I should've listened to the ones who encouraged me to drink it months ago."

Sandra flinched. "You don't mean that."

"You're right."

"The brave woman I met in Stuttgart a few months ago—has she disappeared?"

"I'm not brave. I'm just too outspoken far too often. Headstrong—feisty as Vati called it. The many mistakes I've made. The lies I've told myself and others. A nobleman's disowned daughter with a baby or two in my belly. I'm nothing more than a bundle of pigeon fluff."

"What a lovely picture." Sandra itched her nose. "Do I need to step away?"

"Might be best for all of us."

"Why? Because you choose to let the enemy win—let him steal all your hopes and dreams?"

"Stealing is what the devil does best." Clara shrugged her shoulders, then slid her hands down to rub the chill from her arms.

"You know the rest of the verse, too. The part where Jesus says, *"I am come that they might have life, and that they might have it more abundantly."* Sandra grasped Clara's hands, her eyes pouring love.

"John 10:10." Clara squeezed her eyes shut. "But if I fail to pass the doctors at the gate, they will refuse me entrance into America. Need I tell another lie? The burden doubles in weight with each new one I pile atop the last."

"You have a letter from your Tante Ingrid, correct? And one from Megs? You have a place to build your future."

"I tucked them inside the fairy tale book. I prayed a happily-ever-after would rub off its pages onto the letters and into our lives."

"Jesus has the perfect plan, and He will lead you to it. He writes better stories than we do—true ones, not fairy tales. It's still a wee bit early, but I hear folks stirring." Sandra whispered.

"Ja! Good idea." No need for Clara to whisper her reply.

"You'll lead then with your beautiful soprano?"

Clara cleared her throat.

"HE LEADETH ME: O blessed thought!
O words with heavenly comfort fraught!"

SANDRA JOINED HER.

"WHATE'ER I DO, where'er I be,
still 'tis God's hand that leadeth me."

MANY VOICES JOINED THE CHORUS. The Zwischendeck filled with music and excitement.

"HE LEADETH ME, he leadeth me;
by his own hand he leadeth me:
his faithful follower I would be,
for by his hand he leadeth me."

. . .

By the end of the fourth verse and the sixth chorus of the refrain one passenger declared, "Those in First class surely know we're a spirited group down here ready to enter America!"

Last morning onboard the S. S. Elbe, *Saturday, 22 April 1882*

Tin plates clattered. The passengers gathered for their last meal together, many carried pads and pencils to exchange best-known information for writing to one another. Excitement for their new home created a party atmosphere and filled the travelers with urgency to move up to the deck where they would disembark. They cleared the tables and gathered belongings.

Clara pulled her trunk. The babies pushed her ribs. The handle of her basket cut into her arm where it hung. She secured her reticule to the trunk and tugged it along toward the companionway. The weight of her broken dreams and the lost cameo weighed far more than all of these together.

"We must get you on the upper deck to sketch the view in the harbor. Let me help you with those please, Frau Becker."

She recognized the voice of the one whose help she no longer needed. But she did need him. *Can I swallow my ego, and admit it? Like I have reason to have even a drop of pride left.*

Max took hold of the trunk's handle, nudging Clara's grip loose.

Drat! She slowly let go, savoring the touch she wished to reject.

Clara's waddle set the pace. When they came into the open air. Max parked the luggage to await their turn to enter Castle Garden. He swung his hand cutting a wide circular swath. "Ladies, your new home awaits. Uncle Sam welcomes you to America!"

In front of them, ship workers had rolled a piano onto the upper deck. Talented fingers plunked the keys, and the S. S. Elbe March enhanced the celebration of the day. A mass of people had already assembled on the deck. Clara bumped a few elbows. *Thankfully, I placed the sketchpad and pencils on top inside of the basket. What to draw first? Everything! I want these babies to someday see what I experienced entering this new place — their home — our home.*

Bertha and the children waited toward the end of the line before coming up. Clara was almost as grateful as Bertha for the kind gentleman who offered to help with the family's luggage. Bertha waved from a few yards away, a huge smile on her face. She moved closer to her new friends.

Eliza wiggled her way close enough to tap on Clara's arm. "Mutter let me carry my paper and pencils, too. I want to draw with you again."

"Your Vater will love your drawings. I imagine he sees our ship, and he's ready to give you a big hug."

"Did Louise expect someone to help with her ridiculous-sized trunk?" Bertha turned to Max. "She's sitting on it just outside our berth, holding her stomach and moaning. She ignored my questions."

"Tricky dame!" Max gritted his teeth. "How did she get it down there in the first place? Nothing like a stampede when you are headed in the other direction." He elbowed through the crowd.

Fifteen minutes later Max appeared on the upper deck again, this time with Louise and the heavy trunk in tow. As they approached the little group of folks that she'd lived side by side with for the last ten days, Louise's hands encircled his arm muscles. "Max is my strong man. Thank you, darling."

Clara snorted! "How fortunate for you, he came to your rescue."

"He's escorting me through Castle Garden, too, right Max?"

Max showed them all what his muscles could do when he jerked his arm loose, his elbow nearly punching the man beside him. "Louise, you'll need to pay a deckhand to get this thing off the boat."

Her pouty lip dripped more vinegar than honey.

With his arm draped around Clara's shoulder, Max smiled. "I'm sticking by Frau Becker."

Gulp. Again. Twice this morning. *He needs to understand I'm spoken for, but those touches.* Clara blinked her eyes several times and gave them a rub. *I don't wish to see any other future before me but Daniel.* He will come.

She prayed she was right.

Castle Garden, *Saturday, 22 April 1882*

THE SMELLS, the multiple languages all spoken at once, the colorful array of clothing seen among the crowds, and the man who could send them straight to the medical area. Just like she had been warned, a tag was slapped on Clara's back. "What will happen to me?" Clara's voice shook.

"I've never been here before." Sandra stared straight ahead. "I don't know. Just keep walking."

The man at the next checkpoint spoke perfect German. "Sie schwanger sind, Frau?" He grabbed her paperwork. "A pregnant woman should have a husband. Where is yours?"

A commotion in the next line attracted everyone's attention. A loud wail. The woman clutched her stomach and fell to the floor.

Clara's jaw dropped open. "Louise!"

Louise's body was still. She didn't speak or look in Clara's direction.

"You know this woman?" the official asked. "Anything we should know about her?"

Sandra pinched her lips, her voice hesitant. "I suspect she may have ingested something that didn't agree with her."

"Move this woman to the infirmary." The official pointed to the collapsed body in front of him and motioned for a nearby worker to attend to her. Two men scooted her along the floor into the infirmary.

"You'll let her family know?" Clara asked the official person in front of her.

He took another look at her paperwork. "All I need to hear from you, Frau Becker, where is your husband?"

"He's not with me."

"Where is he, I asked. Give me the truth—now."

"Excuse me, sir."

The very familiar male voice interrupted again. Clara inhaled deeply and held her breath. She fixed her eyes on the man asking the questions.

"Who are you? Her husband?"

"Nein. But I take responsibility."

"Responsibility for what exactly? Who are you?"

"Maximillian Engle. I'm escorting this young woman safely to her Tante's home in Chicago. The woman is a doctor and has invited Frau Becker to live with her."

"What is the nature of your business in America?"

"My home is Germany. I travel often between the continents. I escort cargo for important businessmen. On this trip, I attend cargo more precious than furniture, pianos, leather goods, fabrics, or guns. I am responsible for Clara Becker."

"And how will she support herself and the child once she is with her Tante?"

"Perhaps you should ask her." He winked at Clara.

The golden sparks from his eyes ignited Clara's quick reaction. She jerked Megs' letter and Tante Ingrid's telegram from her reticule and poked them toward the official, then held her breath while he read them.

Max rubbed her upper arm and gave it a gentle pat. "Breathe," he whispered.

The official tapped Clara's papers in his palm. The corners of his mouth finally turned northward. "You are free to be on your way."

He gave Max a sideways stare, then turned and addressed him directly. "You come through here often, and you've never given us trouble. Be sure you keep your word about Frau Becker. Women do not become Doktors."

The telegram from Sandra's daughter proved sufficient, too. Maybe her age spoke for her honesty, or the official chose to avoid another encounter with Max. After all, the lines snaked on.

He waved them all through. "Welcome to America."

"WE'LL HAVE the best seats on the Pennsy." Max promised the ladies an upgrade.

"Any seats would be more comfortable than our crowded bunks and plank benches on the ship." Clara rested on her trunk. "I wish this seat had a backrest."

"The ones on the train will. And padding, too."

"Promise."

"I do." Thankfully, she's not arguing.

"Please don't talk with any vendors. Cheaters and swindlers abound." No more than twenty feet from where he left the ladies Max heard the first of them.

A man on the sidelines of the cavernous rotunda called to Clara. "Exchange your marks for dollars. Right here, Frau."

Max spun on his heels. "I've seen you before. You're among the worst of them, and Officer Morgan here is a good friend."

"Trouble, Max? Shall I cuff him?"

"Good to see you, Ted, and your timing's perfect. Take care of the swindler later. Right now, please guard these two ladies for me while I purchase our train tickets?"

"I'd be honored to. Where are you and these lovely ladies headed?"

"My cargo, my two new friends, and I are all headed to Chicago. I'm accompanying them."

"New friends? Is the younger one meeting her husband in Second City?"

"She's meeting her aunt and her best friend there."

Ted wiggled his eyebrows. "Purchase your tickets. I'll keep a watch on the ladies."

"Bertha, over here." Clara waved to the family of four reunited and headed to their new home in America.

Their bunkmates smiled. Eliza jumped up and down. "Vater, Vater, here is Fraulein Clara. We need to say goodbye again."

Theodor Strauss whistled a happy tune attracting a host of turned heads. He signaled a porter. "Here are a few coins to deliver our luggage to our carriage—the blue one. Our driver placed a placard with 'Strauss' on the door. Let him know the family has arrived. We'll be along shortly.

"The children have chatted of nothing but you two and some fella named Herr Max. Danke! You've made the passage easier for my wife and children." He withdrew a pair of cards from the pocket of his silk-trimmed coat. "Please be in touch when you know your new addresses." With the pomp of a prince, he placed one card in Clara's hand and another in Sandra's.

After hugs all around, he led his family to their carriage. "To our new home. Surprises await!"

The children waved and the ladies blew them kisses until they were out of sight.

Sandra lifted her eyebrows. "Do you think he's a banker? Or owns a fancy hotel?"

Clara stroked her cheek. "Perhaps an attorney. Whatever his highly-respected profession, the circumstances make no sense." She studied the card he placed in her hands, but only his name and a distinguished mark graced it. She moved her fingers to grab the stray tendril and twisted the curl round and round. "If his business or family are of significant importance like royalty or hotels or banks or law, why did he send his family to America via Zwischendeck?"

"A mystery we may learn one day." Sandra tucked his card in her duffel. "Perhaps Bertha chose the steerage accommodations to set an example of humility rather than pride for her children. I'm thankful we met her and became friends. What a kind woman."

Sandra cupped her palm around her ear. "Listen. Tis the familiar jingling of coins in Max's pocket. He's returned with our tickets."

"We board a ferry for Jersey City in two hours. From there we catch the Pennsy rolling toward Chicago. Do we know any train songs?"

Clara noticed a gentleman standing off to Max's left. He was alone and held a hand-written sign: *Herr und Frau Albert*

Schwarz. "Louise's fiancé's name was Albert. Sandra, do you suppose?" Clara kept her voice low.

"If the man is her brother, he must not know the outcome of his sister's wedding story. He expects a married couple. Our friend isn't married, but she is expecting. The last we saw of Louise…"

"…she was lying on the floor holding her stomach and being pushed off to the infirmary. Should we ask if he's related to Louise?"

Max stepped beside them. "Ask who what?"

"The man holding the sign for the Schwarz couple. We believe he may be Louise's brother."

"Her fiancé was named Schwarz?"

"Possibly. His first name was Albert." Clara shrugged. "Could be Albert anybody, maybe Albert Schwarz."

"We'll find out. They never married, right?" Max waited for their answer.

"They never did. Albert passed away two days before the wedding." Sandra sniffled. "Is she even alive back there?"

"Ted, you're still here. Danke for watching these two and keeping them out of trouble."

Clara gave Max a curt sideways nod.

"You're a spirited one, Frau Becker! You keep me ever on alert."

"I don't expect your further protection? I warned you Sandra and I are going it alone from here, but you keep inserting yourself in our affairs."

He held back a smile and scratched his head.

"Ted, any chance you can learn what happened to Louise? She shared the berth with Sandra and Clara. She may be the one the Schwarz family is searching for. She went through a different processing line than we did. They hauled her to the infirmary. If the man with the sign is her brother, it would be kind to advise him what happened?"

"I never denied I'm headstrong, but Louise—now she is a plucky one! Unpredictable, too." Clara fluttered her lashes.

Max winked and jingled those coins again. "And you are most predictable, Frau Becker? You wear a tough front, but it takes only a smile to melt your resolve."

He's right. *Why am I so undone by his smiles and his faintest touch? His kind heart does remind me of Daniel.*

"Since you're also headed to Chicago we can't keep you off the train, but I'll be in Tante Ingrid's care as soon as we arrive in Chicago. I'll wire her when we know our arrival time. She'll be awaiting us at the station. I'm certain she's made arrangements to her home. Megs will be there, too."

"Let's board the ferry!"

The ship's master stood at the walkway exiting the garden for the ferries thanking the departing travelers for coming to America on his ship.

"Of all the luck! You're just the man I need to see." Max extended a firm shake to his friend. He pointed toward the second ferry. That's the one we'll take. He patted Clara on the shoulder and nudged her. "I'll be right behind you."

"You were on the ship? I never saw you on my nightly strolls greeting the passengers." Willigerod shook Max's hand.

"I traded my first-class passage for Zwischendeck to keep a promise."

"Always true to your word. I admire the quality in you, Max."

"A lady lost a cameo down there. Could you alert your crew to be on the lookout when they clean?"

"Come on, now, Max. You worry about a cameo? She must be an important *lady*."

The scuffle ahead of them caught their attention. "Lady down! The one with child."

"See you next time, Willie. I know you'll recover the cameo for me."

If looks could scrutinize to the core of one's being, then Willigerod gained intimate knowledge of my heart. Max took off, elbowing his way through the crowd. It must be Clara. Louise didn't make it through the entrance process.

He watched as another man pulled Clara to her feet. The one who always made unwelcome remarks on the ship. Will he carry her trunk to the ferry? At what cost to Clara? *But she wants to be rid of me.* He clamped his jaw and gave himself permission to forget her. *After all, I am still grieving for Emelia and our baby. I don't need to take on the responsibility of another's child.* She only wants Daniel.

Clara turned her eyes toward Max. He grieved the loss of their sparkle.

She grimaced as the lecherous man's hand jabbed at her side. "Keep walking," he shouted.

Mocking laughter stabbed Max as hard as the guy's hand poked Clara. His next words were far more suited to a bar fight. The louse would regret how he treated Clara these last many days.

To assure himself the two women were safely on the ferry, Max kept his distance while remaining within earshot of the unfolding incident. Eavesdropping paid off. Blade! The jerk's name is Blade.

"YOU WILL STAY WITH ME, Frau Becker. The fella you don't need or want will never find you. I'll relieve you of the burden in your tummy, too. My friends call me Blade. Since we're friends—"

Clara never knew his name on the ship. Now he introduced himself as Blade. There could not be a more appropriate name for the butcher offering sharp slices of intimidation. She choked back the vomit creeping up. This time it wouldn't be the acidic backlash of her condition, but words to bury a man's ego. She argued with the thoughts racing through her mind.

The rules of my noble upbringing remind me of what a lady must not say. This one is worse than Georg. Is that possible? She pressed her lips tight and prayed. *Send me help. Oh, Vater Got, I haven't been repentant of my mistakes, and now I plead for Your mercy. Deliver me safely to Tante Ingrid. Is America full of scoundrels like Blade? Does he travel back and forth on these ships looking for his next victim? Help me, please, O Lord.*

With her life and dreams broken, she'd considered drinking the tea, but the things she'd seen. The things she knew. God's word. They didn't line up with the words spoken by others— it's not a baby until you feel it move. She knew better. She experienced the joy of life inside her, and not a tea or a crazy man would steal her baby's life or babies' lives from her now. One with a name like Blade. What kind of fillet had he prepared?

I need You, God. This scoundrel is forceful and mean, and I've sent every contrary response in the world to Max. He must believe me a dolt—one no longer worth fighting for. Daniel isn't here. The only thing she knew to do now. She screamed!

"Keep it down. Stuff this in your mouth." Blade shoved his snotty kerchief at her.

MAX STRAINED to hear the words Blade shouted at Clara while he hauled her trunk toward the dock. His hands would be busy for a short time offering a wee measure of safety. The crowds chattered and walked toward the ferry drowning out the words. His ability to read lips held no value from the backside.

Remind me, Lord, why I am bothering about her. Keep her safe, please. The man frightens me. He must terrify the women. He breathed easier witnessing them enter the ferry. Sandra followed behind Clara and Blade. *Clara keeps her gaze straight ahead. He probably threatened more harm if she turns around, but there will be time on the ferry. I'll be sure she makes it to the Pennsy. I have their train tickets.* What about all the stops along the way? Would Blade be on the same train, too? Max slapped his palm to his forehead wishing he never walked into Sajou all those months ago.

He was falling for Clara while the memories of his departed wife still warmed his heart and spirit—the girl whose heart cleaved to the love she was forced to leave in Germany. She carried Daniel's offspring. *I'll spend my time on the train agonizing over the dilemma—the one with no possibility of a blessed outcome. One with a promise we'll both lose more than we dreamed possible even a few weeks ago. At least I hope she would believe it a loss, too.*

A feminine hand shook his shoulder and disrupted his thoughts.

"We need your help, Max, despite what my friend told you." Sandra's brows knit together.

"You would have her wound my heart again?" He shook his head.

"Clara's a confused young lady. The oaf—Blade—never knew his name on the ship. He has some mischievous intention up his pants leg." Sandra scowled.

"More like evil intent!"

"I don't trust him, and I can't be gone from Clara's side for long. We'll be in Jersey City soon?"

"Pardon my rudeness a moment ago, ma'am. I disliked him on the ship, and I detest what I saw earlier, but I'm respecting Clara's wishes by staying out of her way."

Sandra pulled her woolen cape tighter. "My fears for the girl, for myself, and for the wounds festering deep in Clara's heart cut through me as chilly as an April breeze. Will you also respect the promise you made to her Onkel when we left? I realize she is a determined young woman. All the more reason Martin sought your help in seeing us safely to Chicago."

"Did Blade threaten her?"

"Threatened to relieve her of her burden. Blade has kept a

tight rein on her since we boarded. The one time he slipped a few feet away, Clara whispered his threat to me."

"A heart battle for me, Sandra. I promised myself just minutes ago I'd assure you two made it onto the train. Clara would rather I didn't interfere, but Blade has been a source of contention since we left Bremen. I'll protect you both, as I promised. I will confront Blade and learn why he's intent on hurting Clara. Pray for our conversation. Pray for my heart. Clara's waffling signals toy with me in ways I can't explain. And she wants only Daniel."

"I believe in your aptitude for persuasion and I trust God for the best answers. For now, let's get to Chicago. Safely."

"Lead on."

SCARED SENSELESS by Blade's callous and evil attitude, Clara welcomed the sight of Max returning with Sandra. His turquoise eyes had turned stone cold. She made no effort to draw a more positive response from him. Quiet subdued gratitude that he traveled with them again was the best she had to offer.

The trio boarded the train without further incident, but Blade followed, sitting across the aisle from them.

"Max, does the train stop along the way?" Clara settled in her seat, twisted her curl, and sucked the pucker out of a lemon drop.

Sheltering his face behind a magazine, Max whispered. "Several times. Please don't wander off alone. Remember our happy little family? Not sure we appear happy, but our best protection is to act like we are. If it makes you happier, pretend you're my sister."

Clara straightened the lace on the sleeves of the blue gown she'd kept clean for the American leg of their journey. She lifted her head high, her smile as wide as the ocean they just crossed. *Max will believe I'm pleased with his plan, but I am pouting on the inside. What would Daniel think of my actions now? And what a poor representative I've been of our noble Gut Apfelhof. What am I saying? I am no longer a part of Kraig Reinhold's world —erased in a blink.*

Max held the most recent edition of the *Saturday Evening Post*. Clara propped her sketchbook on her tummy, shielding any tell-tale signs of her emotions, misgivings, or regrets. She sketched a family pushing a baby carriage. Before flipping the cover shut, she contemplated once again the man with no face. Her true love's blonde hair now replaced by chestnut waves. *Hannah would have a philosophical explanation for my motivation.* She stuck her fingers in her ears blocking echoes of her sister's voice.

"Drat! I missed the first twelve chapters. I'll learn how John Anderson used his revolver, but I'll be left imagining what led to it."

She peeked over the top of the sketchbook seeing those same chestnut waves she sketched moments earlier. "What did you say about someone using a revolver? Another reason to worry?"

"A story. The Post publishes serial stories. I'm reading George Manville Fenn's story *Ships Ahoy! A Story of Land and Sea*. It continues here with John's revolver in Chapter thirteen. I missed chapters one through twelve."

"Why are a dozen chapters missing?"

"The magazine publishes one chapter each week until the story is finished. Well-written serial stories prove effective for repeat sales of the publication. You can go back to your sketches."

"The train sways more than the boat, and oh how it clickety-clacks down the tracks. It's difficult to sketch."

"Are you comfortable?"

"Ja. We will arrive in Chicago soon, right?"

"This time tomorrow, maybe." Max went back to his story.

Clara had carried her pillow rather than pack it back in the trunk. She maneuvered it behind her back easing her discomfort. Rosa estimated July. Three more months. Only three months. She caught a few winks. Megs' possible reactions crisscrossed her dreams. She awoke realizing the trauma of a pending nightmare could supersede the hope of a new dream. The matchbox-sized lavatory on the train created an immediate dilemma.

Max rolled his *Saturday Evening Post* into a tube and poked at the man across the aisle. "Blade? The name fits your attitude well, *my friend.*"

"Well, you consider me a friend. Glad to hear it."

"Sarcasm, Blade, sarcasm. What is it? Jealousy? Meanness? Private story? Why do you harass Clara?"

"I told her I'd take care of her."

"Why would she need you?"

"I need Clara. I promised my sister she would help?"

"Your sister knows Clara?"

"No. They have mutual friends." Blade grinned like he was the luckiest man on earth. His ticking eyelid betrayed his confidence.

Jaw-clenching fury made his pulse race. "I don't want to know anymore." Max leaned back in his seat. He unfurled the magazine and resumed reading. All he could focus on were the terrors awaiting Clara.

A fist jabbed his arm.

"What?"

Blade opened his fist revealing two nickels he had clenched in his hand. "Need a hint?"

Chapter Twenty-One

CHICAGO UNION STATION, *Late afternoon, 23 April 1882*

HUNDREDS OF MILES of late winter landscape sped by. This far north hints of Spring remained at least a few weeks off. Clara shuffled up and down the aisles of their coach stretching her legs and the cooped-up space the babies occupied. Chicago came into view, and the train came to a halt at Union Station.

People meeting their loved ones, businessmen, and an occasional bum lined the platform. Clara clapped her hands. "Hooray!"

Megs waved from the throng and shouted, "Clara! Over here!"

In seconds Clara spotted Gus accompanying her friend. An older couple stood beside them. Tante Ingrid and a stranger. She wanted to push through the crowd, but how improper and rude that would be. Balancing her reticule, her basket, and the load in her tummy reminded her hurrying would not be a good idea.

Max is standing right behind me. He thinks he'll be helping me again. She turned to him. "Max, danke for your attentive care on this trip. My friends and my Tante are here now. They'll help me."

"As I recall your friend was not such a big help in Paris. She needed almost as much help as you." He winked, and the golden flecks in his eyes shimmered.

Sandra spun toward Clara. "First things first. Max and I will both meet your friends and family, and everyone will meet my family, too."

"Of course, Sandra. Where are my manners?"

I dread the impending interrogation from Megs. I remember well her encouragement surrounding Max while we visited Paris. And now I need to consider these babies and their Vati. Daniel will be here for us soon. The quicker I'm free of Max the better.

It was now their turn to exit the coach. Megs glanced at Gus and nodded to Sandra in front of her. Gus helped Clara's friend down. Clara's belly came into full view. With a very large smile and slightly raised eyebrows, Gus offered her his hand and led her onto the platform. Megs hugged her tight in spite of the obvious obstruction.

Sandra's daughter and granddaughter found her quickly. They all stood together, everyone talking at once. Tante Ingrid waited a few moments, then reached around her grand niece's shoulder and placed a kiss on her cheek. "Let me introduce you to my husband, Oscar Gerber."

"Welcome to Chicago!" Herr Gerber offered his hand.

Clara heard Megs over the other conversations. "Max! What a pleasure to see you again. Are you and Clara together—as in married? Tell us the story."

Clara's hand flew to her mouth. "No!"

"The baby you carry—did you marry my brother?" Megs smoothed the silk panels of her skirt.

Max dropped his bag by Sandra and rushed away from the group.

Clara's head shook as much at Max scurrying off as at Megs' question. "The baby is Daniel's."

A sigh of relief gushed from Megs. "He's with you, right?

Ingrid reached to rub the young woman's back. "Megs, she is worn out from the trip. Oscar and I have a carriage to take her to our home and let her settle in. In a few days, I'll bring her to visit your shop. The two of you can catch up with each other's lives."

Megs' facial features were as pale and hard as chiseled stones. *Is Megs disappointed I didn't bring Daniel or that I'm pregnant or both?* "We'll talk soon, Megs. I've missed you."

Waving as they crossed the street, Gus and Megs strolled toward home.

Oscar found Clara's trunk and loaded it into the Gerber's carriage. Max returned offering his assistance to Sandra and her family to catch the street car to the place Belinda and Hilda were staying.

"Danke for all your care, Max. Clara may not admit it, but she needed you." Sandra reached into her duffel to retrieve the card. "While you purchased train tickets, Clara and I met Bertha Strauss' husband—a refined gentleman dressed like a prince. Here's his card. He gave one to each of us. We're perplexed about what his business might be and why he sent his family via steerage accommodations."

Max perused the card. "Not much information for sure, but may I keep this? I'll look him up the next time I'm in New York."

"I hoped you would."

INGRID, Oscar, and Clara boarded the Gerber's conveyance. Their driver gave the signal and the horses moved the carriage toward their Prairie Avenue neighborhood.

"You're not surprised by any of this, are you? Oma wrote you with all the details."

Ingrid frowned. "Dear girl, I'm so terribly sorry for all you've experienced. Dorthea told me about the terrible arrangement your Vati made for you."

"I didn't have to marry Georg. Oma relayed the whole story, right?"

"She did. I was dismayed to hear of the many lies and traps he set to ensure your Vati's dreadful decision."

"Curt always believed the Wolffs' intentions less than honorable. He and Vati secured the help needed to untangle their ill-intended plot. Vati and I reconciled."

Ingrid rubbed tiny soft circles just below the cuticles on each of her fingers, waiting for her niece to continue.

"So many people were involved. It was excruciating to learn some of those we trusted for many years were major players.

But I felt free when Georg was arrested. Curt and Onkel Martin connived a plan for Daniel and me to marry—secretly."

"You and Curt, Megs, Daniel. The four of you were inseparable as children. Did Daniel continue to hide small gifts in the secret spot in the garden for you to find?"

"You remember him leaving those?"

"I do. I despised the rules, too, Clara. When my Vater, your great-grandfather, allowed me to attend medical school, I embraced the freedom. Not an opportunity allowed many women then or now."

"Oma warned Daniel and me our behavior lacked respect. She hated the rules for us. She knew we'd married, but we shamed Gut Apfelhof and the family either way."

"Is Daniel coming to America?"

"He promised he will, but..."

"Until he arrives, you have two doctors to care for you, and to help bring this baby into the world."

"Two? Clara pointed first to Tante Ingrid and then to Oscar. "You're both doctors?"

"Ja. Oscar came from the staff of the highly respected Rush Medical School. My friend, Mary Thompson, and I studied medicine in Boston. Mary, Oscar, and some other doctors started the Chicago Hospital for Women and Children. I joined them. You're in excellent hands, Clara dear. Do you know when the baby might arrive?"

"Rosa believes July."

Ingrid studied Clara's tummy. "Unless this baby is going to weigh fifteen pounds, I would say he or she is coming much sooner."

"What if it's too early?"

She rubbed her temples. "You're a twin, Clara. You know your Mutti had a twin, too?"

"Ja, Tante Adeline told me. She's convinced I carry twins. I've been so sick from the very beginning. The same way it was for my Mutti and her Mutti, too." She lowered her voice to a whisper. "My breasts swelled and my belly grew quickly. I can tell you the exact day this happened, and I was miserably sick within two weeks."

Ingrid's tone was as kind as Rosa's. "Tell me when."

"The sixth of October. Right after Erntedank."

Ingrid extended her hand to hold Clara's restless one. "If you're expecting twins, these little ones will arrive by mid-June, less than two months from now."

"Two months would be too soon, right?"

"I believe God decided twins would come earlier than a single baby. Little ones do a lot more growing their last couple of months in the womb. By July you might just pop!"

Clara rubbed her stomach. "I cannot imagine this spreading further."

"Oh, but it will, sweet Clara. A baby can gain three or four pounds and grow another six inches in the last two months."

"If I'm carrying two of them—" She swallowed the sour taste filling her throat. Already embarrassed by having the conversation in front of Onkel Oscar, Clara refused to ask about the alarming new pain and fullness. Wrapped tightly beneath her crisscrossed arms, her bosom fought to bust through Rosa's most generous accommodations of her garments. *Please, Lord, don't let them ask about my wincing expression.*

"We'll care for you and the babies and make the time pass quickly. We'll feed you well and take walks along the lake shore, visit the animals in Lincoln Park Zoo, and write letters to Oma and Adeline. Do you think they would sneak one to Daniel for you?"

THE REINHOLD FAMILY'S three-story half-timber home suited their noble family well. She never expected to live lavishly again and was unprepared for the home awaiting her. With her mouth agape, Clara struggled for words as they entered the drive of the Gerbers' home. Turrets, arches, alcoves, carved stonework, and fancy windows everywhere. The exquisite mansion covered more than three times the space of the Gut Apfelhof home.

"Only the two of you live here?" It was all she could manage to say.

"Penelope, come meet my niece." Tante Ingrid motioned to a dark-haired young woman. She slipped from the porch swing where she had been reading and joined them.

"Clara, meet Penelope. She lives with us. I know you'll become fast friends."

"Pleased to meet you, Clara."

"And you as well. What are you reading? I love books. We should compare what we've read."

"I would love for us to." She stroked the horses' manes. They nickered their thanks for the sugar cubes Penelope had brought to them. "Mrs. Gerber, may I show Clara to her room?"

"Of course. Do you girls smell those aromas?"

Both of them inhaled. Clara rubbed her tummy. "I'm eating for all of us, and the savory spices filling my nostrils promise a scrumptious meal."

"Meet us in the dining room in thirty minutes. Robert will deliver your things to your room, Clara."

A white ball of fluff rounded the corner and leaped ahead of them onto the stairs.

LAVENDER EVERYWHERE REMINDED her of her Fedderbetten at Gut Apfelhof. Touches of pink and yellow, too. "Has my Oma instructed Ingrid about my favorite things?"

"I believe she must have written to Tante Ingrid." Penelope smiled. "We shopped together for some of the items, and she checked them off on a letter she carried with her."

"Even a cradle." The white Persian cat plopped inside and made herself comfortable.

Penelope rubbed Aster behind the ears until she purred, then lifted her out and cuddled her in her arms. "The cradle's for the baby. You'll need to find another place to snooze." Aster bounded from her arms and promptly brushed against Clara's gown before leaping onto a small pink chest next to the cradle. It was filled with diapers and layettes.

"You're the princess of Tante's home, I do believe." Clara smiled at the royal feline, then wandered around the room with its high windows of beveled glass cut and channeled into designs like the stained glass at St. Luke's. She had a view of walled gardens below. Different from the rural German estate she and Tante Ingrid had both once called home, but the Gerbers did have a garden like the one she loved. "Have you lived here for a while? What grows in the garden?"

Penelope carried the cat to the window. "Roses, lilacs, daffodils, zinnias, Queen Anne's lace, and at least a dozen other varieties I don't recall the names of. In a few more weeks the daffodils will be blooming. Something called pussy willows are blooming now. I love their fuzzy little tufts—almost like a tiny cat's paw." She stroked Aster's soft feet.

"You'll show me those tomorrow?"

"Yes. After my classes."

"Maybe you could tell me about your classes while we look at the pussy willows. We're expected at dinner in a few minutes. But first, one more question. Are there sunflowers in the garden?"

"I adore those bright cheery flowers. I haven't seen one since I left Germany. I remember they often grow very tall and always reach for the sun."

"And they symbolize happiness and joy." Clara cringed regretting those words when mistiness filled Penelope's eyes.

"I could use a ship full of joy."

∼

GERBERS' GARDEN, *24 April 1882*

LONG SEPIA BRANCHES gracefully cascaded and traversed the Gerbers' garden path. Clara held the reed in one hand and stroked the furry catkins. The pussy willow stems were long. She drew one up to her face and let the fuzzy little ball-like flowers tickle her nose. "Our gardens brought me much joy. I pray this one will, too."

Penelope shuffled her feet. She rubbed the sniffles from her nose.

"What has stolen your joy, Penelope, my new friend?" Clara continued petting the pussy willows while she searched the young woman's eyes.

"Since we're friends, please call me Nell. Penelope sounds so childlike. My youth is behind me."

"Nell, what has stolen your joy?"

"In two weeks, it'll be seven years. I shouldn't still be so sad. Here you are having a baby, and you don't even have the Vati with you."

"Sharing our burdens often lightens the load." Clara reached for Nell's hand and walked beside her around the garden.

"You're probably wondering who I am and why I'm living here. Oscar's my Onkel. We're both nieces to this loving couple."

"You've answered one question. I'm happy we're cousins in a way, then. I miss my sisters so much."

"I miss my whole family. Let's sit down while I share my story." Nell pulled a handful of hankies from her pocket as they headed to the swing where she had been sitting when Clara arrived yesterday.

"Did you hear about the German ship sinking in the Isles of Scilly several years ago?"

"I remember. My brother and Vati lost a business associate who was also a good friend when the S. S. Schiller sank. Was someone dear to you on the ship, too?"

"Ja. Me and my whole family. It was awful. Seven years later the nightmares persist." The first hanky was already soaked. "Only 37 people survived. I was the only one in my family who was rescued. Three of my brothers, two sisters, my Vati, and my Mutti who was expecting another baby—they all died."

What do I say, Lord? I've lost so much, but my family lives. Daniel lives. Unlikely as it seems, I have a small measure of hope we'll see each other again. Nell's family is gone. "I'm very sad for you. The ship had been traveling from New York City back to Germany. Your Onkel came to Penzance and brought you back to America?"

"I couldn't travel alone. Our family had visited my mom's brother, Oscar, here in Chicago. We hoped to return in a few years to live here also. I'm so thankful he came to bring me back to Chicago. May 7 it will be seven years since the accident. I long for the family I once had." Nell struggled to stifle her sobbing.

"My baby's Oma—Daniel's Mutter—covered our whole family in prayer and Bible verses. Do you believe in God, Nell?"

"I did, but I'm angry with Him after He took my family away.

I experienced another loss, too. One I can't talk about. I'm afraid of what else might happen."

"Maybe I'm hearing Rosa's voice in my head whispering words to me because I need to hear them, but maybe they're for you as well. May I share them with you?"

With her face resting in her hands, Nell nodded.

"Fear thou not; for I am with thee: be not dismayed; for I am thy God: I will strengthen thee; yea, I will help thee; yea, I will uphold thee with the right hand of my righteousness.

"Maybe God put us together to strengthen both of us. I wonder if God hears my prayers or cares about me, but I know He cares about others. I can't imagine the horrible pain of your loss. I'll be praying for us both."

"Danke, Clara."

"Are your classes at the Women's Medical College?"

"They are, and I'm learning much about what it takes to be a doctor. Our family has many of them, and I'd like to become one too. My dream is to deliver babies."

Chapter Twenty-Two

DOWNTOWN CHICAGO, Thursday, *4 May 1882*

THEY ROLLED and swayed as the car was pulled along by the underground cable. The bell clanged. The conductor signaled the gripman to smoothly bring the cable car to a halt at the next regular stop.

Madison and State just outside Schlesinger & Mayer department store. Feeling more like a roly-poly than a human, with Tante Ingrid's assistance Clara navigated the two steps down to the street. Ornate buildings lined the street in both directions. "I feared there would be no beautiful architecture in America. This is magnificent."

"Chicago is not Germany or Europe, but a host of creative architects are making a mark on the city. Despite all the horrors the great fire brought, it also provided an opportunity to rebuild with attention to creating incredible beauty among the ashes."

Tante and Clara held hands on the short walk bringing them to Megs' shop on Madison. More bells jingled overhead as they entered.

Megs greeted her friend at the door. "You arrived on the cable car, ja? The newest convenience in transportation around the city. Now, come in and see our new modern fashion home."

Two half circles of white velvet chairs edged a platform where fine creations for her clients were modeled and fitted. A mannequin dressed in lace and jewels stood on the Persian carpeted stage. Strategic lighting reflected off the perfectly placed mirrors like glimmers in the night sky.

In a twirl, Ingrid spun around to take in the details of the place. Clara held her hands over her bundle of baby and made the turn with much more caution.

Ingrid tapped her fingers on a wooden box atop a three-legged stand overlooking the platform. "A camera. You offer your clients portraits too?"

"They adore the added touches we've added since moving from our original location."

"You've done well, my friend." Clara pointed to the lace confection. "Is this glittering ensemble ready for your first client of the day?"

"Isn't it lovely? I've boasted of your creativity to our client. She's expecting the two of you to imagine the perfect design for her to share with her milliner. You did bring your sketchbooks, pencils, and pastels?"

"Tante Ingrid, you carried the satchel." She reached for the turquoise and rose striped bag—a gift from this special lady. After unlatching the pearl clasp, Clara withdrew the sketch-pad. "I came prepared to do my part."

"We still have a half-hour before Mrs. Miller arrives. I have water heating for tea. Shall we have a seat, ladies?"

"I'll leave the two of you to chat and enjoy your tea before the lucky lady arrives. I'm due at the hospital shortly. Megs, you'll be certain Clara finds her way to the cable car to bring her home later today?"

Megs nodded.

With a kiss to Clara's forehead, Tante Ingrid made her exit.

Megs strode to the office and returned carrying a tray with their tea. "We've much to catch up on, Clara. Tell me the whole story."

"Maybe another day." Clara tipped her cup and sipped, moistening her dry throat. "Does your client have a preference in hat styles? Feathers? Flowers? Ribbons? Flamboyant? Birds? Something less assuming?"

"You've already envisioned ideas. I see it in your eyes. Interview her. Learn which of your suggestions may excite her most."

A smile spread across Clara's cheeks. "You know me well. Of course, I have ideas. But maybe not the bird's nest. The birds may find the shiny beads of the gown a bit too much of a temptation to add to their little straw homes."

"Silly. I don't think this client would approve of the bird idea, and you're teasing."

"I was. It wouldn't be a live bird anyway." Clara studied the camera. She remembered seeing a similar one back at Gut Apfelhof recently. "Will you show me how to use the camera? I could work on sketches based on photos saving our clients' time."

"I see us adding a full photography studio in the future. I'd love for you to learn."

"This camera is portable, correct? We could photograph our clients in locations of their choosing. Settings which would tell a story while showcasing them and their new ensembles." Her fingertips tingled at the possibilities.

"You could photograph the baby. Send those cabinet cards to Daniel and your family." Megs tapped Clara's shoe with hers and giggled.

Her chest tightened. Revealing Vati had disowned her—had forbidden the other family members from having contact with her—was more than Clara was ready to share even with her best friend. "It would be nice to have photos of the baby or babies."

"Did I hear someone say baby?" The bells tinkled as Mrs. Miller entered.

Clara and Megs stood, and Megs made the introductions. "And, yes, someone did say baby. My friend, Clara, my new partner in the shop is expecting in July."

"Babies are delightful. I'll enjoy lavishing attention on the little one every time I come."

Clara blushed. "Thank you. You're most kind. I pray the baby doesn't become an annoyance around all these pretty and enticing things."

Mrs. Miller waved Clara's comment away. "Let me admire this gown all over again. Wearing it, I'll be the most well-bedecked lady at the party."

"It is beautiful." Clara circled around it again to gain every perspective. "Give me some ideas of your taste in hats."

"I've heard the banter about four-story hats with a basement. Nothing so ostentatious, but I would adore an ivory one to match the lace of the dress and piled high with purple silk flowers and flowing lavender ribbons. More glimmering lights threaded throughout. Could you create the sketch for my milliner to follow?"

Clara's hands moved back and forth over the page. First with pencils and then adding pastels. "Like this?"

"Oh, Megs, you were correct! Your friend interpreted my vision exactly. Clara, this is exceptional." She blew the girls kisses.

Clara dabbed her eyes to stop the sudden stinging. A lightness filled her chest.

"We're sending a length of the fabric and pieces of lace with you. When your crown is complete, we would love to photograph your likeness." Megs had the package prepared, placed it in Mrs. Miller's hands, and walked with her to the door.

Back inside, Megs pulled Clara to her feet and attempted to spin them around. Clara wobbled side to side instead. The bell above the door tinkled again.

A young man from the telegraph office bounded through the door whistling Yankee Doodle.

"What inspires your happy tune today?" Megs giggled as he danced a little jig.

The messenger boy drew the familiar yellow telegram envelope from his satchel. With a touch of pomp, he placed it in Megs' hands. "From across the Atlantic ma'am. It must be important. Shall I wait for your reply?"

Megs handed him two pennies in exchange. "You may be on your way, Archie. I'll find you if I'd like to respond." She slid the message in her pocket.

"Do you know who sent the telegram?"

"Archie said it's from Europe." Megs carefully unsealed the edges of the thin page. As Megs read, her eyes spread wide. All the color drained from her face.

"Has someone died, my friend?"

"Apparently, yes." Megs stared down at the page for a long while. She opened and closed her mouth several times as if to speak. No words came.

"Can you say who it's from?" Clara's fingers twitched. Her insides quivered.

"My Mutter. She's not making sense—unless there's a story you haven't told me. She mentions Daniel as the Vater of Tilly's dead baby. What baby? And Daniel is…"

Megs let the pages flutter down on Clara's lap. "Maybe you should examine this yourself. And remember it is from my Mutter."

Take care, *daughter, about Clara. Daniel seen with Tilly. Both gone together days at a time. I bet Daniel is Vater of Tilly's dead baby. Georg took the fall. Tell C, D does not love her. Handsome man is trouble. Herr R should not trust D unless he is D's Vater. Rudi Feldt driving for Reinholds. Georg was best man for Clara. C is trouble for you. Send C away.*

.   .   .

Sᴡᴇᴀᴛ ᴄᴏᴠᴇʀᴇᴅ Cʟᴀʀᴀ'ꜱ ᴘᴀʟᴍꜱ. Her pulse pounded in her ears.

"Tilly and Daniel gone together? Days at a time?"

∿

Cʟᴀʀᴀ'ꜱ ꜱᴇᴄᴏɴᴅ ᴡᴇᴇᴋ ᴀᴛ Mᴇɢꜱ' shop, *Tuesday, 9 May 1882*

Cʟᴀʀᴀ ᴡᴀᴅᴅʟᴇᴅ through the door of Megs' shop. Megs had claimed them to be partners, but doubts assailed her. *Maybe more like we were partners.*

After reading Frau Wolff's telegram, she owed Megs an explanation. Every time she tried a client entered the shop. *I'll be dropping a heavy weight on my friend's shoulders.* Her legs wobbled. Would the story she prepared to share leave as sour a taste in Megs' mouth as what she tasted right now?

The gown Clara had been working on was draped across the rose-striped settee. *The beauty of this fabric and the design impress me every time I see it.* Megs is nowhere to be seen. *I'll get back to work on the dress's embellishments. Sitting here for very long, I'm not always comfortable. I'm grateful for the fluffy green and white pillows Megs and I positioned to help.* She arranged them to make herself as comfortable as possible and worked on Mrs. Hardy's dress.

With hands planted firmly at her hips, Megs came in through the back door and approached Clara. "I'm waiting for the story." The bells jingled interrupting Megs' foot tapping. "Clara, please do not leave today until you've told me everything."

Clara quickly spread a sheet over Mrs. Hardy's dress.

The door opened with a whoosh. Megs greeted their first client of the day and led her to a seat by Clara. "Mrs. Spalding, I would like you to meet Mrs. Becker, a talented fashion artist. She's ready to work with you to bring your vision to life. The sketch is, of course, the first step."

"Why should I trust her?" The woman crossed her arms over her chest. Her nose inched upward.

Is it the babies having a wrestling match or are my insides quivering? What if I fail this woman? Has Megs set me up for a fall because she's leery of our arrangement?

A vial hung from Megs' chatelaine. She fidgeted with it, tapping its tiny stopper. Two steps away from the women, Megs pivoted. Two steps back. "Mrs. Becker traveled to Paris with me last fall. Impressed with her skills, Monsieur Worth offered her a position with his fashion house had she stayed in Europe."

"Looks like maybe she should have stayed. Is your husband here with you, Mrs. Becker?"

"Mrs. Becker's situation is personal. Please use the good manners your mother taught you, and refrain from being nosy. My friend will be happy to have you exclaim over her little one when he or she arrives."

Mrs. Spalding nodded, but her mouth drew into a tight pucker. She took the seat Megs offered, sitting with her chest thrust out.

Her sketch pad propped on her ever-expanding-middle, Clara listened. Mrs. Spalding pulled a fashion magazine from her satchel and opened to a well-worn page she had marked.

A full-page image of a House of Worth gown. "I would like for your shop to create this for me."

"Let's exchange some of the flowers flowing around the bodice and the skirt." Moving her finger over the sketch, Clara traced the gown's neckline. I'd love to see us incorporate some new laces and ribbons which have just arrived."

"Some new ribbons arrived yesterday. I believe there's a perfect one in the package." Megs headed to her office.

"My husband is a major shareholder in the Chicago White Stockings. I want him to have the most beautiful woman in the room at his side. Can you assure me of that?"

Her chest thudded like a staccato drumbeat while Clara drew the sketch. *Mr. Worth warned us about copying anything of his.* She changed the shape of the sleeves and altered the neckline to flatter Mrs. Spalding's figure.

"Let me see." Mrs. Spalding turned the corner of the sketch pad toward her. With her other hand, she covered her mouth.

Is she hiding a smile? *Have I done well?* Clara's arm muscles tensed and she held her breath as she handed the pad to the client.

Mrs. Spalding nodded. Tears pooled in her eyes. I would rather criticize your efforts because no one ever understands me. I didn't expect you to either, but you've captured my vision."

"You expressed your love of the color aquamarine. I'll need to add the color details. Are you able to return in two days to see my completed sketch?"

"I'll be here as soon as you are open."

Megs had stepped from her office, the perfect lace draped over her arm. "Didn't I tell you Mrs. Becker would create a magnificent rendering of your dream gown? She's also the best at fine detail embellishments needed to give the dress its exquisite finish."

"Then, Mrs. Becker, I plead. Please keep your baby inside you until my gown is complete."

~

"IS MRS. SPALDING ALWAYS DIFFICULT?" Clara wiped her brow with one of Oma's hankies.

Megs scanned the shop. Laughter rippled from her throat. "I had to be sure we were alone before I answered. Truth. Most times she's worse, but your sketches made her happy. You side-stepped her House of Worth request without upsetting her, too. She doesn't smile often. She loves you, Clara!"

"You exaggerate, Megs. She may admire my work, but she insinuated many things when she arrived. Am I an embarrassment to you in my condition?"

"You're married, my dear friend, but I do speculate on what has kept Daniel from joining you as he promised. And why is my brother in prison? I can imagine many reasons he should be, but I'd like details. And Tilly's baby?"

Clara sniffed. Tears trickled toward her chin. "I wish I knew the answer to your question about Daniel. I imagine you wish you hadn't asked me to be part of your business."

"You're my friend, Clara. I trust important matters have created Daniel's delay. He's a man of his word. He'll come soon."

"I pray tis so. The babies and I need him."

"Tilly had a baby? What happened to Tilly's baby?"

Megs handed Clara the lace. She stroked her fingers across it as she prepared to share the story. Finding the baby remains. Curt, Vati, and Daniel chasing clues about betrayal, blackmail, and the mystery which precipitated Vati's agreement with Georg. "It's not a pretty story, Megs. In the midst of a colorful ring of characters and the whole blackmail and coverup, they learned Georg had taken liberty with Tilly against her will. If the tea he had forced down her hadn't worked, Georg would have blamed Daniel."

Megs chewed her lower lip and clenched and unclenched her fists. "Grr. I believe you. He's my brother, but I grow to hate him more all the time. I taste anger and bile." She took a seat beside Clara. They held hands. "My Mutter's message is all lies then?"

She nodded. "But the part about Daniel and Tilly presents new worries for me?"

"Allow me to do what you and Rosa have done for me so often. You taught us Psalm 56 in our Bible class. Meditate on these verses. *What time I am afraid, I will trust in thee. In God I will praise his word, in God I have put my trust; I will not fear what flesh can do unto me.*"

"It's much more difficult to practice what we easily memorize. Thank you for recalling the verse at this moment." Clara dabbed her eyes with her handkerchief.

"God blesses me with good words—and a good memory—occasionally. Now back to your concerns about our shop. My clients have been receiving your presence here with enthusiasm. Your kindness brings them joy before you even sketch their ideas or embellish their gowns."

"And when I'm birthing this baby or babies and I'm not as available our plan crumbles. I disappoint you and your ladies. Mrs. Spalding will be the first to remind you of her misplaced trust."

"I can handle her. I'm headed out to get supplies. I'll bring us treats when I return. You're in charge of greeting our clients. Mrs. Pullman's gown is ready for beads and embroidery. Will you begin your artistry on it while I'm gone?"

Clara settled in with the gown across her lap. She balanced a dish with the beads, needles, and shiny floss fibers on a tray just within her reach. She waved to Megs as the bell above the door signaled her departure. A wallop inside her abdomen, while she reached for the embellishments, caused Clara's hand to tip the container. Sparkles flew and rolled all over the floor.

Megs had left for *supplies* more frequently than Clara believed necessary. At the moment Clara was alone and needed to clean up her mess. She risked her slipper sliding on the little round pieces of glass and her feet splaying out from under her. She carefully moved the gown to an empty area on the settee. She pushed herself up and stepped gingerly clearing a path as she went into the office looking for a broom.

When Clara bumped a stack of materials on Megs' desk a paper box slid from beside the pile, falling into an open drawer. She didn't need to retrieve it to discover its contents. It landed with the label visible. *Women's Pills—Preventative Powders.*

"Preventative? Hardly. They might end a pregnancy, but they won't prevent anything." Clara wrung her hands and averted her gaze. They were fortunate to have an indoor toilet in their shop. Clara made it there just in time to empty her stomach. This time her babies had not caused the illness. *How do I even discuss this with Megs? She told me when we were in Paris, she wasn't sure she ever wanted children.*

They had lost the first one. Did she lose it? Or had it succumbed to Women's Pills? Why? Clara found what she needed and returned to clean up the catastrophe of findings. She would pray for the right words and timing.

When Megs returned, she sashayed past Clara handing her a waxed paper bundle with tea cakes inside. "Would you prefer I make tea or coffee to enjoy with them?"

"Tea today, please." *Hopefully, more settling to my stomach.*

Megs hurried off barely waiting for Clara's answer. Papers crinkled. Gentle clicking sounds like pebbles shaken in a cup could be heard from the office area. What interesting tea is she brewing back there? Not Earl Gray, chamomile, or lavender. Clara fought back tears. If Megs had added crushed Ladies' pills to her tea, would Clara begin laboring too soon?

∿

WEDNESDAY, *17 May 1882*

"IN THE SPRING *a young man's fancy lightly turns to thoughts of love.* Alfred Lord Tennyson penned it well. Wedding bells would ring all over the city in the next few months. Clara, you've always amazed me with your talent. Our ladies will outshine all their friends because of your finishing touches. They'll gather all the compliments."

"If Mrs. Palmer attends in her Charles Worth original, our creations will not compete."

"Your sketches impressed Monsieur Worth enough that he offered you a position sketching for him." A smile breezed across Megs' lips. "I adore these pale pink silk roses with their beaded stamens you're creating for the mint green gown. Mrs. Pullman asked to come by this afternoon for a peek at it. I'm hoping other clients don't come through the door while she's here."

"Didn't you tell me you believe it is an excellent idea for the clients to be here at the same time—get ideas from each other's new gowns?"

"Perhaps not such a grand idea after all. I've learned these women prefer keeping their special attire guarded secrets until the event. We're creating gowns these women will show off when they attend a wedding at Second Presbyterian Church—the Lord's house chosen by the wealthy and influential people of the city.

"Mrs. Spalding's husband is the owner of the Chicago White Stockings baseball team. I believe she'd like to outshine the beauty of the church. It may not rival the cathedrals of Europe, but it is stunning. She requested I obtain a large supply of Swarovski crystals for the aquamarine confection. Be visualizing how you'll incorporate them."

"If my babies soil her gown or come early and keep me from completing it, I'd acquire as black a spot on your shop's reputation as if we'd spilled an inkwell on someone's finery."

The bell jingled. Megs stepped to the door. "Good day, Mrs. Pullman."

The lady gushed as she cast her gaze toward Clara covered in mint green fabric. "I love what I'm seeing!"

"You must view it up close." Clara motioned her closer.

Mrs. Pullman tiptoed almost reverently toward Clara. "Silk roses! The freshest shade of pale pink in the morning sky. And you've set them off with tiny star beads. I'll have the most stunning ensemble for Josefine's wedding." She studied it carefully. "If only I could hold the picture in my mind forever." She skimmed her fingers over the roses as if to caress them. "How soon will you have it ready, ladies?"

"I believe Clara will have it ready in one more week."

"Excellent. And now I'll be on my way. My daughter and grandchildren will be waiting for me."

How I wish for my babies to know their Omas.

Mrs. Pullman oohed and ahhed over the confection one more time. "Thank you."

Megs walked their pleased client to the door.

Behind them, Clara's smile evaporated. Robert, the Gerber's butler, strode through the door as Mrs. Pullman exited. "May I have a word with you outside, Mrs. Becker?"

THE GERBERS' home, *Wednesday Evening, 17 May 1882*

DISCOVERING MEGS' pills already has me frantic with worry. I'm seething about Frau Wolff's telegram. Now what's urgent enough Robert was sent to fetch me home?

Clara scurried through the front door Robert held wide for her. "Tante Ingrid, have you received difficult news from your family in Germany? Is it your sister? Or her son—the one who disowned me? Or something worse?" Clara crumpled onto the sofa and pressed her shaking fists over her ears.

Eerie shadows from the wall sconces deepened Clara's fear. She thought it was just her and Tante Ingrid. She jumped and slapped a hand to her chest when someone whistled a jaunty tune from the kitchen.

"It's Oscar, dear girl. He's been planting seeds in pots on the veranda. He enjoys cultivating a few horticultural specimens for us to enjoy while we swing."

"Oscar, I left mail on the kitchen table. Could you bring it to us please?"

Ingrid took the fat packet from her husband. "This is addressed to you, Clara. I've already read the thin one from Dorthea addressed to me. Your family's well, but there are concerns. You should read these as soon as possible. If you'd like to be alone, I understand."

With the pearl-handled letter opener Tante offered her, Clara slit the large envelope revealing letters from home. A note from Onkel Martin topped the stack.

Dear Clara, These letters were left on the seat of our carriage. We found them when Tante Adeline and I returned from accompanying you to Bremen. I pray you find encouragement and hope in their words—and sweet reminders of home.

Daniel must have left them when he returned the Walthers' carriage, but how was he able to collect them without Gut Herr Kraig Reinhold's knowledge? After Frau Wolff's accusatory wire, whose letter should she open first? Frau

Wolff could be trusted almost as little as her son, and why did she find a need to send the telegraph at all? Instead of hope and encouragement would these letters all contain wild incriminations against the man Clara loved?

She eenie-meenie-minie-moed the three before deciding to keep Daniel's for last. At least his happy thoughts will soothe fear and agitation arising from the words of the others.

What concerns had Oma expressed to Tante Ingrid? Clara would open hers first.

2 April 1882

My Dearest Clara,

How are you and my great-grandbaby faring? It's Palm Sunday. We rejoiced with the little children and waved palm branches in church this morning. This afternoon, I'm particularly missing our chats in the garden. The beauty of the foliage and flowers gentles difficult conversations and enhances the lovely ones. If only this could be a conversation, but alas a letter must suffice.

Has news reached you of Rosa's condition? Her feet and her fingers are not behaving properly, resulting in clumsiness and pain for her. I applaud your Vati's commitment to her care. When he learned of a Doktor in Paris who has discovered much about her disease, sclérose en plaques, he determined Rosa would have the best care this man and his fellow neurologists could provide.

Your Vati assigned Daniel to accompany her on the monthly trips to Paris. Since Rosa is Daniel's Mutter, the arrangement makes sense. I'm thankful for any help she receives there.

Yours and Daniel's little secrets have encountered consequences.

You're suffering separation from Daniel so close to your time of delivery. Expect his arrival in America to be greatly delayed.

It saddened me the choices you and Daniel made. It saddens me more how those choices have separated you and put an ocean between you and the family. Now I must tell you of another concern. Your Vater hired Tilly to assist in Rosa's care. She travels with Rosa and Daniel on every trip to Paris. As well, she helps him tend to Rosa's care and needs each day back in Gut Apfelhof.

Your young man has held a special place in my heart, and you've heard me tell him he is Gut Apfelhof's best carriage driver I've known. The sneaky way the two of you handled yourselves lowered my opinion of him a notch. Now he spends much time with Tilly. It's always been in her eyes when she's around him. Tilly loves Daniel. He cares a great deal about Tilly as well. This is merely a hunch, but a pretty well-founded one.

It's very likely your marriage to Daniel has been annulled. In your Vati's eyes, Daniel and Tilly make a better-suited match. A man's heart deviseth his way: but the Lord directeth his steps. Your Opa quoted this proverb often—a reminder God has the final say in our plans. I once made the suggestion you ask God to help you find a new dream. Is this the time?

Love, Oma

OMA'S WORDS from the long-ago day flooded back. 'Imagine a new dream. Pray about it, meine Kind. Watch God work.'

She hadn't prayed about it—she had no desire for a new dream. She needed God to work out her plans her way. *Everything will be all better when I get to Daniel's letter.*

Who is this one from? The shaky penmanship on the envelope gave no indication. Clara lifted the flap with care to keep the sky-blue stationery pristine. She scanned for the signature first. *Rosa* in crooked broken letters. She wanted to deny what Oma had written about Rosa's problems. When had this happened?

With the writing so unsteady Clara read slowly being certain to glean every word correctly.

Dear Clara,

How are my grandbabies? You'll be holding them soon. If my fingers were working better, I would sew delicate layettes for the little ones. As you can see from my handwriting, stitching anything has become very difficult.

I've disappointed your family by being unable to complete my seamstress responsibilities quickly and with the same skill. I'm disappointed in myself and afraid. I cling to this verse from John: Peace I leave with you, my peace I give unto you: not as the world giveth, give I unto you. Let not your heart be troubled, neither let it be afraid.

To the point of the seamstress work, Tilly has blessed us all improving daily in all the skills required. God gifted her to do this work, and she is developing her craft with excellence. She also attends to me well. She and Daniel together ensure all my needs are met. You may be worried about Daniel and Tilly spending so much time together. I know she's always had her eyes on him. She might act on her feelings if it weren't for the two of you being so in love.

My son would never betray you. You believe me, don't you, sweet Clara? I desire to cuddle our baby in my arms. Daniel promised to bring me to America to meet the baby or babies, but I'm not sure my body could endure the trip. He's saving money for the passage and

*to help with the children, but your Vati has made his leaving very
difficult—almost impossible.*

I'm praying he finds a way.

With much love and affection,

Rosa

Poor Rosa. Will she be able to travel with Daniel to visit the
babies? If they came would Tilly accompany them? 'She and
Daniel together...' to quote her words. *Is Rosa being naive to
assure me again of Daniel's commitment to me? Am I being naive
to believe Daniel has no interest in Tilly?*

She has, as Rosa and Oma have both written, always had eyes
for him. *Tilly had not acted on her feelings for him because she
respected me. At least she did while I was in sight. But I'm nowhere
near, and apparently, I'm not married anymore either.*

Clara held Daniel's letter. Her belief it would all be happy
news drained from her heart. Her pacing rocked the babies
and stilled them. Reverie mingled with fear. She jumped
when Aster rubbed against her legs. "Will you sit with me,
kitty, while I read this? If the news is bad, I'll stroke your tan
ears and under your silky chin. Your purring will relieve
tension from my quaking body."

The cat looked at her as if to say, "Only if it's bad news?"

She snatched her up and cuddled Aster while she read. The
purring already eased the tension. She grabbed the letter
opener and reached around the kitty to slit Daniel's envelope
open with extra care. She patted Aster's head. "I can always
trust Daniel to send beautifully decorated missives."

10 April 1882

My wife, my lovely lady, you and our baby or babies keep my mind so distracted from performing my services to your family at Gut Apfelhof. I see everything through the cover of hearts and stars. I've just stopped by to leave this and other letters at the Walthers' home.

Seeing you today made the pain of separation even more unbearable. I apologize I was unable to travel with you to America as we had planned. How soon will our little one or ones arrive? I trust you've been treated well by your Tante and Megs and lack nothing save for my presence there with you.

In the past. Georg was at the center of our troubles. Even with him in prison, new challenges have presented themselves. Your Vati, of course, forbids communication with you for any of us at Gut Apfelhof. My Mutter gave me hers and your Oma's letters before we left for the Easter festivities at Tante Caroline and Onkel Knut's home. Our visit made it easy to leave them where Onkel Martin would find them.

In the future, Curt and I have found a way around the problem. With Lillian's help, he'll sneak letters between the Walthers' home and Gut Apfelhof. The esteemed Gut Herr will do nothing to compromise the relationship between Curt and the Viscount's daughter even if they were to be caught. I trust the Walthers to send my letters—all of our letters on to you. How long it takes for you to receive them, I cannot say. I pray they arrive quickly.

The news I must tell you is so difficult because it causes me pain in more ways than just being an ocean away from you. My message about it was quite mysterious earlier today when you asked. My Mutter has developed problems with her feet and legs. She stumbles often and tires easily.

Curt heard from your sisters, they have seen her fumble often with the needle and thread. She's so skilled with those that I can't imagine her frustration. Her fingers have lost dexterity. Everyone here is quite worried about her, especially your Vati. He learned of a Doktor in Paris who is researching and has named a disease that matches her symptoms. I fear this Doktor has no cure. Nevertheless, the Gut Herr insists Rosa be placed in his care.

The responsibility of accompanying her to Paris for monthly appointments has been placed squarely on my shoulders for as long as Doktor Charcot is attending her. Her visits with him could be for a very long time, Clara, my lovely lady.

This condition has been noted with interest in England, too. The Doktor has named it sclérose en plaques. *I don't believe he has helped anyone improve, but perhaps a slower advance of disease for those who have sought his care. Maybe they will learn something to help others in the future.*

My heart is torn as I know yours will be, also, upon reading these words. We both love my precious Mutter. How can I not stay in Germany to help her?

When not traveling with Mutter to Paris, my time is occupied by my role as the carriage driver for your family and helping with Mutter's care. Your Vati has hired our friend Tilly to help Mutter when we are at Gut Apfelhof, which of course, is most of the time. She also travels with me to Paris to help with Rosa's care. Tilly's faith and needle skills have grown tremendously as she assists Rosa, as you can imagine.

I've been so grateful for Tilly's assistance. She's always been a good friend. Her kindness and her smile bring joy to our days and make the sadness of Rosa's health so much easier for me.

My forever promise of love stands. I continue seeking the first opportunity to come to America and to you and our babies. I wish I could tell you when, but as is Rosa's habit, she reminded me of this verse from Romans: Rejoicing in hope; patient in tribulation; continuing instant in prayer.

My patience has worn thin, I pray less, and there seems little prospect for hope.

All of my love,

Daniel

P.S. My sunflower sketches each have seeds at the center. If our sunflower box and I never make it, I've sent pieces of both our hearts—pieces that will grow and flourish for generations like here at Gut Apfelhof.

CONSIDERING the news of the first two letters and Frau Wolff's wire, Clara read a million possibilities between the lines of Daniel's. Which parts would she trust? Nothing was better at all.

Her throat constricted and pain like a vise squeezed her whole head. Worry tugged from every direction. Denial wouldn't serve Clara well. Every one of the letters and Frau Wolff's telegram insinuated Daniel and Tilly—her husband and one of her dearest friends had betrayed her.

Onkel Martin promised Vati couldn't annul the marriage, but had he? Or had Vati declared it to Daniel as if it were true? *Could it be he is still my husband?* Could Vati do this? Oma and Rosa are right. Tilly has always had eyes for Daniel. *Daniel seeks to assure me he and Tilly are working together only to help Rosa.*

Traveling together, though, presumes close proximity and time away from eyes holding them accountable. Kind-hearted Daniel sees the best in everyone, and he bragged on Tilly— maybe overly much. He even said 'Her kindness and her smile bring joy to our days and make the sadness of Rosa's health so much easier for me.' *How should I interpret his words? I doubt Frau Wolff's nasty accusations, but all of this together on the same day. Fear rips its tentacles through every cell of my body and the body or bodies of the little one or ones I carry inside. My life —our lives—a tattered heap of frayed promises.*

Clara tossed the letters across the room and then sank onto her bed. She pulled a pillow over her face. Sobs racked her body. A hammer-like sensation joined the vice inflicting further pain in her head. Little hands and feet punched and poked. Instead of answering the knock, she would have preferred to get up and kick the door. "Come in," she mumbled.

"I'm unsure what to say or ask." Tante Ingrid tiptoed to the bed. She stroked Clara's curls the way she remembered her Mutti had always done.

Clara's sobbing eased. "Danke. You remind me of my Mutti. I need her."

"I wish I could arrange for her to be here for you." Ingrid sighed. "Would you like to talk?"

"Later. My thoughts are stampeding like wild horses. I need to harness them first."

"I'll send your caller on his way for tonight, then."

"Caller?"

"Ja. Said he was a friend of your friend Max from the ship. He told me he has a surprise from Max."

"Send him away!"

❧

ALONE AGAIN, Clara picked at the seeds on Daniel's letter. She reread the words.

MY SUNFLOWER SKETCHES each have seeds at the center. If our sunflower box and I never make it, I've sent pieces of both our hearts—pieces that will grow and flourish for generations like here at Gut Apfelhof.

WHAT DID THIS EVEN MEAN? He knew how much she enjoyed the sunflowers. *We always added the bold yellow flowers to the Erntedank carts and wove them into the ribbons on the horses' bridles.* The ones decorating the beautiful box Daniel had carved to save their coins for America delighted her. The box she had been unable to retrieve before leaving Gut Apfelhof on only a moment's notice.

Her delight over the sunflowers she and Curt had discovered by the abandoned cottage had dampened with the discovery of the remains of Tilly's baby buried among them. Yet those same sunflowers had helped chase sadness away knowing they would bloom like rays of sunshine over the grave of Tilly's tiny babe each year.

Tilly, Daniel, Tilly's baby. *Tilly's smile and kindness bring me joy.* Is it only her smile and kindness bringing him joy? Or something more? All these messages. What meaning do the seeds bring today? They may grow and flourish for generations, but whose generations will they be? *How should I respond to Daniel's letter? To any of these letters? Oma—a new dream?*

Shakespeare's line from Hamlet wove through her deliberations. *There's a divinity that shapes our ends, Rough-hew them how we will.* The words echoed the same message as the Bible verse Oma had quoted again.

If their marriage had truly been annulled, had it been the doing of Vati? Had Vati listened to their Heavenly Father directing this path? God hated divorce, but by marrying the way they had, they had stepped out of God's instructions to honor their parents. What had become of their marriage reeked of consequences.

Oh, wise Oma. How I long to talk to you. I need your wisdom to sort through my dilemma.

SHE PRESSED the seeds into her palm. Would the flowers' stems grow straight and strong or twist each in a new direction? Clara carefully picked three seeds from the paper and wrapped them in the corner of her handkerchief.

She stepped into the hall. Her cumbersome load made stealth impossible as she descended the stairs. Clara was two steps from the bottom when Onkel Oscar entered the foyer.

"Clara, is all well?"

"How fortunate for me. I was coming to find you." Standing two steps from the bottom her eyes were level with his kind ones.

"Oh." He winked.

"You planted seeds in pots on the veranda earlier today. Would you have another pot for these?"

She untucked the corners of the handkerchief and dropped the trio of seeds into Onkel's now extended palm.

With his index finger, Oscar poked at the seeds in his hand. "Sunflowers. Symbolic of loyalty and admiration."

Clara nodded. "An experiment, I suppose." *O Lord, if they grow and bloom, let them be a sign Daniel's gift honors those attributes and carries the sunflower's promises.* "Please pray over them when you plant them."

"I'll tend to them well and pray for God to make them soar and bloom."

Chapter Twenty-Three

MEGS' SHOP, Wednesday, *10 May 1882*

CLANG, clang, clang. The sound of the cable car and its bells along the tracks kept Clara alert. After a sleepless night, a nap on the way to work would have been a great respite. Instead, she held on to the upright poles and jostled along as they traveled through the curve in the track halting at the Madison Street stop.

As she stepped from the car, a man whistled from the street corner, then jumped and waved his arms catching her attention. How could it be? Hadn't this man caused enough trouble already?

How did Blade know where to find me? Can I get to Megs' shop unharmed?

She stared straight ahead, refusing to turn her head even an inch lest she encourage him. She moved as quickly as her extra load allowed. Just before she entered the shop, he slapped a hand on her shoulder and turned her to face him.

"You don't have time for an old friend?" His cocky grin sickened her.

She trembled uncontrollably on the inside—or were the babies attempting to kick the louse away from her?

"Where's your man? Not here to protect you today? You were such a happy little family on the ship."

Clara jerked away. "I'm late for work. Leave!"

"I know where to find you, Clara. I'll be watching for an opportunity to spend time with you." He leaned toward her and winked.

Realization struck. She had been certain no friend of Max' was at Tante and Onkel's door last night. Now she knew for sure! *I hate to admit this, but I need Max right now. He would know what to do about Blade. But he isn't here. I'm strong. Daniel will come.* She shivered while holding the sunflowers' promises.

She dropped her satchel on the floor as she bumbled her way into the shop. Before she could head to the settee, Megs stepped in front of Clara.

"What's happened to you? Have you seen a ghost?"

"Of sorts, ja." Clara wiped her sleeve across her damp forehead. "A crass character from the ship found me here in Chicago. I never saw him again after we disembarked the train until this morning. Calls himself Blade. The name should give you a clue about the kind of man he is. Not a gentleman. He found me. Max can handle him. Last night I sent a friend of Max away. I'm sure it was no friend. Probably Blade. And I asked Onkel Oscar to plant sunflower seeds.

"And Daniel is spending time with Tilly, but maybe to help Rosa. Yes, to help Rosa. But it could be something more. And Rosa is sick with some disease—*sclérose en plaques*—doesn't have a cure. Treatments might slow its progression. And Daniel can't come yet. Will he come at all? Tilly's traveling to Paris with him for Rosa's treatments. Is traveling *all* they're doing while going back and forth? Oma still thinks I might need a new dream."

"What?" Megs raised a hand. "Slow down. Stop. Clara, Unravel all your run-on thoughts please."

"I'm so confused and so pregnant. Robert came for me because three letters awaited me at Ingrid and Oscar's. Tante had already read hers from Oma. She decided I needed to find out quickly what was going on. I read the letters, but they've left me with many questions and doubts and little reassurance."

"You mentioned Max. What a handsome gentleman. And, yes, he is a gentleman. You turned him away—again?" Megs scoffed, shaking her head and frowning.

"Max's *friend*, not Max." Clara rubbed the tension from her throbbing forehead before rattling her response. "Your opinion certainly gallops all over the place. First, you claim what an honorable man Daniel is and assure me he's coming. Now you're chiding me for not paying more attention to handsome Max. Again, it was Max's supposed *friend*, not Max. He told Ingrid he had a surprise." She patted her tummy. "The only surprise I want is Daniel arriving here to be with us."

"Time to work on the gowns." She pointed in the direction of the platform where the day's project lay ready to be tackled. "And Clara, maybe Daniel will never be able to come."

"Are you suggesting a diversion or discouraging my hopes?"

The bell clanged over the door as Blade stepped inside.

"Didn't I tell you to leave? What do you want from me?"

"I believe you know." Blade spawned a cocky grin before reaching into his pocket and pulling out two coins. He rubbed them together. "My lucky nickels."

Lucky nickels? What are this man's intentions? Clara's heart pounded.

"How may we help you?" Megs strode toward the door.

"I'd like to order a gown for my sister."

"Let's make an appointment for her."

"At her home. Not here." The man demanded.

"We don't make home visits. Women come to us." Megs studied their calendar.

Does Megs notice my quivering fingers and the perspiration staining my sleeves?

"Our first available appointment will be June 19th at 3 pm."

He fidgeted with the buttons on his coat, then turned to leave. The hairs on Clara's arms stood at attention from the assault of his words edged with a demonic laugh as he headed out.

"We'll be here."

∾

LATER THE SAME evening

ASTER SPRUNG onto Clara's lap and batted a fuzzy white paw at her pen. "Don't you tip the inkwell, silly cat. Maybe you could offer inspiration for my letter to Daniel instead."

Purr. Purr. Purr.

Clara rubbed under her chin. "You suggest sweet nothings?"

"Merrooowww." The cat stretched into a humped-back pose.

"I see. You're confused too, girl?"

DEAREST DANIEL,

Our babies have become quite a load but they are active which Tante Ingrid claims means they are healthy. Megs and I see several clients each day. Most are very kind. They are excited to meet the little one. One or two are as cantankerous and self-absorbed as Frau Wolff. Megs handles them well. My tasks at the shop include beautiful embellishments to the ladies' gowns. I had the opportunity to envision and sketch a hat design for one. Thankfully, she wasn't into the birds and bird cages on top of her head.

The Gerbers' home is in the Prairie Avenue neighborhood south of the city. Both of them are Doktors. Onkel Oscar came from the prestigious Rush Medical Center. He helped Tante Ingrid's friend, Mary Thompson, found the Chicago Hospital for Women and Children. Tante is a Doktor also.

Tante and Mary are among the first women Doktors. The babies' and my care are in excellent hands, and I'm living in luxury. Please don't let the luxury part frighten you. Anywhere you and I make our home will be perfect.

The letters all arrived yesterday. I saved yours for last praying for news of your plans to travel to America—maybe you would already be on your way as I was reading. Hope fizzled reading your words. Of course, none of it surprised me after your vague hint when you drove us to the Stuttgart station and after reading Oma's and Rosa's letters before yours. The babies and I need you, Daniel.

My pleading sounds very selfish when your Mutter is hurting. I had noticed moments when Rosa's movements faltered. It didn't occur to me illness was to blame. And there is no cure? There isn't a treatment yet either? The Doktor is seeing her to observe the course of her disease and hopefully be able to find a treatment for others in the future. Kind-hearted Rosa would be pleased if her trials proved to be beneficial for others.

I'm thankful Tilly is helping her and pleased Tilly's improving her skills, but now I must share further concerns.

You and Rosa both speak of your faithfulness to me, but I read between the lines. Rosa and Oma both noted Tilly has always had eyes for you. She respected our love when I was there. But I'm not there. I don't know if we're even married anymore. Annulment? What has Vati done?

You write of the joy Tilly brings when you're together. Then you assure me she's nothing more than a friend, and you'll be coming and bringing your Mutter. Will your Mutter have the strength to travel when she's becoming weaker and weaker? Would she live with us here? Vati is keeping you there to oversee her care. What should I believe?

The same day as the letters arrived, Megs received a telegraph—not a letter— from Frau Wolff advising of your shenanigans with Tilly. I put little stock in anything any of the Wolffs say, but combined with the letters I can't help but wonder. Have I been back-stabbed by the love of my life and one of my dearest friends? By the rules, you two do make a better-suited match.

I'm so torn between my love for you and the distance between us. Everything about our union seems very wrong and like more of a charade than a marriage. Perhaps Oma is right to suggest I need a new dream. She quoted the verse from Proverbs again in her letter. Daniel, I need you. We need you. You—not your reassurances.

Onkel Oscar is planting a few of the sunflower seeds for me in their lovely garden. If they grow, I pray they are a sign our love will thrive and we will be together soon. If not? I do not want to even consider the possibility.

I pray I am still,

Your (one and only) Lovely Lady

Chapter Twenty-Four

A BOARDING HOUSE in New York City, *Friday, 2 June 1882*

HE STRUGGLED to throw off the blanket wound around him like a concrete cocoon. His pulse roared like a hundred galloping horses. Black spots danced before his eyes as Max realized the bleeding woman and a man with a knife battled in his nightmare. Awake now, he tentatively pushed himself up and placed his feet on the floor, his weak legs barely promising to hold him. The woman in Luke—with the issue of blood. *She's the woman I saw, but she had Clara's face.* The man with the knife had been frantic to cut off the tassels of Jesus' robe.

A breakfast bell tinkled from the floor below him at the boarding house just across the water from Castle Garden. Close access to the ships and the city, and the kindest innkeeper made his endless journeys across the Atlantic more bearable than he deserved. This morning the nightmare had stolen his appetite, but the savory aromas of sausage, eggs, and sweet delicacies mingled, wafting a trail up the stairs. His stomach growled with its desire for him to join the other guests.

As Max groomed and dressed, he puzzled over the bizarre vision. *Lord, it was Clara's face I saw. You'll take the best care of her. She must be so frightened. And it was me who shared the awful stories of my wife and my mother both losing their lives giving birth. Emilia's and my baby, too. Clara has made sure I know she doesn't need or want me—only Daniel. Are you asking me to go where I'm not wanted? How do I finish my business here?*

Max headed down the stairs and collided with his friend, Officer Morgan, at the bottom.

"Looks like we both know where to find the best breakfast in town. The best except for my wife's cooking, but she's off visiting her sister in Pennsylvania."

"I've completed my business here for this trip, but there's a personal matter. Willigerod anchors the Elbe back at Castle Garden in two weeks. Would you deliver this bundle to him? I'll include specific instructions for him once he's back in Bremen."

"Let's go find a seat. I'll take care of everything you need done. We can talk about it over breakfast."

A large serving of the inn's version of Bauernfruhstuck on a red plate was placed in front of his place at the table. The hostess poured his coffee in one of the inn's signature red cups. The dishes' hue only added another reminder of the images plaguing his sleep last night. The farmer's breakfast threatened to come back up. *Poor Clara. Nothing she ate stayed down while we were on the ship. Of course, it wasn't for the same reason.*

"You don't look so well, my friend."

Max sipped the coffee with his eyes closed. "I'll be fine. Nothing a time in the outdoors won't cure."

"Hope you're right. This ill-feeling of yours—does it regard the young woman I met at Castle Garden?"

"You meet many young women at the castle."

"Ahh—but you requested my care with one in particular."

"Clara's married."

"A wedding ring doesn't stop some men from pursuit."

"You know I'm honorable in all my dealings—business and personal. Promise you'll come back in the morning. I'll have the package ready."

"On my word." Morgan wiped his face and laid the napkin on the table. "See you in the morning. Almost time for my watch."

Max asked for a refill on his coffee and drifted to a solitary seat on the back porch. The swing swayed freely. Flowers lined the fence around the small yard. Birds sputtered chirps and chatters from the lone tree standing sentinel over the house. He had enough thoughts to ponder without their added intrusions. A solitary spot, but not a quiet one.

He prayed —for Clara, for himself, for direction, for Daniel, for the strange circumstances winding around and through his life—almost like he should be able to keep the world from fraying. No. The responsibility belongs to God alone.

When he'd returned to his room, he packed his belongings. He visited Theodor Strauss yesterday. After the solicitor welcomed him and thanked him for caring for his wife and children on the ship, he produced an envelope with an embossed motif Max recognized at once. He recounted Herr Strauss' words. 'For Clara. I hope you will be seeing your friend. I've promised this will reach her.' The mark is Gut Apfelhof's. What news does it carry and who and why by way of Theodor Strauss? Max assured Strauss he would see it safely delivered to the intended recipient. He patted his chest. The envelope rested securely inside his jacket pocket.

He'd do without lunch today and spend the time writing out all the details to attach to the package Morgan would collect in the morning. With one of his belts, he tied the whole delivery securely. The park down the street always provided a cheery respite. Children played tag and threw sticks to their puppy friends as he walked up. Instead of engaging with the children as he had on the ship, he found a vacant bench, plopped down, and observed.

Fragrant red roses lined a path beside him. Does Clara enjoy flowers? What are her favorites? A question he never considered on the ship. Maybe because there were no flowers on the ship, but why now? Never mind. She only wants Daniel. Reaching into his pocket, Max succumbed to the temptation niggling at him. Thankful the envelope wasn't sealed, he withdrew the contents.

A note on top would confirm Clara's fears. Her father had disowned her. He shoved it back in the envelope. *I can't show her this.* His mind meandered through a maze of disjointed reasons why he should or shouldn't, before returning to his disturbing dream. The sun dipped toward the tree line while he prayed for Clara and whatever predicament was causing turmoil.

Before leaving the boarding house, he paid for the extra week he'd registered for. He headed for the train station and the beginning of the journey back to Chicago. Telegrams he sent from the station would advise clients and family of his delay. Details wouldn't be necessary—he didn't have them if they were.

He grabbed the latest edition of the Saturday Evening Post. At least the continuation of the serial story he'd been reading would give him another place to focus his attention.

But then another thought seemingly out of nowhere—*Blade!*

Chapter Twenty-Five

MEGS' Shop, Monday, *5 June 1882*

CLARA'S ABDOMEN now grew at an alarming rate reminiscent of how quickly her bosom had expanded in the beginning. She imagined herself 1000 times larger than an obese duck, shuffle-waddling her way along. Less than a week until the wedding extravaganza of the season. I'm thirty minutes late arriving at the shop and moving like a slug. Mrs. Spalding has requested a thousand more jewels be added to her gown. She'll outsparkle the bride.

As she stepped through the shop door a popping sensation where a baby's head should be resting preceded raindrops sliding down her leg—and then a full downpour. Water everywhere.

Pain gripped her midsection below her waist. "Megs! Come quickly! Bring towels!"

Megs spread a towel across the nearest seat and helped Clara lower herself. "What's happened?"

"I believe my waters have broken. Get a message to Tante Ingrid, please."

"Didn't Rosa count, and this should not be happening until July? And the wedding? How will we get everything ready?"

"Megs, my friend, right now Mrs. Spalding needs to be very grateful I did not leak this on the wedding gown or her gown."

"I'll share your *blessing* with her." Megs had a wire delivered to Ingrid's private receiver, then mopped the mess.

Messenger Archie arrived with a response less than ten minutes later. "She's on her way and bringing a carriage to get you back home."

"I'm grateful they are doctors and willing to help me."

"Are you comfortable? Did we get you cleaned up well enough? Does this mean the babies may be too early?" Megs paced in circles around her friend.

"I'm comfortable until the next pain comes." Clara pressed the pleated ruffle on her sleeve. "Curt and I are twins. Mutti was also a twin. Her brother died at birth. The way this pregnancy has gone, I'm absolutely certain two babies live inside of me. Everything about how I have felt perfectly reflects what Tante Adeline told me Mutti and her Mutti experienced." Clara pointed to her belly. "Twins usually arrive a few weeks sooner than just one baby."

Megs rocked forward and back, gazing down at her feet. She rubbed the bend in her neck. "Have you heard more from Daniel? Is he coming soon?"

As she choked on her sobs, another pain came. She held her breath, willing the contractions to stop. She took a few deep breaths when the discomfort eased. "Do you know how long it was between the pains? Tante Ingrid told me to time them. And I remember now she said to breathe while I'm having them, not after."

"It's ten minutes past nine now. And you were late. You arrived at 8:30. Can you figure it out?"

"You were always better at arithmetic than me."

"My arithmetic has me wondering how we're going to finish trimming the gown in time. You didn't answer. Is Daniel coming soon?"

"My body and my heart are breaking right now, and you are worried about the beads on a gown? And reminding me Daniel is not here when I need him most."

Tante Ingrid rushed through the door. "Hush, Megs. I heard your words and concerns, and they're almost as insensitive as your brother's motives are reported to be. I remember you as a kinder soul." She brushed Clara's fiery curls back from her forehead.

"I'm so sorry. I'm just nervous for my friend."

"You'll be fine, Clara dear. This is how babies join our world."

Her smile, angelic voice, and kind gestures nudged Clara to calmness.

"Have you two measured the time between your pains? When was the last one?"

"Ten minutes past nine—a mere fifteen minutes ago." Megs grimaced. "The first two were about thirty-five minutes apart."

"The ride home may be a bit uncomfortable. I expect you'll have at least one more contraction before we get you settled into a bed. Megs, Robert is waiting outside. Let's help her get in the carriage."

Megs went back for the bolsters Clara used in the shop and situated them on either side of her friend to cushion the ride. Ingrid spread a feather-light baby blue quilt across her lap for modesty.

"Megs, I'm very sorry about your client's gown. I suspect it's more than dazzling already, but give her our apologies."

"You're correct, of course, Ingrid, but not in my difficult client's opinion. She's been determined Clara and these babies will ruin her ensemble one way or another. And now the babies are early, the shop is a mess, and Clara's leaving. How will I ever complete the extra beadwork by myself?"

"Hire someone to finish it. I'll cover their fees."

"I've decided babies are inconvenient."

"Megs, please note babies come when God's ready for them to make their entrance into our world. Their timing rarely bows to our convenience."

"I mean, babies are an inconvenience any time."

Ingrid pursed her lips as if squishing in words fighting to spew out. With Robert's helping hand, she climbed aboard and seated herself comfortably across from Clara.

Robert shooed away the pigeon sitting there and hopped into the driver's seat. With a light slap of the reins, the horses moved the carriage forward, gently merging to share the street.

Clara's face constricted with the next pain. "You're Vati did this to me." She poked at her round middle. "I wish I'd never met him."

∿

Gerbers' home, *5 June 1882*

Ten long hours of labor later, a little girl slipped into the world all rosy and with hearty lungs. Clara smiled through her exhaustion.

Nell washed the wee one, diapered her, and swaddled her in pink flannel. "I'll rock her for you, *Mutti*. It appears you have more work to do."

"A second baby is on the way, Clara." Tante's smile encouraged her. "Work with us—the baby and me. I know you're tired, but you'll find the strength. The second one usually comes more easily."

Contraction after contraction continued into the night. Clara prayed and clutched the sheets as the twist and clench of each pain wracked her.

Oh, Jesus, is something wrong? I'm reaching for You like the woman reaching for Your tassels. Help me. Help my baby.

A cuckoo clock in the hall announced the midnight hour.

"Push, Clara."

Nell had settled the baby in a cradle at the side of the room before climbing into the bed behind Clara to help her push. "Your baby's almost here. You're doing fine, Clara. One more time."

"You've done it." But other than those three words, Ingrid was quiet. So was the baby.

"Nell, please prepare this one." Ingrid spoke through her tears.

"Prepare for what?" Clara's voice was as weak as her exhausted body.

"Clara, you brought your little boy to us, but he's left us too soon."

"Like Mutti's twin." The world spun about her.

"Ja. I'm terribly sad for you, but you still need to deliver the afterbirth. Don't give up. Baby girl will need you for a very long time."

"As soon as we're finished here, you may hold your darling little girl, or you might let her sleep. You could get some rest, too."

Clara's body shook. "But what happened to my baby boy?" Tante rubbed Clara's feet. "I wish I could tell you, meine Kinder."

"Can I see him?"

"Nell, keep him here until we're finished."

Ten minutes later, the afterbirth came. "All done and with no tear to repair."

"I can hold him now?"

"He's not pink like a newborn, Clara. You may be further distressed when you see him."

Clara's chin and lips trembled. "I need to see him. Please."

With a nod from Tante, Nell handed the wrapped bundle to Clara. "Tante and I will step out and give you privacy. We'll be back in a few minutes with clean sheets and night clothes, and we'll give you a sponge bath."

"Danke." Clara unwrapped her baby as the two women closed the door behind them. "Oh, little baby, your Vati will never see you or hold you." Clara stroked his tiny head. Tears streamed down her cheeks. "I'll name you for your Vati, but I'll call you Danny—my little Daniel. I'll love you forever, and I'll tell your Vati I held you and hugged you for both of us." The baby girl whimpered in her cradle and began to stir.

Clara barely heard the doorknob turn when Tante Ingrid and Nell came back in.

She reluctantly placed the baby into her aunt's arms. "I named him for his Vati."

"A name your baby boy would have been proud of, and Daniel will be honored." Tante smiled.

Nell lifted the other child from her crib and handed the hungry girl to her Mutti. "Make sure her tummy's full before we give you that sponge bath."

Clara snuggled the baby close. "Do you miss your little brother already? You and Danny would have been best friends like your Onkel Curt and I are." Through her tears, Clara began to sing her favorite lullaby. *Lullaby and goodnight! With roses bedight!...*

Tante rocked her head side-to-side to Clara's tune. "The song your Mutti sang to you and Curt."

"Ja. A few months ago, she sang it when things looked so bleak with Georg. It always soothes my fears." Clara smiled. "I'm ready for my bath and clean sheets."

Clara bit her lip, "And one more thing."

"What's that?" Nell crossed her arms and edged closer.

"Allow me to grieve a while. No visitors, please."

Chapter Twenty-Six

THE PALMER HOUSE, 5 *June 1882*

MAX WASTED no time getting from Union Station to the Palmer House. He checked into his favorite room at the fancy hotel and made plans to visit Megs' shop tomorrow. She had liked him since Paris and would be thrilled to give him the Gerbers' address. He'd inquire about Clara from Megs. His most pressing matter of the moment—Blade!

His mind entertained flashbacks of Paris, the Westminster, and the pathetic bloke harassing Clara. Georg and Blade, both sorry characters cut from the same cloth. Has Blade created similar disturbances for the Palmers here in Chicago as Georg had at the hotel in Paris?

Nervous energy pushed Max toward the billiard room. If Blade frequented this establishment, he wagered his time would be spent gambling away his assets.

"Anyone here gambling with nickels." Max flipped one in the air. Tails he called to himself. Heads it was. Probably as good as his chance of finding Blade here on a whim.

"We play for higher stakes."

Clara had detested Georg's gambling habits. Max offered a backward wave and headed for the grand lobby with its marble, chandeliers, and promise of a light meal.

The little boy climbed upon his knee. Max couldn't help but grin as they bounced in time to the piano player's frolicky tune.

"Arthur!" The woman pinched the boy's shoulder and scolded him with her look. "What have I told you about children being seen, but not heard?"

"As far as I can tell, he hasn't said a word. He climbed up, and I'm delighted to give him a horsey ride. If smiles are noisy, then maybe he's at fault. I say, no harm done."

"Thank you, mister. Arthur, we'll be going." She plucked two nickels from her reticule handing them to the boy. "Pay the nice man for his services."

Max held a hand up as a refusal. "Never. I love children. I'm insulted you would think to pay me."

"Very well. Thank you, again."

"I do have a question. Is there a significance to the two nickels?"

"My brother gave them to me. They're the only coins I have."

Two nickels. Most likely pure coincidence. The child looked back over his shoulder and waved to Max as the woman tugged him toward the exit. Max followed at a distance—too far a distance. The pair stepped onto a cable car just before it pulled away.

~

TUESDAY, *6 June 1882*

TRUE TO HIS PLANS, the first order of business in Max's quest today focused on an address for the Gerbers' home. Whether she thought she needed him or not, he would warn Clara and return the cameo. He stood outside the door to Megs' shop to take a few deep breaths and calm his racing heart. He peered in before opening the door. Megs toyed with a bottle of pills. As he entered, she tossed it behind the counter like a hot potato.

"Hello, Max. If you're looking for Clara, she's not here."

He bowed toward Megs. "Then I hope you will share her aunt's address."

"Clara had a baby yesterday. It's doubtful she'll welcome company."

"Only one baby? She had been certain she carried twins."

"A baby girl. I'm told her head is covered in tiny golden curls." Megs shrugged. "One should be trouble enough."

Rubbing his jaw, Max felt the heat flaming in his cheeks. "If you please, may I have the address?"

Megs reached for a sheet of stationery. She dipped the fountain pen in the inkwell and scrawled on the paper. "Here. The address and their private telegraph line. Contact them first. Unless there's something else you need, I have extra work with Clara at home. This baby came a month earlier than I anticipated."

Max' eyebrows shot up as he turned to leave. "One more question. Have you seen Blade since Clara arrived in Chicago?"

She offered no response, but she fiddled with her necklace.

What's she hiding? "I'll let you get back to whatever had your attention when I came in."

"Max. Wait."

"He visited the shop a few weeks ago terrifying Clara. He commented about his lucky nickels. Wanted a dress for his sister. Became jittery as we discussed it. I offered him an appointment for June 19th. He was displeased we wouldn't make a home visit but said he'd bring her."

"Where can I find him?"

"Stalking Clara."

Chapter Twenty-Seven

THE HESS HOME, 6 *June 1882*

MAKE IT STOP!" Arthur buried his head in Sandra's lap.

Screeches from Zilla's glass armonica pierced Sandra's ears, too. With her hands covering Arthur's ears, she turned his face up to hers. Slightly uncovering one of his ears, she whispered to the lad. "Would you like to play outside?"

A grin spread across the boy's face. "Can we fly my kite?"

Belinda's arrangement with the Hess family to live here required tasks of both mother and daughter. Sandra thanked heaven that caring for the Hess' grandson, Arthur, for a few hours each day fell to her. Tree limbs waved in the breeze outside the window. "You've chosen a perfect day for kite flying."

At that moment Hilda came running toward them snuggling her Oma in a giant hug.

"Can Hilda come with us?" Arthur grabbed the girl's hands in his, and the two bounced together.

"Please, Oma?"

"What a splendid idea!" They gathered the kite and hurried out the door. A large grassy lot up the street provided plenty of space to run and loft the red and white stripe paper-covered frame with its blue and yellow tail.

"It's up!" Arthur shouted, and the trio sat in the tickly grass.

Sandra transferred the ball of string to Arthur. "Slowly let out some more line."

The boy grinned as he untwisted the next several feet of line.

"Can I try to pull on the string, too?" Hilda tugged on Arthur's jacket sleeve.

They took turns lofting the kite higher and higher.

"I wish I could fly like a kite."

Sandra laughed and tousled Arthur's hair. "Maybe someday someone will invent a way for people to fly, but we can travel by streetcar, cable car, trains, and boats. We have many ways to go places."

"But none of them are in the sky like a bird."

"Hilda and her mom and I all traveled on boats and trains to get here. Our trips took almost two weeks."

"Uncle Egon told me he goes on big boats a lot. He's always gone a long time. How long is two weeks?"

"Let's count to twelve. That's how many days it took me to get here. Hilda, hold the string. Arthur, use your fingers. One. Two. Three…" They counted all the way.

"I ran out of fingers."

"I knew you would. I slept as many times from Germany to Chicago."

"Where's Germany?"

"We could look on the globe in Aunt Zilla's room."

"I hope she stopped."

"Me too. Hilda, I believe your mom has lunch ready. We'll look at the map after we eat."

"Before our naps?"

"Yes."

As they plodded up the back steps, they heard harsh voices coming from the carriage house. Zilla's and a man's—one Sandra found vaguely familiar—arguing about a package.

The Gerbers' home

"The baby's hungry, Clara." Tante Ingrid snuggled the swaddled newborn in the crook of her arm. She bent down, kissed Clara's curls, and laid the girl in her niece's arms.

Clara grabbed a clean diaper from the table next to her and dabbed her eyes. Her shoulders shuddered. "Why didn't her brother live?"

"How I wish I could take the pain away for you. Only God knows the answer to your question. I won't pretend I can answer for Him, but God's word often comforts me when I'm distraught."

"I haven't found God to be very kind to me lately. Now He's allowed my baby to die. How could the Bible possibly help? No. Just let me cry." Clara's head hung limp.

She had remained silent, but Nell rocked in a corner of the room. "The Bible verses you've shared with me the past few weeks have been a balm for my soul. While I sat watch with you and your little girl last night I searched for one for you. All your troubles made me think of Job. Do you remember the words Job spoke to his friend when his world had fallen down around him?"

More tears ran down Clara's cheeks. She loosened her gown, and the baby latched on. "Please read it, Nell. I'm sure I don't want to hear it, but contrary to what I just said, I'm equally certain I need to."

Nell opened to the page she had marked with a leaf from the garden. *In whose hand is the soul of every living thing, and the breath of all mankind.* I needed to hear it, too. When little Daniel didn't take a breath last night, I was painfully reminded of how my baby was never given a chance to live and breathe."

Clara gasped. "You lost a baby?"

"Have you shared your story with Clara?" Tante hugged Nell's shoulder.

"Only a tiny mention about it, but it's time. My husband also lost his life when the Schiller went down. I didn't know I was pregnant until I miscarried the baby two months later."

All three women's eyes leaked.

"This baby lives and breathes and needs you."

"And she needs a name." Tante Ingrid's eyes glimmered.

Peering into the baby's barely open eye slits, Clara declared, "You need a name all your own—one we won't borrow from anyone. Do you like the name Esther?"

She made gurgling sounds as she filled her tummy.

"Contentment. She likes it. Esther, I'll pray for you to live up to your name." Clara smiled at her daughter—their daughter —hers and Daniel's.

"What purpose does God have for you in our world, little one? In this time?" Ingrid reached down and squeezed the end of the blanket with Esther's toes inside. "How happy I am to be in the audience for your story."

Nell stood when dits, dots, and taps sounded from the telegraph in the kitchen. "Would you like me to collect the message, Tante?"

"I'm grateful you can decipher those codes."

Clara watched and listened. From the look of sheer terror on Nell's face the messages couldn't be good.

"Your hands are shaking, Nell. You have as little color as a specter. What's happened?" Tante Ingrid hugged the girl to her side.

"The first one was short and to the point.

To: Clara.

Pregnant. Took the pills.

M.

· · ·

Ingrid guided Nell to a bench in Clara's room. Tante rearranged the pillows and the two sat down. "Poor girl. Your insides are shaking, too. I can feel the trembling."

"But why has Megs done this?" Nell looked from Clara to Tante Ingrid. "My mind winds around a labyrinth of ideas, fears, anger, and helplessness while looking for hopefulness. Unlike your little Daniel and my baby, hers has a chance for life. I've been praying asking God how He can use me and you, too, Clara, to work in Megs' situation. Let's pray the pills do not work."

Nell balled up her soaked handkerchief and dabbed her eyes once more. "Before I crawled too deep down into a hole of despair over Megs' message, I grabbed the next string of code and decrypted it." She handed the note to their aunt.

Mrs. Gerber.

Megs shared your address and wire. Ask Clara to see me, please. It is about Blade. When may I come?

Max.

Clara's chest constricted. She gasped. "Blade! No!"

"Who is Blade?" Deep creases appeared between her aunt's eyebrows.

"A vulgar and disgusting man on the ship and the train! I don't want to hear about him or from him ever again."

"Max knows your feelings about this man?"

"He does. He protected Sandra and me from the beast. I

resented his help, but without Max, I'm not sure we would have survived the journey. The man is evil."

"Shall we put Esther down and talk in the other room? We'll hear her when she awakens." Ingrid pointed to the cradle.

Rocking the cradle a few times, Clara had little Esther settled. The three of them tiptoed to the kitchen and gathered around the table. A pot of tea, cups, and warm shortbread cookies awaited them.

"My cook—always attentive to the little things." Plop, plop. Ingrid dropped two sugar cubes in her cup and stirred.

Clara could almost feel the intensity of Tante studying her face and looking into her soul.

"You admit you needed him when you traveled. Would Max ask to come if he didn't believe his message was important to your welfare and the life of your baby?"

"THIS ARRIVED FOR YOU." Tante Ingrid handed her an envelope.

"A letter from Daniel? I'd much prefer Daniel standing here beside me on this day after our babies arrived. Is the envelope filled with words of hope or doubt?" She recalled Daniel's words of despair from the last letter. He lacked hope for them and admitted his prayers faltered. The events of the past 48 hours had scuttled Clara's mind and numbed her emotions. Her throat felt like sunbaked grit on a hot summer day. She sipped a few mouthfuls of the juice Tante Ingrid offered.

"Would you like me to take Esther? I'll change her. You'll have privacy to read the letter."

"Danke."

Ingrid leaned the baby on her shoulder and gently patted her back singing *Lullaby and Goodnight* as they left the room.

When she heard me singing the tender song, had Tante remembered Mutti singing it to Curt and me? Memories of Gut Apfelhof are bittersweet. Clara tugged at the sealed envelope and withdrew Daniel's single-page note. No decorations. No seeds. No *my lovely lady* greeting.

DEAR CLARA,

So much has happened to us over the last ten years? Do you ever wonder what God tried to tell us when your family and the rules warred against our union? Were we so determined to have our way, we missed God's plan? Why is our world crumbling around us? Do you feel it as strongly as I do?

I wasn't completely honest in my last letter. Your Vati has had our union annulled. Your Onkel Martin assured me he could not get the annulment, but Gut Herr Reinhold's influence—along with a portion of his wealth perhaps—persuaded those with the authority to declare it invalid to do so. Clara, we're not married.

The fact should make me angry enough to leave for America without looking back or contemplating the above questions and more. There's my Mutter's health. Herr Reinhold provides every means possible to help Rosa. He allows me time whenever needed to tend to her needs. Rudi drives for the family on those days allowing Tilly and me to provide faithful loving care.

For all my Mutter has endured with the fire, losing her husband, and raising me without a Vater, I feel a deep responsibility to her. And your Vati has always treated me like one of his sons. In his eyes then, I see him thinking 'Siblings can't marry.' The challenges and

307

implications have grown into a massive whirling storm. My first responsibility should be to you and our children. The conundrum wrenches at my loyalties. How will we ever manage to traverse the Atlantic Ocean and the sea of problems our decision has created?

Tilly's friendship becomes dearer each day. She and I have discussed how long Rosa may have suffered and kept the symptoms to herself. She's grown so attached to Rosa while she's assisted her. Tilly has learned and improved her sewing skills and her faith while caring for Mutter. Tilly has learned to comfort me with Bible verses and a listening ear much like Mutter has always done. I'm often quite a dunce and reject the truths of God's word she begs me to embrace. I appreciate her effort.

I don't know where my friendship with Tilly is headed, but it's only fair you hear it all from me. I must end my message now. Curt and Lillian await my letter to post it when they meet in Stuttgart tomorrow. They are doing well. They will marry in August at Viscount Denzler's estate on the Neckar.

I'm not praying much. My efforts feel futile. But I do pray you and the babies will be well cared for always. I want to meet them and let them know their Vati loves them.

Sending my love,

Daniel

CLARA USED the letter to fan the heat from her face before she crumpled it into a ball and slung it against the door. Nausea bubbled up as it did in her early days with child. Anger shook her to the core of her being.

Who's tapping on the door? *Who cares about me anymore?* Not Daniel. Not anyone.

"Your sobs can be heard out here. May I come in." Tante's voice was gentle. "Esther's asleep. It's only me."

"Ja."

Ingrid stood behind the rocking chair. Her hand rested on Clara's shoulder. She waited.

"My world is crushed. My dreams sunk into the sea. It's over. Esther and I are on our own. Oma wins. Vati wins. Tilly wins. Even Daniel wins. The baby and I are the losers in this fairy-tale disaster turned horror story."

Stepping from behind the chair, Tante reached for the paper ball, then rolled it around in her hands. "This ball looks like a globe—the world—and it's definitely crushed."

Not even a tiny sprout of a smile from Clara.

"Whenever you would like to talk about it, I'm here. I'll listen. Until then I'll ask Jesus to begin healing your heart."

Anguish rolled down Clara's slumped shoulders. "It's hope-less. One torment piled on another. My heart is wounded beyond even His ability to restore."

"I don't know what Daniel wrote in this letter, but I see a deeply hurt young woman in front of me. In time you'll believe you can trust Jesus for your future—and Esther's."

Clara raked her fingers through her curls desperate to scrape Oma's words from her mind. No matter how she tried, the message persisted. *Imagine a new dream. Pray about it, meine Kind. Watch God work.* She had trusted Daniel. She had trusted their love. She had trusted their plans.

She hadn't prayed—not for a new dream!

Chapter Twenty-Eight

HESS TRUST BANK, Wednesday, *7 June 1882*

MAX PULLED open the massive wood doors of Hess Trust of Chicago. He unfolded the Hess Trust Bank's advertisement he had clipped from the *Illinois Staats Zeitung* early this morning. He had an idea for a new business, and they were offering loans to begin new companies.

The bankers all served other customers when he entered. Max took a seat in a brown leather chair. He held the folded advertisement in his lap, closed his eyes, and prayed silently. *O Lord, is this idea from You? Have You placed the heavy concerns about Blade on my heart? Is Clara in trouble from this man? Is starting a transportation company here in Chicago an idea from You?*

I could move here. Be near Clara, but then you know she doesn't want me, Lord. She pushed away my concerns again. She has made her wishes known since we boarded the Elbe back in Bremen. She's waiting for Daniel. Is he coming, Lord? Am I here to protect Clara until then? How do I find this Blade character? Was he really another immigrant from Germany traveling on the same ship? Does he live here? What's his motive?

"Sir." A man dressed in a navy frock coat with matching slacks stood in front of him. "If I may interrupt your deep thoughts, I'm Mr. Egon Hess at your service. And you are?"

"Maximillian Engel, but you may call me Max." He stood to shake the man's hand. "You're Mr. Hess. The Mr. Hess to see about my new business plan?"

"The one. Yes." Hess' smile spread across his face. He motioned to Max. "Follow me to my office then. I hope your idea is a grand one."

"I believe it to be, sir."

Hess directed Max to his office and pointed to a burgundy leather armchair then took a seat behind his massive cherry Louis XVI desk. He lifted the peacock-decorated lid of a tin on the corner of the desk. Aromas of cherry tobacco floated through the roam. He tamped the crushed leaves into the bowl of his pipe and waved it in a circle. "What enterprise are you hoping to build, Mr. Engel?"

"A shipping empire, sir. Chicago is well-situated on the Great Lakes and is served by the developing railroad industry. A company assisting businesses to move their goods efficiently from one city, state, or country to the next holds great promise for Chicago companies, for the employees of those companies, and for the investors."

"You don't lack confidence, young man. What qualifies you to begin such an endeavor?"

"I've spent the last five years serving businessmen in Europe doing business in Britain and the United States escorting their goods over land and sea. I'm currently in Chicago because I accompanied a shipment of wine from Southwest Germany. My services are in demand. I have several other clients and believe I could merge them with new ones here to create a rapidly expanding shipping conglomerate."

"Your customers would lose a great asset in their businesses if you choose to start this company."

"I've built a network. The telegraph makes international communication easy. I believe I would be expanding the work I currently do. Not only would it benefit my current customers, it would create a business Chicago will be proud to claim."

"I like your idea." The banker's eyebrows inched up his forehead. "Do you have a plan for your business and have you anticipated the amount needed to begin?"

"May I bring you the information by the end of the week?"

"I'll be expecting you." Hess struck a match, set it to the tobacco, and puffed on the stem of his pipe.

Leaving Hess' office Max nearly collided with a familiar little fella running toward Mr. Hess with outstretched arms. "Grandpa!"

"You're Arthur, right?"

"You two have met?"

"Let's say he entertained me a couple of days ago at the Palmer House." Max patted Arthur on the back. "Have fun with your grandpa."

On his way out the door, he passed the woman he'd seen with Arthur before. He smiled, but her expression remained as dour as her attitude at the hotel. Whether or not she was Arthur's mother remained a mystery.

FRIDAY, 9 June 1882

"CLARA, YOU HAVE A VISITOR," Tante Ingrid held the door open for the caller.

Clara descended the stairs. Her heart just may beat out of her chest. His turquoise eyes held hers as she led them to the parlor. She patted the babe clutched in her arms. "Would you like to hold Esther?"

"May I?" He moved closer.

Pleasant tingles ran up her arm as their hands touched when he took the baby.

"She looks like her beautiful Mutti."

"You flatter me, Max. Are my cheeks all rosy?"

"I'm happy to see you smiling, pink cheeks and all."

"How did you find me?"

"I visited Megs' shop. She gave me your Tante's address and told me about the other twin. I'm so sorry you lost the little boy, but Esther is blessed to have you for her Mutti." He reached an arm around her and folded the three of them into a hug.

Clara melted against him. Like the little family he spoke of on the ship.

They sat together on the settee in the parlor. Max pulled his handkerchief from his pocket and blotted Clara's tears. He kept his arm wrapped around her.

She finally stopped sobbing. "You bring news you believe I should hear?"

Her mind spun as he filled her in on the rest of the reason for his visit.

"Nickels? I have no idea what you're talking about."

"Megs mentioned nickels, too, Clara. And there's something about mutual friends?

"I agreed for you to visit because you referred to an important message about the madman. Why are nickels so important?"

"It's the only clue Blade gave me. I'm certain he's up to evil well beyond the mischief we've experienced from him on the trip. He rubbed two of the five-cent coins together in front of Megs, too."

"I'm staying in Chicago, Clara. At the Palmer House. I answered Hess Trust's ad in the *Illinois Staats Zeitung*. I've inquired about a loan to start my business in the city. Leave a message with the front desk at the hotel if you need me."

"I will, but we'll be fine here at the Gerbers' home. And what do you mean by starting a business in Chicago? Why?"

"I like this city full of opportunities. My past and present experiences would contribute to building my own shipping company."

"But your family is in Germany?"

"Word is on the way to them. I hope they will join me here in America."

"And you think you'll be better able to keep a watchful eye on me. The baby and I are well-protected here with Tante Ingrid and Onkel Oscar."

"I'll be far more concerned when you venture beyond the safety of your aunt and uncle's home."

"Blade referred to a mutual friend?" Hairs prickled on the back of Clara's neck. "And nickels?"

"Ja. He emphasized the nickels as the only hint we would get. And something about his sister."

Breaths were hitching in her chest. "I've only met them once and they are no friends of mine. The Nickel brothers are friends of Georg's. The eccentric duo played an unscrupulous role in the trouble precipitating my Vati's awful agreement with Georg. Do you believe they're involved in whatever wicked scheme Blade's concocted?"

"I intend to learn his intentions. Nickel brothers? I'll keep them in mind. And thank you for allowing me to cuddle baby Esther." He handed her back to her mother.

"Thank you, Max."

"Before I leave, this is for you." A card picturing the S. S. Elbe hung from twine wrapped about a brown paper package.

Her heart raced. "This isn't a bad joke from Blade, is it?"

A smile lit his eyes. "It's safe to open it."

She worked the strings toward the corners inch by inch until they fell away. Unfolding the paper from around the box a surge of hope filled her. She lifted the lid and smiled.

"A young woman handed it to one of Willigerod's crew on her way off the ship. From his description of the Fraulein, it was Louise."

She closed the lid again, her smile fading.

"What have you not told me, Clara? Losing your baby is just cause for your sadness, but something else is tormenting you. You're hiding your pain behind the shades of those chocolate brown eyes of yours?"

How should I feel about the cameo now? I love Rosa like my own Mutti, and she is Esther's Oma. But I can no longer look at her gift without being reminded of my shattered dreams for Esther—for us —for our family. "Not today, Max. Since you and Megs both heard about some nickels, let's compare stories. Megs expects the baby and me to visit the shop next Friday morning. Meet me there. Nine-thirty sharp."

Chapter Twenty-Nine

THE GERBERS' Home, *Saturday, June 10, 1882*

THE THREE SUNFLOWER seeds had not only sprouted, but the seedlings were eight inches tall. Clara recalled her words in the letter to Daniel. *If they grow, I pray it's God's sign that our love will last, and we will be together soon. If not?*

She planted her foot stopping the porch swing from gliding her and Esther gliding to and fro. Hugging her little one tight, she whispered to the wind. "The seeds are thriving and growing, but after Daniel's letter should I pray death over them?"

"Pray death over what?"

"Good morning, Nell." Clara patted the space next to her on the swing.

Nell sat, then pulled her feet onto the swing and curled her legs to the right. "Praying death over what?"

"Those silly sunflowers"

"But you love sunflowers."

"I also made a bargain about those sunflowers. Like a pact with God, I doubt it was a wise decision." Clara's throat quivered with a quiet laugh. "If the seeds grew and thrived, it would mean that Daniel and I would be together. They're growing, but the likelihood of Daniel and me being reunited here in America is shriveling."

"I joined you here to tell you the rest of my story. Maybe you would rather not hear it."

"From what I know, yours ended in tragedy. We can console and encourage one another. Please do tell me the rest."

"My husband and I married on the ship. His family owned a castle in Ludwigsburg and ran a prestigious inn along the Neckar River. We met here in Chicago. We were completely taken with each other from the moment I stepped on his toe dancing at a wedding of mutual friends. We had arrived here in Chicago at different times, but we traveled on the same train back to New York City and boarded the S.S. Schiller together.

"What a delightful opportunity when the captain offered to officiate weddings on the ship, our second day at sea. We each had a room on the ship, but after the wedding, I slept in his for the rest of the trip."

Clara chewed her lower lip. "Then disaster. You lost all your family. Oh, Nell."

"All but Onkel Oscar. He came and brought me here. It was two months later when I miscarried."

"You poor girl." Clara pulled her close. They rocked together, the baby between them. "I was in a family way immediately, too. My condition made keeping our marriage a secret from our family impossible."

"Our families were happy for us to be married. Yours weren't?"

"Not at all." Clara filled Nell in on the details of her secret marriage.

Nell reached over and stroked Esther's fuzzy head. "We've both lost so much. If Megs succeeded with those pills, she's lost even more. She intentionally eliminated her baby. I believe a couple of women at school have also experienced losses. How can we help Megs and them and ourselves?"

"My Oma and this baby's grandmother both dripped well-timed Bible verses into every situation. I taught our ladies' Bible class before all this happened. You've been searching the Bible for verses to encourage us. Could we invite these women to a Bible class?"

"I love your idea. I've seen some of your sketches, Clara. Would you write and decorate some pretty invitations? You could deliver one to Megs when you visit her next Friday. I could invite the two students."

"What Bible verse do you suggest I put inside the invitation?"

Nell's pointer finger rested against her cheek. "The one from Job."

"The Job verse is an excellent one, but I have another idea. We could use this verse from 1 Thessalonians. *'And the Lord make you to increase and abound in love one toward another, and toward all men, even as we do toward you.'*"

"Let's say we're hosting a ladies' friendship group to be more enticing to the shy ones. They may share their sorrows more easily. The first meeting can be on Saturday afternoon, June 17, here at our Onkel's home."

"I'll pray the ladies we invite receive our invitations with enthusiasm." Nell pushed to her feet.

Esther stretched her arms and legs. Her eyes fluttered open. She nudged toward Clara's bosom, looking for nourishment.

"Let's change your diaper first, little one."

Nell helped Clara to her feet and sang. *"Hey diddle diddle. The cat and the fiddle. The dish ran away with the spoon."*

"I sure hope Aster doesn't have the spoons. Or the forks either" As they entered the house, Clara inhaled the mingled scents of cinnamon, fresh bread, eggs, and coffee. "I'm famished and ready for breakfast."

Nell joined Ingrid at the breakfast table. Clara returned with Esther and covered the baby with the sunflower quilt while she nursed her. Nell handed her a plate with a cinnamon roll, and Tante Ingrid filled her coffee cup.

"Your sunflowers are growing." Onkel Oscar called from the doorway. "So, a happy experiment?"

Nell's eyes widened.

Clara groaned.

Chapter Thirty

MEGS' SHOP, *Friday, 16 June 1882*

A LIGHTNESS CIRCLED Clara's head and her stomach churned as Robert drove the horses and carriage around the corner off State Street and onto Madison. A few moments later they parked outside Megs' Designs. Robert took the baby from Clara and laid her in the buggy he'd just unloaded. The apple border of the quilt peeked over the edges. He held a hand out to Clara and helped her step to the sidewalk. "Mrs. Gerber supplied me a list of errands when we left the house. I expect to be back for you in about two hours."

"Thank you, Robert." She rubbed the baby's head, let Esther grab her finger, and then smoothed the edges of the quilt. "I'm in no hurry to face Megs after her telegram." She took the tiniest steps toward the door but still arrived in only a few seconds. She steadied the buggy with her hip and pulled hard on the heavy oak door's brass handle. The bell jingled. She pulled the buggy into the shop.

The only hanky she had was one of Oma's embroidered ones. She would need to remember to retrieve it when they left. For now, she wadded it up and stuffed it around the clapper of the bell to silence it before Max's arrival. Esther would sleep while she talked to Megs.

"How are you and the baby, my friend?" Megs' smile seemed forced.

"I'm devastated about her baby brother, but Esther and I fare well. Would you like to hold her?"

"Does she favor you or Daniel?" Megs peered into the buggy. "She is cute, but I might break her if I hold her."

"She's ready for a nap. She'll be comfortable there. Maybe you'll change your mind and hold her when she wakes up."

Megs cleared her throat and peeled her eyes toward the office. "If she'll be ok here we can talk in there."

A shiver prickled up her spine. Max warned about venturing away from the Gerbers' home, but this is Megs' shop. *I assured him we'd be fine, but uneasiness creeps around me.* The shop's not open yet, and Max will be here soon. She rolled the buggy back and forth for a few minutes. Esther dozed off. Clara followed Megs to the office.

"I don't want one of those, but these didn't work!" Megs clenched the bottle of women's pills in her hand and pitched them into the wastebasket. Her shoulders collapsed and she began to weep. "I'm pregnant. I'm going to have a baby who will be in the way and keep me from serving my customers. It'll pee all the time and other stuff, too. It'll have a drippy nose and cry."

"Like you are now?" Clara couldn't help but giggle.

"It's not funny, Clara!"

"You're right, but your dramatics made me laugh. Are you sure you're expecting?"

"If my time doesn't start tomorrow, I'll have missed five times."

"Oh, my friend, you haven't been sick at all. Do you know how lucky you are?"

"I'm not lucky. I don't want this baby! I was counting on you to be the extra hands I needed to finish all the work for the busy summer season. Esther got in the way. Oh no. I take back my awful words. I know you love your baby, but I don't want this one."

Clara leaned her head forward looking into her lap. She fiddled with the buttons on her bodice. *Lord, I need words. I'm struggling with my pain. How do I comfort Megs?*

"Did you find someone to finish the work I couldn't complete? I know Tante Ingrid was willing to pay."

"Your friend Sandra, the one I met at the train station, came by one day. Ever since she's been collecting the gowns needing work and returning them a few days later. I must admit, she and your Tante have been godsends."

"I'm happy to hear you're pleased with their help. Where is Sandra living?"

"She only said Belinda and Hilda had stayed at the Briggs house for only a couple of nights. A family they met there invited them to be a part of their staff and live in their home. She didn't say where the home is. As long as she picks up the work and returns it, where she lives doesn't matter to me."

"I'm relieved for you and Sandra, that this arrangement has worked out. She was such a kind friend on the ship."

"But now neither you nor I will be able to meet with the ladies coming into the shop. I don't want this baby, Clara. Why didn't the pills work?"

Clara pulled her lips between her teeth. Her head shook slowly. "I know very little about the pills. Some women you and I both know drank the pennyroyal tea by force or by choice. They all either lost their lives, or their hearts are overwhelmed with grief. Forgiving ourselves is more difficult than forgiving others."

"But it says on the bottle they will be effective within two weeks at restoring a woman's time."

"Maybe if the woman isn't pregnant, but merely late?" Clara tilted her head and lifted her eyebrows.

"You're not going to yell at me and tell me I'm being a selfish brat? Or worse, I'm acting like my brother?"

"Nein." Clara swallowed hard. "Nell, Onkel Oscar's niece who also lives with them—she and I are starting a friends' circle much like the Ladies' Bible class back in Gut Apfelhof. We would like you to join us tomorrow at the Gerbers' home. I have an invitation for you tucked in the side of the buggy."

Clara shrieked as she stepped out of the office to grab the invitation. "The buggy is gone!" *When am I going to heed those prickly feelings stabbing at me? If I hadn't stuffed Oma's handkerchief in the bell, we would have heard someone come in.* "Hurry Max." He'd help her.

Clara lurched into his arms as Max entered the shop a few moments later. "Help!" Her whole body shook.

"Someone, please explain what's happened."

"Someone stole Esther!" Megs chewed her knuckles.

"No! It's not true! Are you sure?" Max's face paled. "When?"

"A few minutes ago." Megs explained what happened. "Find her, please!"

Sandra peered over the gowns she carried as she entered the open door "Such dour faces? Clara, where's your baby? Megs, you told me if I came by this morning I would meet the wee one."

Megs grabbed the gowns from her arms. "I'll take these to the back."

"This looks more like a funeral gathering." Sandra's eyes broadened.

"I arrived a short time ago and two minutes too late to foil the kidnapping." Max's fists clenched at his side as tightly as the hard set of his eyes. "Blade's noxious stench permeates this crime."

"Someone kidnapped your baby!" Sandra clasped Clara's shaking hands in hers. "Max, you think it was Blade? Have you heard from him? O dear, Lord, help us find Esther."

"She's inconsolable, Sandra, as she should be. The baby was asleep in her buggy right here." Max pointed to a spot by the settee. "Megs wanted to talk to Clara in the office. When they came out the buggy and the baby were gone."

"Why are you suspicious Blade took her?"

"He's been leaving a trail of threats. And something to do with nickels. I hoped we had lost him for good when we disembarked the train in April."

"I left a quiet and almost abandoned house this morning. I expected the only excitement today would be meeting baby Esther and bringing this little gift for her." Sandra pulled a handmade doll with yellow yarn curls and a lavender dress from her pocket. She laid her gently in Clara's hand.

"Your pregnancy was so difficult. Those characters on the ship! Well, God knows about them. Now your baby is gone. We'll find her, Clara. God knows where little Esther is. He'll keep her safe. He's collecting all your tears in His bottle."

Clara leaned her head against Sandra's shoulder. "May I rest my fears right here, dear friend?"

Sandra hugged Clara even closer.

Megs took her time rejoining the others. "Blade visited the shop a few weeks ago. He wanted us to come to his sister's home for a consultation and measurements for a gown. We see our clients here. We don't make home visits. Our next open appointment was on June 19. He agreed, and said they would come."

"Maybe if you had agreed to go to her home, we'd have the address now." Clara's lips curled as she glared at Megs.

"And you were terrified he was even in the shop and were grateful he left quickly."

Max took a few deep breaths. "Megs, could you bring us a tablet to take notes of what we know?"

Clara twisted knots in the handkerchief in her hand—the one she had yanked from the bell.

"Hello!" Archie called from the shop entrance. "Your door is wide open."

"I don't know who you are young man, but if you'll summon the police for us, there's a reward in it for you." Max stood and shook the lad's hand. "Hurry on your way."

"We should have sent for help immediately. We weren't thinking very clearly." While Clara massaged her temples, she took several deep breaths hoping they would relieve the tightness in her chest. "Thank you, Max. I'm grateful you've come."

"Megs, you're appointed secretary. Bold letters. Top of the page. **Missing. Two-week-old infant with downy blonde curls**." Next, Max directed questions to Clara. "What color is the buggy?"

"White."

"Any special designs on it?"

"Some lavender flowers were painted on the front."

"Was there anything else with the baby? How was she dressed?"

"A white smocked day gown. The apple quilt lined the buggy. And a little elephant from my Mutti."

"The ones you showed me on the ship?" Sandra teared up. "Your loss grows and grows."

Archie returned with the officer. Megs and Clara relayed the chain of events. Max added their detailed notes. He especially filled them in on the threats from Blade and his past behavior toward them. Toward Clara in particular, beginning with the first days on the ship.

"Chicago is a big place. This isn't much to go on. Could you give us a description of the man you suspect?"

"Sloppy. Smart aleck. Crass." Max let loose of a slurry of sleazy descriptive terms, but they could refer to hundreds of men.

"Greasy mouse brown hair. Stocky build. Thick fingers." Sandra chewed her lip. "Would these things help?"

"It's not much to go on, but there's a missing baby out there. We need to find her."

Max pointed a finger toward the officer. "We are all counting on you to find the scoundrel."

"And you say his name is Blade?" The officer tapped his pencil on the side of his head.

"Blade's the only name we have." Deep furrows stretched across Max's brow. "He never gave us one on the ship. He cornered Clara after we had disembarked and reintroduced himself by the strange name."

The police officer shook Max's hand. "One more question. Are you the baby's father?"

"I'm not. Clara's husband is still in Germany."

The authority blinked a few times and shook his head. "Be sure to leave an address where we can locate you, Mr. Engel. We'll be in touch." His hand flicked an Auf Wiedersehen as he headed out the door.

Clara twisted her curl and sucked her lips between her teeth. "Max, would the banker you've been talking to know Blade?"

"A fellow like him would be an unlikely customer of a place like Hess Trust."

"I'm reaching for any possible link for locating the man we

believe has stolen my baby, and you're judging whether he has money to put in a bank?"

"Did you say Hess Trust?" Sandra's hands trembled.

Clara sat with her head down dabbing at her sniffly nose. "I did. Do you know Herr Hess?"

"Belinda and I are living and working at his home."

"I'm confused." Clara rubbed tears from her eyes. "Aren't you working for Megs?"

"Ja. My duties at his home allow time for both."

"I met Mr. Egon Hess recently. He and I finalized our business plans just before I arrived this morning." Max tapped his fingers on his forehead. "Sandra, would you ask Herr Hess if he knows the creep? If he does, please ask if he will help us find him."

"I'll head home now. Here's their address on North Kenmore."

Megs wrote it on the tablet. "The cable car will get us within a short walk. We'll be right behind you as soon as I have put up the gowns and locked the shop. We'll flag down an officer to send a wire from one of those street boxes to the Gerbers' home."

Max let out a bottled breath. "If these pieces fit together, I see a glimmer of hope. A woman and a young lad came into Mr. Hess' office as I was leaving after my first visit with him. I had met them both at the Palmer House one afternoon. Mr. Hess is Arthur's grandfather. I don't know the woman's name or her relationship to Mr. Hess, but she tried to hand me nickels in payment for giving Arthur a horsey ride on my knee. She mentioned the nickels being from her brother."

"What is it about nickels? Common coins. We couldn't make up a stranger or sillier story if we tried." Megs rubbed her head.

Clara's voice was raspy, "Find Blade."

～

THE HESS' home

"MATTHUS LIED TO ME AGAIN. I hate him!"

Chet, the English Setter, followed as Sandra tiptoed to the bench just outside the carriage house. She rubbed his head and his long orange ears. "Shhh." Sandra's finger crossed her lips. She often heard arguments coming from the outbuilding. Most days she ignored the discord. Today all conversations, especially heated ones, demand an eavesdropping ear.

"He lied about what?"

"He promised to deliver a package, Father." Zilla stomped her foot. "He wearies me with his failures to act on his words. Do something!"

"What I'm going to do is have a great laugh about your child-ishness. I'm certain he had a good reason for his most recent blunder." The deep cackling startled Chet. Sandra pulled his face toward her legs to muffle his whimpers.

"Father!"

"You're entertaining guests at the Palmer House tonight. Your time would be better spent practicing. And play the piano— not that screechy other thing."

"But…"

"This conversation is finished."

Zilla stomped right past Sandra as she stormed for the house. What's this young woman's story causing her to be so disagreeable?

Mr. Hess exited through a side door. Chet bounced after him.

A few moments later, Sandra approached. "Chet and I were walking. He caught a glimpse of you and took off. May I have a word with you, sir?"

"As long as it's not about the argument I'm sure you heard."

"It's about a man Clara and I met on the ship. I think he stayed in Chicago. He created many problems on the ship and found Clara recently at her work. He's made recent threats toward her again. With your position at the bank, I wonder if you might know him?"

"Does this man have a name?"

"The only one we know him as is Blade."

"A first name or surname?"

"Could be either." She rocked in place from one foot then the other, in time to her racing heart.

"I'm unfamiliar with anyone by the name. What was the threat?"

"He's followed Clara a few times and threatened to hurt her. This morning her baby was kidnapped from her friend's dressmaking shop."

He gaped and took a step back. "What terrible news." Chet

had climbed his front paws up Mr. Hess' leg. He pushed him down. "Were there witnesses?"

Sandra went over the details. "They were expecting a visitor before the shop was officially open for the day, and she didn't want the bell waking the baby when he came in. He arrived two minutes after they realized the baby was gone."

"And everyone is pointing fingers at a guy named Blade?" Mr. Hess scratched his shaking head. "And you arrived after the expected visitor?"

"Yes, sir. Since Clara's baby arrived early and kept her from finishing the work Megs needed by a specific date, I brought some of it here to complete during my free hours. She and I both benefitted from the arrangement. I was returning gowns she had asked me to work on the last time I was there. I hope you don't mind. I did ask Mrs. Hess' permission first."

"I don't mind at all. I'm worried about Clara and her baby, though. Who was the visitor at the shop?"

"Mr. Max Engel. Clara never wanted his help on the ship or after we disembarked, but…."

"Mr. Maximillian Engel? The young man involved in the shipping business?"

"I believe he could be the same one. You know him, Mr. Hess?"

"We've met recently. A brilliant and inciteful young man. I'm sorry I interrupted what you were saying about him."

"Clara's Onkel arranged for him to travel with us on the ship. He protected her many times, especially from this Blade character."

"You said the police are searching?"

"Yes. Max sent for them immediately."

"Where is Clara's husband?"

"A whirlwind of circumstances prevented him from traveling with her. She expects him to join her soon. I pray he does. The poor girl has suffered grievous losses in her short life. She, my daughter Belinda, and her Hilda—all three of them have."

"And now her baby has been stolen." Mr. Hess' eyes misted.

"Will you help us identify this man?"

"I won't rest until we find this Blade or whoever kidnapped the child. I'll personally recommend a very stiff punishment."

Mr. Hess led Sandra to a particular seat in his home. Sandra imagined what a tiny mouse felt like while she rested against gigantic pillows on the oversized lounge. He hurried to the next room over from the large and extravagant parlor. She had a limited view but witnessed him give the bell pull a commanding tug. She overheard the conversation when Mr. Hess and the family secretary spoke.

"Ask Matthus and Zilla to meet me in the parlor. Now."

As she waited the steady tick-tock of the grandfather clock reminded her every second was precious with Esther missing.

Have Clara and her friends prayed? *I ran off on my search. I haven't prayed either. Prayer—our most effective weapon against the devil's plans and often we reach for it as our last hope. We think we have the best plan, oh but God.* Sandra folded her hands, closed her eyes, and cried silent tears to the God of heaven and of their lives.

Mr. Hess' voice broke her reverie. "Mrs. Blum, meet my son Matthus."

Sandra observed a tidy and polished young man. Every brown hair in place. His tie and waistcoat perfectly complemented his morning coat with its long lapels. His pinstriped trousers gave the strapping man the appearance of additional height. He might have extended her a hand, but they remained stuffed in his pockets. Something about this guy bode strangely familiar. Their eyes locked for the briefest moment. It can't be. "Where have you been young Mr. Matthus Hess, that I'm only now meeting you?"

"Hiding out from my sister and her histrionic outbursts."

"You must be the brother Zilla's been complaining about?"

"I am, but as you can see, I'm the perfect gentleman."

"You remind me a lot of someone. Can't be though. The guy was much less refined."

Zilla strode into the room, a sure-to-be fake smile plastered across her face. "Hello. Father, you called for us."

Mr. Hess motioned for Sandra to stand with them. "I think better standing on my feet. An important matter needs our attention. A baby has been kidnapped this morning, and Mrs. Blum requested our help. Have either of you heard of a guy named Blade around town?"

Zilla shuffled about in a little circle, evil glares darting from Sandra to her brother.

Matthus swallowed repeatedly. "I don't know anything. This is ridiculous. How are we supposed to know some seamy character? Our family is too affluent to associate with riffraff."

"You're right, Matthus. Your family is higher class than the despicable character I remember. I doubt you would know him." Sandra shrugged. "Mr. Hess, I'm sorry to have bothered you with my friend's problem."

Freeing a fist from his pocket, Matthus pressed it against his heart. "I hope the baby hasn't been harmed and your friend finds her."

Sandra knew she had recognized the voice when Zilla argued with a man about a package. Now Sandra recognized the thick fingers. "Matthus, you're not too affluent and refined to avoid harassing women on a ship in third class. Why would you care about Clara finding her baby?"

"Why would you be on a ship in steerage?" Mr. Hess' eyes widened. "But answer Mrs. Blum's question!"

"I travel back and forth to Germany, Father. It's entertaining to change my habits."

"Did you make your sister travel steerage when the two of you took your European holiday?"

"Of course not. Did she feed you a tale claiming otherwise?"

Belinda emerged from the kitchen with a bundled baby crying on her shoulder. "She needs her mother. Matthus, maybe you know who she is. Agnes from next door banged at the back door. Said she heard a baby's cries coming from the carriage house. When we checked, we found a note attached: *To Zilla from Your Loving Brother*."

Matthus sprinted toward the door. "Not so quick, son! Sandra is this Clara's baby?"

"I was planning to meet the baby today for the first time. I don't know."

Belinda brought the baby to her Mutter. "Mutter, look at this lovely quilt she's wrapped in. I love the apples cross-stitched around the border. Didn't Clara come from someplace with Apfel in the name?"

"Ja, she did. She showed me this quilt on the ship—a family heirloom." Sandra huddled Belinda and the baby close.

"How does a quilt prove anything?" Matthus smirked and snatched the infant from Belinda's arms. "Father, even you know Egon means blade, after all, it's your first name. My middle name—a useful tool when I need a clever disguise."

"Son, hand the baby back to Belinda."

Blade tucked her into Zilla's arms instead. "Run!"

Chimes announced visitors at the front door.

"Run out the back door Zilla. No one will get hurt if nobody follows us." Blade swung the blade in his hand.

Sandra spotted Mrs. Hess and the neighbor coming from the kitchen.

"Matthus! What's happening?"

"Stay back, Mother." Blade screeched.

"Your mother may stay back, but we won't. Two police officers barged through the front door. "Hand us the baby."

Clara, Megs, and Max stood behind them.

"Oh, the happy little family, and you brought a friend." Blade grinned.

"Matthus, Blade, whoever you are, there are more of us here than you and Zilla can handle." The officer kept his revolver sited on him. "Give yourselves up."

The other officer spoke to the older Mr. Hess. "Your son's in serious trouble. It would be best if he set his knife down without us using force."

"Matthus, do as the officer asks."

He whirled it around once more, then dropped it. "I could still use it."

"Thank you for putting it down, son. Now no more threats. Zilla, the baby's mother is here. Please give the infant to her."

Max stood beside Clara as Zilla shoved Esther into her arms. He hugged the shaking mother and her baby. "Is there somewhere private Clara might tend to her baby?"

Belinda showed her to a small nook with a comfortable chair around the corner from the big parlor. "You'll have privacy here, but you'll be able to hear the conversation. Call my name if you need something."

"Danke, Belinda." Clara's quivering body calmed as she softly brushed her hand over Esther's cheeks. She covered the two of them with the quilt, then fed her hungry baby."

"With the officers' permission, I'd like to hear this whole sordid tale before they haul you away, son. It's not bad enough we lost your sister and her husband."

The officer closest to him nodded.

"You're stuck with Arthur, though." Zilla retorted. "Little trouble-maker."

Ignoring his daughter's outburst, Mr. Hess hugged his wife. "Frances, I don't know how you pulled this rescue off, but thank you."

She squeezed Agnes' hand. "Only with our neighbor's help. Thank goodness she was so observant. We didn't raise our son to be a criminal. After Clara finishes tending to the baby's needs, I believe we all need to hear all sides of this story."

CLARA'S STEPS swayed with the sleeping baby in her arms as she rejoined the group. Max rose and led her to the seat beside him. She was grateful for his strength and support despite all she had declared about not needing him and making it on her own.

Mr. Egon Hess rubbed his balding head. "Where do we even begin? I'm struggling to imagine how or why my children concocted a plan to carry out this atrocity. Max, in the short time since we've met, your character, competence, and kind heart have impressed me. It's more God's sovereign hand bringing us together than your mere chance response to my advertisement.

"Clara, you've endured much from my family today. I won't ask you to give me the details. Max, I trust you know her side of this story well enough to steer this conversation on a logical path, if logic in this case is possible."

Max squeezed the front of his neck and took a deep breath. "I'm not sure logic is possible either, sir. But there has been a common thread throughout the sordid tale. Blade, help us understand about the nickels."

Esther squirmed and whimpered when Blade howled with laughter. "Eccentric pair. Friends with Clara."

Heat rose in Clara's neck and face. Max's hand rested on the baby. His smile reassured Clara. *I detested when he spoke for us on the ship, but I'm trusting him now.*

"As I understand the story," Max began. "The meddling pair spread rumors that nearly destroyed Clara's family. They further consorted in illegal activities to manipulate her family. Not the attitude of friends of Clara's family. If you told us they're friends of Georg Wolff, we would believe you."

Zilla and Blade both eyed the exits. Zilla chewed her fingernails. Her toes kicked at the ottoman in front of her chair.

"Don't know a Georg." Blade's eyelid twitched.

"Where did you meet these Nickel men? Maybe we can connect them to Georg. Something inside me makes me believe both of you have met him." Max glanced back and forth between Zilla and Blade.

"Monte Carlo." Zilla slumped over bawling into her sleeves. "I met Georg there. He broke his promise to me."

Clara's throat burned. Dread crawled up her arms. Another woman he bamboozled with those dimples of his.

"The secret trip you and Matthus made to the French Riviera when I granted you permission for a summer in Europe? A slight omission in your proposed itinerary?" Egon pounded his fists on his knees. "I'm no fool. The less-than-upstanding activities of the place are well-known. Who is this Georg, and what happened?"

"He played the part of a gentleman. He treated me like a lady. He invited me into his private suite overlooking the water."

Clara's pulse throbbed in her neck. That year the Wolffs traveled about Europe. All Georg's bragging.

"He got Zilla in a family way, then broke his promise and left. His was the baby Zilla lost." Matthus smirked. "The Nickels told us Georg was in love with Clara."

"Inviting you into his private suite hardly sounded like a gentleman!" Egon's neck and cheeks flamed.

Max scratched his head. "Matthus, Blade, whoever you are. You did your best to embarrass Clara and me on the ship. Sandra can attest to your snide comments and detestable behavior. I'm afraid I'm embarrassed again by the direction of this conversation. How do we make it more palatable for mixed company?"

Matthus plowed ahead anyway. "I promised Zilla I'd bring her a baby. That's what she wanted. I wanted to hurt Georg or someone he loved. You said yourself, the Nickels meddled in other people's business. I met up with them again in Stuttgart on my recent trip to Germany. They told me to follow Clara on the ship.

"I set my goal to hurt her because Georg loved her. How convenient to learn she was pregnant, and her baby could fulfill Zilla's wish. I followed you, Clara, until I could deliver Georg's baby to my sister."

Frances sniffled and dabbed her eyes. "Did Zilla know how you planned to get this baby?"

"No, I kept the details from her." He jutted his chin toward his mother.

Egon stared at his palms.

Clara held Esther close, her lips pressed to the baby's head.

A palpable tension engulfed the room.

Megs broke the silence. "I've listened to all of this. I've been Clara's best friend since before we ran through the apple orchards and grain fields of our families' estates in Germany. Georg is my brother. I hear the truth in your claims. Since we were young teens, Clara and I have both been on the receiving end of his disrespectful and indecent behavior toward women.

"Clara's present circumstances and her family's story are far more involved than what the untrustworthy Nickels relayed. You allowed them to pull you into their evil schemes. I promise you Georg never loved Clara, and Esther is not Georg's baby."

"Officers, my son is guilty." Egon's shoulders slumped. "Do whatever you need to do?"

The front door chimes whirred and jingled as the officers escorted Matthus Hess out. Egon rose to greet the visitors. "Drs. Gerber and Gerber, my fine friends, you've arrived at an inopportune moment."

Clara nudged Max. He joined Mr. Hess at the door. "Mr. Hess, you are friends with Clara's aunt and uncle?"

"They are friends and customers of Hess Trust."

"We received word Clara may be here and her baby had been kidnapped." Oscar pulled a handkerchief from his breast pocket and wiped the sweat from his forehead. Is this a mistake?"

"Friends, I'm happy you came. My children have mortified me by what they've done, but your niece and her baby are here, and they are well. Come in, please." He shared the shortened version of events.

"If all is well now, we'd like to take Clara back home."

Max stepped back into the parlor and helped Clara to her feet. He steadied her steps as they moved toward Tante Ingrid and Onkel Oscar coming into the room.

"Thank God." Tante Ingrid reached for the baby. "May I, Clara?"

"Ja, please." Clara took Max's hand. "Will you come with us to the Gerbers' home? There's a private matter for us to discuss."

"Let me collect the baby's buggy for you. I'll meet you by your carriage." Belinda scurried off.

"Mr. Engel—Max, come by my office Tuesday morning. I'll have papers ready for us to make our business official."

Clara turned to Megs before she headed to the cable car. "I think we can squeeze us all in the carriage today."

Onkel nodded to Megs to climb aboard. He drove them and pulled the carriage to a halt in front of Megs' shop. Max helped her down, then climbed back in, settling himself beside Clara. "Is this private enough? Can your Tante and Onkel hear whatever you have to say?"

"Nein. But I'd like to hear about Matthus' and Zilla's sister and brother-in-law. Tante, since you know the family, do you know what happened? And who is Arthur?"

"Another sad story, dear Clara. Valentina and her husband were driving their carriage home from the Briggs House annual New Year's celebration. They were hit by a street car. Both of them perished from their injuries. Mr. & Mrs. Hess took their grandson to raise. Much of the responsibility falls to Zilla. She resents Arthur because she'd rather have a child of her own."

"Oh, I'm so sorry that happened to her, but so much loss. I can't believe my Danny didn't live, and then Esther was almost gone, too." Tears filled Clara's eyes again.

"Enough sad talk for today. Let's get you home and be thankful Esther is back home, too."

Clara hugged the baby tighter and kissed Max's cheek. "Thank you for always being there for us."

Chapter Thirty-One

THE GERBERS' home, *Friday afternoon*

CLARA WAVED to Nell sitting on the swing, as Onkel Oscar tugged the reins and brought the horses and conveyance to rest at the Gerber home. Seated closest to the carriage door, Max stepped down and helped the ladies.

"I'm relieved you have Esther with you." Nell pressed her hand to her heart before staring at the fellow she didn't expect. "Max?" Her eyes shifted between Clara and the gentleman.

Clara winked to Nell.

"Max!" A smile slowly crept up Nell's cheeks. "Come join us. Cook and I have lunch prepared for everyone. And a letter for you, Clara." She slid an envelope in Clara's pocket when they reached the top of the steps.

"Please excuse Max and me. We'll join you in the dining room shortly." She took him by the hand and led them into a side parlor. "We'll leave the door open for the sake of propriety, Tante."

O Lord, give me wisdom for the conversation ahead with Max.

She spread the apple quilt in front of the fireplace, snuggled Esther between pillows from the sofa and then gestured for Max to have a seat in one of two chairs positioned across from each other. She hoped she could look him in the eye— those distracting gold-flecked deep turquoise eyes.

"I've been very prideful and selfish with you. You've shown nothing but kindness and concern for me and the baby. Will you forgive me?"

"I've never held a grudge against you, Clara."

Her knee bounced in time to her thumping heart. "Since Esther's birth, I've pondered Oma's words, Sandra's words, the words between the lines of Daniel's letters, and words with Curt months ago. Except to say, I'm waiting for Daniel, and he's the only man I ever want, I haven't shared details of conversations and recent letters. I'm taking the next steps today—steps to trust God for the road ahead."

Without a word, Max smiled and leaned toward her.

My Vati has had Daniel's and my marriage annulled. Onkel Martin said he couldn't, but Vati has money and influence. I'm an unmarried mother. I promised Curt I would pray to release Daniel to pursue future love with another if he chooses. Caring for Daniel's Mutter in her illness has pushed Tilly and Daniel together. She has always had eyes for him. He writes how she has been a godsend in his life. His feelings for her have grown.

He has no idea when he might be in a position to leave for America, if ever. I've asked God to help me let go of the pain of the betrayal I've endured. Oma reminded Daniel and me our decisions have consequences. We plan our way, but He directs the path that our lives will follow.

Max waited patiently until her words came.

"I proclaimed for all to hear—at least anyone listening—that I never wanted another man in my life besides Daniel. But God has a sense of humor, Max. He placed another most kind-hearted man in my life, and I've been too foolish to open my eyes. Think of all the times He's put us together since we met in Paris nearly a year ago. You once asked me to be a part of your family in whatever way I was willing. I wasn't willing."

He reached across the space between them to hold her hand, then took a deep breath and exhaled. "May I dare to believe you are willing now?" He tightened his grip on her trembling hand.

Tears stung her eyes. "You'll never replace Daniel as Esther's Vater, but the way you stood up to Blade on the ship, I've known you would love and protect us both without hesitation. Letting go of my pride, and admitting it to myself and to you is one of the most difficult things I've ever done. Even more difficult than forgiving Georg. And now I pray I can forgive Blade."

"We could work on that together." Like the time on the ship when he had invited her to be part of his family, tears welled in Max's eyes again. "Clara Reinhold Becker. May I ask your Onkel's permission to court you?"

"He's peeking in the door. He's probably hungry as a bear and ready for us to join them for lunch."

"But you haven't answered my question yet."

"Ja. Ja. You may. Ask him now."

Onkel waved an arm motioning everyone through the door with him. "We know you wanted privacy, but we were hopeful and praying and listening for the good news." He extended his hand to Max. "Don't court her too long. Make it an official engagement soon. And we'll hide our eyes while you kiss."

Thunderous applause ignited Clara's new dream.

Epilogue

CHICAGO, *1883*

IMPRESSED with her gown and the service she received, Mrs. Spalding joined Mrs. Hardy, Mrs. Miller, and Mrs. Pullman in spreading the word about the fashion salon. **MEGS & CLARA— FASHION & DESIGN FOR THE MOST DISCRIMINATING** thrived. Clients sought out Clara's ideas, sketches, and attention to detail. Sandra kept baby Esther one day a week while she met with the ladies. Clara brought the work to Sandra when she came to get Esther. Along with Megs, the three women made a great team. Mrs. Hess delighted to love on Megs' little August like he was her own grandchild. He stayed with her every day.

The growth of Max's business more than pleased both he and Mr. Hess. On a trip to Germany in the spring Max introduced his new and expanded services to his existing clients. He visited family and invited them to America for the wedding. He hoped they would choose to stay and live in Chicago, too.

Clara and Max spent many an evening with Sandra and Mr. and Mrs. Hess at their home. Max's coin tricks and the couple's storytelling entertained Arthur, and he often invited his friends to join them. Having collected all the editions of *Young Folks* magazine, each week Max read a new chapter of Captain George North's *Treasure Island or the Mutiny of the Hispaniola*. It became Arthur's favorite. Hilda played patty cake with Esther. The little one squealed at a popping jack-in-the-box and enjoyed punching towers of blocks watching them tumble.

The friendship group grew. Megs attended the first one. She, Nell, Belinda, and Clara invited others. Zilla had mellowed toward Arthur since she had joined the ladies. The group became a close circle of support and encouragement for each other in their times of trouble. They celebrated all their joys together, too. When Clara and Max announced their July 14th wedding, the ladies planned together to make the day everything Clara could imagine.

The grandeur of the Second Presbyterian Church in the Gerbers' neighborhood hosted the nuptials. Mr. and Mrs. Hess and Max's father shared the seats for the groom's parents. Tante Ingrid sat in the seat of honor in the stead of Clara's Mutti. Both Nell and Megs stood where they would be at Clara's side as Maid and Matron of Honor. Arthur carried the rings. Megs' husband, Gus, sat in the front row with Tante Ingrid. August Schmitz, Jr. squirmed in his lap giggling and reaching for his Mutter as the wedding party waited for the bride to enter.

In the narthex, Onkel Oscar offered Clara his arm to escort her down the aisle. Before the church's inner doors swung open, the entrance doors creaked behind them. The pair turned to see who the latecomers might be. Clara's eyes widened in disbelief.

"May we?"

Clara threw herself into Mutti and Vati's outstretched arms. "I thought I would never see you again. I'm not sure why you're here, but I'm so happy you came."

"Max invited us. He's a godly man, Clara." Vati whispered in her ear, then stepped back, handing his daughter a bouquet of sunflowers tied with turquoise ribbons, a small gold key dangling from one. He placed a kiss on her cheek. You know what goes with the key. It's waiting for you at your new home."

Mutti pulled two white embroidered handkerchiefs from her reticule. With one she dabbed her own eyes. The other she offered to Clara. "Every bride needs to carry one of these. Dry your eyes, too, before you join your groom."

Vati turned to the man beside his daughter. "You must be Oscar. I learned your name from my Mutter, and Max assured me you would do the honors."

Onkel Oscar nodded.

"Please do a different honor. Please escort Clara's Mutti to her seat."

Oscar extended his arm to Lydia. "Shall we."

Kraig took Clara's hand and placed it in the crease of his elbow.

With Clara squeezing her Vati's arm, they floated down the aisle to the strains of Mendelssohn's *Wedding March.* The ivory, turquoise, and gold beads of her coral silk gown sparkled in the light of the bright summer day. Esther hugged her well-loved elephant. Dressed in her dreamy gown matching her mother's, the little one took tentative toddler steps walking alongside her.

Tante Adeline had provided a generous amount of the lovely fabric confection. Megs insisted on designing the gown for her lifelong friend. Her magnificent design and Sandra's attention to detail for the matching mother-daughter ensembles would be the talk of Chicago's fashionable women for a long time to come.

Following their vows and a reception in their honor at Tante Ingrid and Onkel Oscar's home, the couple finally made their exit and hurried to their waiting carriage. Max carried his bride across the threshold of their new home. He allowed her feet to touch the ground in front of the Apfel-engraved piano she and Vati had commissioned from the J.P. Sauer company back in Germany—now a wedding gift from him and Mutti. Frances and Egon Hess had a spacious and airy cottage built on their property. One day it would be a caretaker's home. For the foreseeable future, Max and Clara would begin their life together here as husband and wife.

"Welcome home, Mrs. Engel!"

The beauty of this day is not what I envisioned for my future, but God has given me a brand new start, better than any new dream I could have imagined.

The End

Author's Notes

With historical fiction, questions arise about what's true and what's not. Here's a brief overview.

Clara's story continues to be inspired by tiny snippets of my great-grandmother's story. She was the daughter of a Baron in southwest Germany. Rules for nobility forbid marriage to a servant. According to what's been shared with me, in the Spring of 1882 because of his daughter's pregnancy by the *carriage driver* (outside of wedlock) her father sent her to America alone. My grandmother was born in August. To my knowledge, my great-grandmother and the baby's father were never reunited. A year after Grandma was born, my great-grandma married a man she met in Chicago. Their family grew, and he loved my grandmother as he did all their children. Did my great-grandmother and her family ever reconcile? I don't know, but I want to believe they did.

The Ratskeller restaurant, St. Peter's Cathedral, Muhle am Wall, and The Romantishes Haus are all real places in

Bremen. Bremen was the port of departure for many European immigrants sailing to the United States. The S.S. Elbe was a fairly new and modern ship only in service for 1 year at the time of the April 1882 sailing. The Elbe March was written a few years later, but I took the liberty of including it as part of the story. William Willigerod was its captain. Babies born on a ship were often named for the ship or the ship's captain.

Dr. Jean-Martin Charcot was a French neurologist. In the 1860's he discovered and named the disease *sclérose en plaques* (Multiple Sclerosis).

Marbach is the oldest (over 500 years) equestrian stud farm in Germany. Stuttgart is a prime area for horse breeding. The city derived its name from this activity. The accident that took the life of Sandra's husband in the story is fictional.

The Pennsy (short for the Pennsylvania Railroad Company) was one of the largest railroads in the world at the time. It traveled from the east coast into many cities including Chicago with connections along its routes.

The Saturday Evening Post published serial stories. Max was reading George Manville Fenn's story, *Ships Ahoy! A Story of Land and Sea. Young Folks* magazine published Captain George North's *Treasure Island or the Mutiny of the Hispaniola* as a serial story as well.

Mary Thompson was a woman doctor, educated in Boston, who along with other doctors from the Rush Medical School in Chicago established the Chicago Hospital for Women and Children.

The Spaldings and the Pullmans are a part of Chicago history. The White Stockings, a professional baseball team, later became the Chicago Cubs. (My grandmother was an avid fan.) Al Spalding, a former pitcher for the White Stockings, became the owner of the club in 1882. George Pullman's company manufactured railroad cars. The Pullman sleeping car was his invention. I have no idea about Mss. Spalding and Pullman's personalities. Their appearances and personalities in the story are fictional.

The Palmer House opened in 1873 and was destroyed 13 days later by the Great Chicago Fire. Potter Palmer quickly had it rebuilt (it had been a wedding gift to his wife Bertha Honoré Palmer). Throughout its history, the hotel has hosted dignitaries, entertainers, and notables from all over the world. Its glory and grandeur continue today.

Prairie Avenue neighborhood was home to many of Chicago's wealthiest citizens. Many of them attended the historic Second Presbyterian Church. Since I imagined Clara's aunt and uncle, both doctors, living in the neighborhood I set Max and Clara's wedding there.

The Lincoln Park Zoo was founded in 1868. The second oldest zoo in the United States still boasts free admission.

Cable cars like those in San Francisco, were introduced to Chicago in 1882. Inaugural service began on January 28, 1882. A main stop was at State and Madison just a few doors down from where I envisioned Megs' shop. The iconic Carson Pirie Scott store, which has since become Target, is located at this intersection. In 1882 it was the site of Schlesinger & Mayer's department store. That one was leveled to erect the easily recognizable Carson Pirie Scott building with its unique and ornate facade.

On April 1875, the S.S. Schiller wrecked in the Isles of Scilly. In one of the worst disasters in British maritime history, of the

372 passengers and crew aboard only 37 survived. One was a woman. I created Penelope (Nell) to represent that one woman. Her story is fictional.

Margarete Steiff, a seamstress in Stuttgart, Germany, created a felt elephant that sold well in her shop. Originally intended as pincushions, they were such a hit as children's toys, that she went on to add many other animals to the line. The company is still in operation in Germany creating high-quality plush toys.

Looking for a game for the Reinhold family game night, I happened upon Das Königliche Gänsespiel—The Royal Game of Goose— as a favorite during the period. It delighted me that a game our family had enjoyed has a long and lasting legacy and could be incorporated into Frayed Promises. My children and grandchildren are grown, but I still have our game set.

Clara and Megs visited Haus of Worth and Sajou, both in Paris on one of Megs' buying trips for her Chicago shop. (Tangled Promises, Book 1). For those who read the first book, you'll remember them meeting Max while shopping at Sajou.

The reasons women throughout history have chosen abortion are the same as today. Learn more in the discussion questions. I am an advocate for life, actively support *Life Choices of Memphis, Inc.*, and have dedicated *Frayed Promises* to their loving staff and volunteers. From their website:

We care. So, you talk and we'll listen.

Life Choices is a safe, confidential, and FREE pregnancy help medical center offering factual information about all your options so that you can be educated and empowered to make the best decisions for your life.

https://lifechoicesmemphis.org

https://lcfriends.org

Discussion Questions

1. Because of their different social classes and the rules for nobility, Clara and Daniel married in secret. Until they could leave for America, they hid their marital relations without much concern for the possibility of needing to hide a pregnancy too. They lived a lie and reaped the consequences. Have you ever found yourself in a situation where you were conflicted between your heart's desires and the challenges you would face following your dreams anyway? What did you do? Do you think Daniel and Clara should have waited until they could leave Germany together before marrying?

2. Throughout history women have faced inconvenient pregnancies and wished to *abort* their babies for the same reasons women today cite: financial, too many children already, interference with their dreams and plans, family/peer pressure, threats, etc. Throughout history, women have been aware of ways to bring back their time of the month. In Clara's era, there were teas and women's pills. Some women drank

turpentine. Sometimes these worked. Sadly, these methods also were responsible in many cases for the loss of the mother's and/or the child's life. Clara chose to carry her baby despite of how her and Daniel's dreams unraveled. She received advice from several people—some suggested she could "drink the tea" and others reminded her that *it* was a baby. What advice would you have offered her?

3. Clara witnessed the evidence of life when she and Curt found Tilly's baby buried behind the old cottage (in Tangled Promises). This was way before ultrasound showed the baby's movements. Women who miscarried may have seen the same evidence of life if the baby lived a short time after delivery. Beliefs about when new life started were beginning to change around the time Frayed Promises is set, but many people still held to the adage that until the woman felt the quickening the baby was not alive. There was no stigma for drinking the tea or taking other actions to "bring back menses" until they felt the quickening. How do you think they reconciled that belief with the evidence many had seen? Today we can find information everywhere that claims it's not a baby, it's just a blob of cells. How is this the same/different?

4. Tante Adeline was pregnant out of wedlock. She shared with Clara her regrets about her decision to drink the tea. While Sandra's story did not involve aborting her baby, she raised her child for several years without a husband in an era when women had few opportunities. God enabled them both to use their experiences to encourage other women. When have you faced regrets or challenging circumstances that were out of your control, but used them for good

to help another like we're instructed in 2 Corinthians 1:3-4?

5. Clara and Daniel made their plans. Decisions they made and decisions that were made for them took their lives in quite a different direction than they expected. Clara often lamented that she didn't believe God was listening to her or cared about her, and she told Him. Early on she even blamed God for allowing her to become pregnant too soon. When have you felt like your prayers were being ignored by God?

6. Rosa's health may have been a convenient way on Kraig Reinhold's part to keep Daniel in Germany, but her condition was serious. Multiple Sclerosis studies and treatment were very new at the time. Daniel worried about his mother. As he suggested in his letter to Clara, he knew she would be worried too. Do you think he made the right choice staying behind hoping his mother would get well first before he traveled to America?

7. God had another plan for both Clara and Daniel. It took Clara a long time to trust Him with her future, but she learned He never lets us down. When have you felt abandoned and your dreams squashed, then realized God was moving in your life the whole time to bring His best for you?

8. Oma shared her disappointments as a young woman and encouraged Clara to dream a new dream. Who in your life has offered you advice you rejected, only to discover or at least admit later they were right?

9. Clara lost one of the twins. Then she discovered her baby girl had been stolen. What emotions did this tragic scene evoke in you?

10. How would you have ended this story?

Acknowledgments

The writing journey is filled with people who encourage and uplift authors in so many ways. Here are a few of those I'm privileged to have in my corner for this book.

My husband for putting up with all the inconveniences being married to an author presents. I love you, and I'm grateful for you. You (the reader) are holding his artistic genius in your hands. He's the talent behind the beautiful cover.

Shannon Vannatter thank you for editing Frayed Promises. You were the first editor for Tangled Promises. I felt the cohesiveness of having your expertise for Frayed Promises, too. Your suggestions and "catches" made the story better than I ever imagined it.

Robin Mokry, Shannon Leach, and Erin Veliquette your friendship and your honest suggestions are appreciated more than you know.

My ACFW Memphis tribe, you're great encouragers. My Book Therapy Huddle members, Becky Yauger, Denise Colby, Becca Kinzer, CJ Myerly, and Wendy Galenetti, what a ride we've all been on. I'm thankful we're here for one another. New Hope Christian Church Women's Class, I love how we hold each other in prayer year after year. Thank you all so much for the countless prayers you have prayed over this book. And my little Ladies of Hope group—we may only meet in little message chats, but you are the best! Thank you for your prayers, too.

Chelsea Stern, because of your curls on the cover – Clara has the perfect 'do'. Thank you for saying *yes* to my crazy request.

To you my readers, Thank You! You are special! You are loved! And you are in my prayers!

Thank You, Heavenly Father, for Your infinite love and salvation. Thank you for the snippets of inspiration you kindle into beautiful stories. I pray those I write make You known. TO GOD BE THE GLORY!

About the Author

Award-winning author, Lynn U. Watson is the great-great-granddaughter of a baron from Southwest Germany. From stories whispered down generations to the vibrant threads of her own life, Lynn's journey is a testament to creativity and compassion. Nurtured by her grandmother's love of needle-work, Lynn built a thriving custom clothing business, and with her husband, Steve, they created The Lynn'n Butterfly Collection (cross-stitch designs). In 2007, Lynn became a certified reflexologist, opening Footsteps in Eden, a haven where she uses touch therapy and prayer to relax her clients. She combines her passions and heritage *Stepping through Time Stitching Stories of Faith*. Lynn, Steve, and their feline overlord, Jasmine, call Bartlett, Tennessee home.

Your reviews are the best way to support your author friends. Thank you for counting me as one of yours.

Have you enjoyed Frayed Promises? I would be forever grateful for you to share your thoughts. Even a sentence or two make a world of difference.

Here are a few places where you can leave reviews:

Goodreads

Bookbub

Amazon

Come along with me as I continue on this writing adventure.

My website: https://lynnuwatson.com

Subscribe to my newsletter – Inklings from My Pen

https://bit.ly/LynnUWatsonJoinMyCommunity

Join my Facebook readers' group – Coffee, Kuchen, & Good Books

https://www.facebook.com/groups/1108709330081009

I would love to hear from you. I can be reached by email: Lynn@LynnUWatson.com

You can find ALL my links at my Link Tree: https://linktr.ee/lynnuwatson

My Gift to You

YOU'LL RECEIVE this original full-color cross-stitch design pattern when you subscribe to my Newsletter. (PDF format: includes pattern ONLY.) Click on image or use this URL

https://bit.ly/LynnUWatsonJoinMyCommunity

Books by Lynn U. Watson

Coffee Cottage Inspirational Collection for Women

The Essence of Courage: Cultivating the Fruit of the Spirit

The Essence of Joy: Filling Your Heart
with the Aromas of Jesus' Nativity

The Essence of Humility: Live and Love Like Jesus

Promised Destiny Series

Tangled Promises (Book 1)

Frayed Promises (Book 2)

Planted Promises (Book 3) — Spring 2026

Pretzels & Pirouettes (Bonus to Promised Destiny series)

Lynn U. Watson
Stepping through time
Stitching stories of faith.